the
MR & MRS
mistake

BRIGHTON WALSH

Edited by Lisa Hollett of Silently Correcting Your Grammar, LLC
Cover Design © Brighton Walsh
Illustration by Newton Henrique

The Mr & Mrs Mistake is a work of fiction. Names, characters, places, and incidents are either products of the author's imagination or are used fictitiously, and any resemblance to actual persons, living or dead, business establishments, events, or locales is coincidental.

Digital ISBN: 978-1-68518-057-7
Paperback ISBN: 978-1-68518-051-5
Special Edition ISBN: 978-1-68518-052-2

CONTENT NOTES

Please be advised that this book contains content that may be upsetting for some readers. Should you prefer detailed information in order to have the best reading experience, please visit the author's website or scan the QR code below to view a full list of content notes.

For my fellow chronic pain warriors.
You deserve someone who handles your pain
as well as they handle your orgasms.
Don't settle for less.

CHAPTER ONE

LINCOLN

IT WAS BARELY ten thirty on a Wednesday night, and I'd already served a dozen screaming orgasms, dodged a swinging tentacle vibrator, and had a woman tell me my ass was juicy enough to start a riot.

Honestly? Not even the weirdest compliment I'd gotten today.

This was pretty much a normal evening at One Night Stan's. The vibe at our family-owned bar was mellow, for the most part. A few regulars sat nursing their drinks. Two tables of flirty twentysomethings tried to get free shots with bad pickup lines. And Mabel, Starlight Cove's horny, elderly menace in a bedazzled tracksuit, was waving an alien dick and loudly discussing the merits of toys that featured both clitoral *and* G-spot stimulation. She didn't have to sell me that truth. I was already a believer.

Everything was completely normal. Well...everything except me.

I'd been restless for weeks. Months, even. Uneasy in a

way that had nothing to do with caffeine or tequila. I was unsettled deep in my bones and frayed at the edges.

And the worst part was, I didn't know why.

I had no idea what the hell my problem was. I was living the life I'd always wanted—running the bar how I saw fit. Well, mostly. Sleeping in and working late and flirting like it was my job because it was. Once I was done for the night, I'd head upstairs to my apartment with more numbers for women than I could reasonably entertain in a week. Not that I'd been doing much—or really any—of that. And then I'd do it all over again the next day.

But it still felt...off, somehow.

Like I was fine with what I had, but I *wanted* something else. Something more.

More than filling in for anyone who called out. More than fixing the bar's POS system for the third time in a month. More than being the brother everyone called for a laugh or a good time.

I just wanted something more fulfilling than being the best bartender in New England and the guy known as the unofficial emotional support himbo of Starlight Cove.

I shook off the thought and got back to work because morose bartenders didn't get good tips. I closed out a group's tab. Flirted with Mabel when she asked for another round for her table. Refilled someone's gin and tonic and shot them a smile that had worked for me as long as I could remember.

And then the door opened, and I did a double take at the person standing there.

Willa Jameson. Former partner in crime, current sparring

opponent, best friend's little sister—if eight minutes counted as *little*.

She walked in like she had a vendetta against my sanity and self-control, and she had no problem challenging both. Dark hair pulled back in a messy braid with wisps framing her face, those lush curves hidden beneath a pair of faded overalls that would be my undoing, and boots that had seen some shit. Topping it all off was a faint flush on her cheeks and a pinch between her brows that meant she was tired, irritated, in pain, and trying like hell not to show any of that.

It wasn't the first time she'd come to the bar this late. Wasn't even the first time she'd looked like she wanted to murder everyone in her path.

But what made tonight different?

Willa was drunk. Not tipsy, not buzzed. *Drunk.*

I clocked it immediately. She moved slower than she usually did, even on a high pain day. Like her bones were too weary to hold herself up. She usually kept those kinds of tells locked up tight. Which meant, if I could see them from across the room, she was disarmed. Off duty in a way she never allowed herself to be. Not around anyone.

Sure as hell not around me.

She didn't stroll up to the bar. Didn't even glance my way. She just dropped into a booth in the back and waved down Lisa, who'd once served an entire bottle of merlot in a margarita pitcher because she didn't believe in limits.

As I grabbed a refill for someone at the bar, I narrowed my eyes on Willa, trying to get a deeper read on her. Something was definitely up. Because even with all our antagonism, she still came straight to me to order, every time. And usually delivered her order with a side of *fuck you*.

She didn't come to me tonight, though.

If I had to put money on why, I'd say it was because she knew I'd notice exactly what state she was in. That I'd never serve her past her limit. That I'd ask what was wrong and she'd dodge my question with a scathing response, and then I'd walk her home anyway.

So whatever the hell was going on with her wasn't normal.

After Lisa dropped off her drink, Willa pulled an old paperback out of her tote bag, opened it, and leaned back into the booth. Settling in like she wasn't clearly falling apart. Like maybe no one would notice a fissure had already formed in her foundation. But I did.

I noticed everything about Willa Jameson.

In between other customers, I kept an eye on her, clocking when she started to droop a bit more, laugh a little too loud, and had trouble locating her straw.

She didn't flinch when a group of guys stumbled past her booth, loud and obnoxious, shoulder-checking one another like a bunch of fucking middle schoolers. One bumped her table hard enough to slosh her water glass, but she didn't even glance their way. Like she hadn't noticed.

Okay. That was it.

I handed the bar off to Tasha—my right-hand woman— grabbed a cold bottle of water, and made my way toward the booth like I wasn't strolling up to a ticking bomb I had no idea how to disarm.

"Evening, hellcat," I said, keeping my voice light and

easy, waiting for the inevitable bite-my-head-off greeting I'd come to expect from her.

It took Willa a second to glance my way. Her eyes were glassy, her cheeks flushed, and her braid had started to unravel. She wore one of her dad's old, threadbare flannels—the same one she always threw on at the end of a really long day. That in itself was telling enough, but the smile she shot my way was entirely unexpected and nearly knocked me on my ass.

It was wide, vibrant. Unguarded in a way that Willa never was around me. Not anymore.

It was a smile she hadn't sent in my direction in years.

"Linc," she breathed. *Linc*. Not Lincoln. Not jackass. Yeah, this was definitely not the girl who'd hated me for years. *This* was the girl I'd been best friends with most of my childhood. The one I'd shared secrets, scraped knees, and inside jokes with. The one I hadn't seen in almost two decades. "Why are there two of you?"

"Jesus Christ," I muttered, bracing one hand on the back of her booth and the other on her table. Leaning toward her, I darted my gaze over her face. "How'd you get here?"

She lifted a single shoulder in a shrug. "Arthur."

Starlight Cove's one and only non-Uber driver who was older than dirt. But better him than herself—I was surprised she'd been able to walk across the room let alone drive.

"How much have you had to drink tonight, hellcat?"

She pursed her lips and squinted one eye. "Mmm... maybe one or two?"

I snorted. "The only thing you've had one or two of is

entire damn bottles, and I wouldn't put it past you. That means it's about time to get you out of here."

"But I was reading." She pouted—actually *pouted*. The girl who'd once broken a guy's nose for calling her sweetheart and told her brother to get over himself when he'd fallen out of a tree and broken his arm when we were twelve. "And the farm's *so* far away. Can't I just sleep here? The booth is cozy."

"You're not going to the farm. And you're sure as hell not sleeping in the bar. You're going upstairs to my place. You can keep reading when you get there."

She squinted up at me, trying to figure out if I was telling the truth, before finally nodding. "Okay, but you have to *promise* me, Linc. I just got to *the good stuff*," she stage-whispered, not at all discreetly.

I glanced at the well-worn cover featuring a half-naked man with lots of lube—er, oil—covering his chest and grinned. "Deal. Now, let's make sure you don't fall on your ass."

Willa stood from the booth, a bit off-kilter but cooperative as she leaned into me. I grabbed her bag off the seat and tucked her well-loved paperback inside, all without her putting up a fight. Oh yeah. She was *definitely* shit-faced. I hadn't yet encountered anything at all in her presence where she *hadn't* put up a fight with me.

"All right, hellcat." I steered her toward the back stairs that led to my apartment, ignoring how soft she was and how good she smelled and how perfectly she fit right under my arm. "Time to go."

Tasha caught my eye, one dark brow raised, her afro bobbing as she tilted her head to study us. "Need any help?"

"Nah. I've got her."

"Yeah, he does. He's *so* strong." Willa sent Tasha a dopey smile and leaned into me, running her hand all over my chest and down to my stomach. "He's *definitely* got me."

I huffed out a laugh as Tasha's brows flew up her forehead, nearly disappearing into her dark, fluffy curls. She glanced at me with wide eyes, her expression very clearly broadcasting, *Oh shit, has she been body snatched?* I could understand the confusion since the only thing my little hellcat usually hurled my way were insults, death glares, and threats of murder.

Willa was going to absolutely lose her shit if she ever found out her streak of public hate against me had been broken.

By the time we made it upstairs and into my apartment, she was barely standing. She tried to sink down onto the couch, but I guided her toward my bed instead. No way was she sleeping on the sofa and fucking up her back even more than it already was. She'd been wrecked ever since that hayloft fall years ago—and the Great Tractor Incident last summer sure as hell hadn't helped—so I had no intention of letting her suffer more than she already did.

"Not that I think I'll get much out of you now, but you wanna tell me what tonight is all about?" I crouched in front of her while she sat on my bed, glancing up as I unlaced her boots before tugging them off.

She blew out a heavy sigh, her shoulder slumping, and shook her head. "Grant..."

My gaze snapped to hers, my entire body flushing with a burst of anger, thanks to the mention of someone I was apparently going to have to kill.

"Who the fuck is Grant, and what the fuck did he do to you?" I asked, voice low and deceptively calm. Because I sure as hell felt anything but.

Instead of answering me, she tipped sideways on the bed, curling her knees up to her chest and sinking into my pillow with a satisfied sigh. "I'm so tired, Linc. And this pillow is so soft and smells *so good*..."

If she hadn't just dropped a bomb on me, I would've laughed at her reaction. As it was, I had too many questions and not enough answers.

And unfortunately, that was how it was going to stay. At least for the foreseeable future.

Willa was snoring softly before I'd even pulled the blanket over her, her face relaxed and peaceful for the first time in a long time. Like the weight she'd been carrying on her shoulders for years—grief, pain, pressure, control—had finally eased.

I set a bottle of water and some ibuprofen on the nightstand before slipping into the bathroom and changing into sweats. After grabbing an extra pillow and blanket, I flopped down on the couch with her worn paperback and flipped it open to the earmarked page.

"Don't stop," Mara breathed, her hips bucking back to meet each of his thrusts. "Come inside me."

Silas growled and fucked her harder, sinking deeper into her, working them both toward their peaks. "You think I'd waste a single drop outside your sweet heat, mate? This body was made to take my seed."

My brows rose as I scanned the rest of the page, and they hit my hairline when I got to the part where Silas shoved his come back inside his mate. This wasn't my first rodeo in the spicy romance department—wasn't anywhere near close to the spiciest I'd read, actually. But somehow, knowing my little hellcat read this? Read and very obviously loved, based on the cracked spine and soft pages?

Well.

That definitely should not have made me hard enough that my dick was trying to fight its way out of my sweatpants. But I couldn't deny that was exactly what happened.

I adjusted myself, knowing I was in for a long night of absolutely zero relief while my visitor was here. But I flipped to the front of the book anyway and started from the beginning.

Maybe reading this would give me some clues into Willa's mind. Because fuck knew that girl hadn't told me anything for years.

But one thing was for sure—tomorrow morning, she'd be telling me what the hell was going on. Starting with just who the fuck Grant was and where I could find the dead man walking.

CHAPTER TWO

WILLA

I WOKE up like I always did—body sore, mind racing, and already feeling like I was five hours behind on things that needed to be done.

But something was off.

This bed was too soft, the air smelled like bacon and coffee, when no one had made me either in years, and there was a low hum of music coming from somewhere outside my pounding skull.

I opened one eye to take in my surroundings. Then immediately wished I hadn't. In that brief moment, an ice pick had tried to stab its way through my temple, and I'd realized I was definitely *not* in my bed.

Or my home, for that matter.

A hoodie I—unfortunately—recognized hung over a definitely-not-my chair in the corner, where a pair of scuffed boots had been kicked off. A beat-up acoustic guitar leaned against the wall beside a record player and a stack of vinyl half buried under three coffee mugs. And then there was the low rumble of a deeply masculine laugh coming from somewhere nearby.

A laugh I'd recognize even if I had a full-blown concussion.

Perfect. This was just fucking *perfect*.

The *one* time I'd decided to drown my problems in a bottle, I somehow ended up spending the night in Lincoln fucking Steele's apartment.

Because, apparently, my life *could* get worse.

Lifting the covers, I took quick stock of the situation—my boots were off, but my clothes were still in place. Well, at least I hadn't completely lost my damn mind.

Unfortunately, that did exactly nothing to calm the screaming spiral of humiliation rising in my chest. I didn't remember much about last night. Just an overwhelming sense of dread, hence the need for alcohol and lots of it.

But how the hell did I end up *here*?

I flopped back onto the pillow and groaned toward the ceiling, certain that however I'd landed here, mortification had been on the menu.

Lincoln chose that moment to stroll toward me from the kitchenette. He had a spatula in one hand, his abs on full display, and a grin aimed at me from that stupidly handsome face. Like the man hadn't spent the night babysitting my drunk self. The jackass.

If I was dead, this was a *very* specific version of purgatory. All it needed now was for him to say something mildly goading just to irritate me.

"Before you ask, yes, you can absolutely pledge your

undying love to me for saving you from performing a live reading of *Bred by the Moonlight* last night."

Annnnd, there it was. Fuck me, this *was* hell, wasn't it?

I wanted to snap back at him with one of a hundred retorts like I usually did, but all I could manage was lifting a certain finger in his direction.

He chuckled lowly, his bright blue eyes dancing as he stared down at me. "There's that biting spirit I missed so much last night."

I didn't know what the hell that meant. Wasn't sure I even wanted to. Because if there was some realm of reality where I *didn't* bite Lincoln's head off every chance I got, well... I didn't want to hear anything about it.

He gave me a quick once-over, that smile slipping just the slightest, before he met my gaze again. "I made breakfast."

I side-eyed him. "What about coffee?"

"That too." With a grin deep enough for his dimples to say hello, he walked backward toward the kitchenette. "C'mon, hellcat. I can't *wait* to talk about last night."

Groaning, I forced myself upright and grabbed the bottle of water from the nightstand. After downing a couple ibuprofen, I shuffled toward him like a zombie. *Wishing* I felt dead inside.

Lincoln stood in front of the stove, wearing nothing but a pair of low-slung sweatpants and a smirk. His thick, dark hair was a tousled mess. His abs, that perfectly stubbled jawline, and those ridiculous dimples were not.

All the more reasons to hate him. I'd been stockpiling them like gold for years.

"Sleep well, sunshine?" he asked brightly, shooting me a grin.

"Why are you like this?" I mumbled, falling into a chair at the small, round table and dropping my head onto my folded arms.

"Perfectly pleasant? Dunno. I've heard it just comes naturally to the most gifted among us." He set down a coffee cup on the table, nudging my elbow with it, before turning back to the stove.

I lifted my head and stared at the mug suspiciously, because one could never be too careful while ingesting things given by a nemesis. It *looked* fine. Actually, it looked more than fine... It looked like the perfect shade of caramel and exactly how I usually took my coffee.

But poison was colorless, and looks could be deceiving.

"If I wanted to kill you this morning, I could've already done it. And it would've been more creative than poison," he said, eyes locked on mine as he drank from my coffee cup like a smug little asshole.

"That's not what I was thinking."

"Liar."

I grabbed the mug from him, not even dignifying him with a response. Instead, I brought it to my lips and sipped hesitantly, face already scrunched in a grimace as I readied myself for shittily prepared coffee.

But as soon as the perfectly made elixir hit my tongue, the expression cleared. I couldn't stop the contented sigh that left my lips as I took another sip, larger this time.

When I felt halfway human, I slid my gaze to Lincoln in all his insufferable, shirtless glory. "Should I file a restraining order with Sheriff McKenzie since you've clearly been stalking me?"

"If I were stalking you, hellcat, I'd have found you before you showed up at the bar at ten thirty on a Wednesday night." He slid me a glance. "Already smashed."

Embarrassment washed over me, heat blooming in my cheeks as snippets of last night filtered in.

But that was fine. Totally, completely *fine*.

Especially when I was just going to go ahead and ignore that and pretend it had never happened.

"What other explanation is there for you knowing *exactly* how I take my coffee?" I asked, skating right over his statement.

He raised a brow in my direction. "Because you're a creature of habit, and you've taken your coffee like this since you were fourteen and sneaking it from my house before school."

Without allowing me to process that little history lesson, he dished up scrambled eggs, bacon, and toast onto two plates.

After placing them on the table, he took the seat across from me and tapped my plate with his fork. "Eat. It'll soak up the shame."

"There's not enough food in the world to soak up last night," I mumbled.

I stabbed a bite of eggs, chewed slowly, and tried not to let my eyes roll back in my head.

Goddammit. Sonofabitch. Motherfuck.

The eggs were fluffy and light and perfectly seasoned

with just the right amount of cheese. Because of course they were.

"Good?" he asked, and I could hear the smile in his voice. Sure enough, when I lifted my gaze to his, he was grinning at me. The little bastard.

"They're fine."

"Oh, come on. They're better than fine. With the way you're biting back a moan, some might even say they're... mind-blowing." He paused, letting those words land. And then, "Kind of like chapter fourteen in *Bred by the Moonlight*, am I right?"

I choked on the bite I'd just taken. Coughing, sputtering, almost dying, thanks to a piece of perfectly crisp bacon and Lincoln Steele's unfiltered mouth.

He very calmly reached over and thumped me twice on the back, his full lips turned up in an amused smirk. "You good?"

"Fine," I bit out, eyes narrowed on him because I knew that look. And that look said he was just getting started.

"Quite the interesting reading material you have there. I wasn't going to read the whole thing, but when I saw the page you had earmarked, I couldn't help myself. Those are some kinks you're into, hellcat. The one that surprised me the most was when Silas said he wanted to breed—"

With a glare, I reached over and slapped my hand over his mouth. "You are the actual worst. Do you know that?"

He stared at me, his eyes sparkling before I dropped my hand and clutched my fork like a weapon instead.

"You've told me once or twice." He took a sip of his

coffee, his gaze intent on me in a way that made me shift in my seat.

Lincoln was always like this—teasing, annoying, and deeply allergic to taking anything too seriously. But right now, I saw something else just beneath the surface.

Something that looked an awful lot like determination.

"So," he said, all faux casualness. "About last night's shame..."

I exhaled a heavy sigh and rolled my eyes to the ceiling. "Thought this breakfast was supposed to soak it all up."

"Yeah, how's that working for you?"

I didn't answer him, just took another bite to buy myself some time.

"You wanna fill me in on what's going on, or should I start digging to figure it out myself?"

And there it was—that determination that I didn't see often from him. In middle school, when he'd refused to give up on his bedraggled science fair robot. During senior year, when he'd rebuilt an engine just to win a bet. And now, apparently, with my life.

I didn't want to tell him what was going on. Didn't want to tell anyone, actually. And I definitely didn't want Lincoln calling my twin brother to ask questions he wouldn't have the answers to anyway.

But the look in his eyes said he wasn't going to drop this, no matter how much I attempted to avoid it.

Maybe I could placate him with just enough information to get him off my back but not enough to spill just how much trouble I was in...

"I didn't mean to get that drunk. It was a rough day."

"Yeah, I got that much." He braced his forearms on the table and leaned toward me, a hard glint in his eyes I wasn't used to seeing. "Now, who's Grant, and where can I find the motherfucker?"

I froze. Blinked. Blinked some more. Shook my head to try to make sense of his words, because *what?*

"I don't—"

"Last night, when I asked you what this was all about, you said Grant. And I want to know who the asshole is before I get his DNA on my knuckles."

"Okay, first of all, settle down, Rocky. Second of all, you think if a *guy* was bothering me, I wouldn't be able to hand him his nuts?"

"I know you can. Beau and I made sure of that. But I still want to know who the hell Grant is so I can pay him a visit."

"Not a *who*. A *what*."

"I'm not following."

I exhaled a deep sigh and sank back in my chair, knowing he wouldn't stop until I'd spilled it all. "I'm fucking up everything."

"I highly doubt that."

"It's true. Everything's breaking—the farm, my back, our bank account. I'm drowning."

"I know." Lincoln leaned forward, his gaze intent on me, and I didn't dare look away. "You about ready to let someone else help?"

I would've laughed if I weren't close to tears. No, I wasn't. Even with everything that was happening, I wasn't about to ask for assistance. I could do this on my own.

"Not someone, but I thought I found some*thing* that could help. A grant, specifically for small farms."

His brows lifted. "That sounds perfect. What can I do? Fill out forms? Make copies? Mail some shit?"

I breathed out a humorless laugh and shook my head. "There's nothing you can do unless you can rewrite my entire life."

"That sounds a hell of a lot more dismal than what you just said. Spell it out for me."

"I read the fine print last night, which led to me drinking my weight in tequila. Turns out the grant isn't available to solo applicants. They want to invest in family farms run by *families*. Couples, at the very least. And since Dad died and Mom left, I don't have anyone."

"Your brother would be pretty pissed to hear that."

I rolled my eyes. "My brother is halfway around the world playing hero with vaccines and IV drips. Besides, I'm pretty sure they mean a spouse or children. And I've got neither."

Lincoln leaned back in his chair, scratching his bare abs, and shrugged...the picture of ease. "So, we get married."

This time, I choked on a sip of coffee, my eyes wide and watering as I stared at him.

"Excuse me?" I managed to croak out.

"*Married*," he enunciated. "You need a family? I'm a family. One whole legally eligible husband, right here."

"You *cannot* be serious."

"Why not? We get hitched, you qualify for the grant, and I get the insider hookup on your fucking delicious jam. Sounds like a win to me."

"Sounds like *insanity* to me."

"I prefer to call it resourcefulness. You need help. I have a Ring Pop and no commitments." He leaned forward, his brow quirked. "Unless you'd rather go about it another way..."

"You mean, not at all?"

He grinned, wide and teasing and completely unrepentant. "I mean, getting married isn't the only way to make you a family. I could also do what your latest book boyfriend excelled at and breed you..."

My mouth dropped open on an incredulous breath. "You did not just say that to me."

"Oh, I absolutely did. And I'm ready to put my mouth—and my swimmers—where my money is."

"You're an idiot *and* a jackass."

"I don't know, hellcat." He tipped his chair back onto two legs and took a sip of coffee, like he hadn't just offered to get me pregnant for a grant. "Seems like this idiot jackass just came up with *two* solutions to your current predicament."

With a huff, I stood and strode straight toward the front door, grabbing my bag along the way. As I slipped on my boots, I said, "If I stay here another second, I'll stab you with that fork."

"Ohhh...forkplay. I didn't read about that in *Bred by the Moonlight*, but I'm up for trying anything with you."

I shot him a scowl—and the finger—before storming out of his apartment and slamming the door behind me.

Hell would have to freeze over before I even *thought* about marrying Lincoln Steele.

CHAPTER THREE

WILLA

I WAS GOING to burn this entire office to the ground. Not with, like, a vat of gasoline or anything quite so dramatic. But I could definitely get a good smolder going by lighting up one overdue bill at a time.

Slumped in my dad's old chair, I cradled my head in my hands. Partially from the lingering hangover and partially from the overwhelming dread of...well, everything.

Piles of papers and stacks of mail surrounded me, all of them saying the same thing in slightly different fonts.

You're failing.

Between the past-due notices, the rejection emails, and a co-op application I'd spent two nights filling out just to learn the farm "didn't meet the long-term viability benchmarks"—translation: *you're too broke to bet on*—I'd been nearing the straw that broke the camel's back territory.

But after what I'd discovered yesterday? I was fully entrenched in that territory. Hell, I was the damn leader.

My ancient laptop whirred as loud as a jet engine, the

grant site that had been my last hope displayed on the screen. The cursor blinked on the line that had sealed my fate last night and sent me into a downward spiral—*open to family-based applicants, defined as couples or households; individual applicants will not be considered.*

So that was just fucking great.

Meanwhile, the stack of overdue bills had grown so large, I'd had to split it into two because it kept toppling over. Just another mess to match the rest of my life.

Outside, everything looked deceptively perfect. The farm glowed in the fading June sun. The fruit bushes were lush, the chicken coop was calm, and the golden light hit the evergreens just right—like the farm was posing for a picture on a brochure I couldn't afford to print.

But inside—buried deep in my heart and my head and my body—everything was barely held together with duct tape and pure spite.

I caught a glimpse of the mock-up I'd sketched a couple months ago for the farm's rebrand. Stone & Bramble was supposed to be a fresh start. Something I could make my own...something to build on.

But I couldn't even keep what was already in place from drowning in debt.

Anger surged through me like a match to dry tinder. I grabbed the nearest pen, scribbling over my dreams until the nib tore through the page.

Fuck, why was this so goddamn hard? And why was I near the point of *tears* over it? I didn't cry. Sure as hell not over a hurdle in the road.

Except losing the farm that had been in my family for five

generations was a lot more than just a hurdle. It was failure. Pure and simple.

I pressed the heels of my palms against my eyes until everything went black, and then stars burst beneath my eyelids. If only the rest of the world were so easy to filter out.

My phone buzzed on the desk, the screen lighting up with my brother's contact picture. In it, he was sleeping, dark hair a disaster, his mouth hanging open with drool dripping out. Had to keep the objectively handsome, annoyingly accomplished man humble somehow.

I answered the video call on reflex, realizing after I'd hit accept that was probably a stupid thing to do, considering I'd just been on the verge of tears.

Beau grinned through the dim screen. His skin was deeply tanned, his hair windblown and wild, and even with the dark circles under his eyes, he still looked like he could model for a *Doctors Without Borders* calendar.

"You look like shit," he said without greeting.

"Gee, thanks. Remind me why I answer your calls?"

"Because you love me and you miss your twin."

"Right now, I'm not so sure."

"You know my insults always come from a place of love." His grin widened. "How's the farm?"

"Fine," I said without hesitation.

Truth be told, my back could be having an active spasm and shooting pain down my legs, all while I was trying to put out a barn fire, and I'd still say everything was *fine*.

The silence that followed was short but pointed, along with the look he gave me.

"I know that tone. It's the same one you used when you'd

just thrown out your back. Again. And continued harvesting the honey like it was no big deal."

"It *was* no big deal. I got it done, didn't I?"

"Willa."

"Don't. I'm fine, really. How's life on the Ivory Coast?"

He narrowed his eyes on me like he was deciding whether he wanted to push, but something in my expression must've clued him into the fact that I wasn't talking. Not yet.

"Busy. Chaotic." He smiled then, soft and satisfied. "But rewarding. I trained three local doctors in neonatal resuscitation this week."

"Wow. It wasn't enough to be a doctor? Now you're a teacher too?"

"Purely out of necessity. That way, they can train others when I'm gone." He scrubbed a hand down his exhausted face and let out a sigh. "Speaking of... I fucking love my job, but I can't wait to be home."

Home.

The word dropped a boulder on my chest, and I swallowed against the rising lump in my throat. A home I'd had to rent out for the summer just to bring in some much-needed cash flow.

"We'll be here, waiting." I hoped.

"I know you will." His teeth flashed bright on the dark screen as he shot me a tired smile. "I'm beat, so I'm gonna call it a night. But I'll talk to you next week."

"Sounds good."

"Love you."

"Love you too," I murmured as the screen went black, the silence returned, and I was alone. Again.

My chest suddenly felt too tight, this space too fucking small and the reality of what I was facing breathing down my neck. Heart pounding, breath caught somewhere between a scream and a sob, I shoved back from the desk and paced the small office.

"Fuck," I bit out, wanting to yell and kick and punch my way to a different future. One where I wasn't watching the legacy my dad left circling the drain. One where I wasn't failing. "Fuck, fuck, *fuck*."

One of the stacks of overdue bills toppled, and I glared at them, only barely stopping myself from shoving them straight into the shred bin.

I grabbed the calculator again, punched in the numbers I knew by heart. The numbers I'd been trying to finagle into something I could make work. But the totals didn't lie.

Neither did the pit in my stomach.

Exhaling a deep sigh and closing my eyes, I braced my hands on the desk and hung my head. It was time I faced the truth of the situation—I was between a rock and a hard place with no way to fix this on my own. No matter how desperately I wanted to.

Which meant I had exactly one option.

"Are you seriously doing this?" I whispered to the empty room, and I answered myself as I reached for my phone with a trembling hand.

I clicked on my messages and scrolled to the name of the one person I knew would make everything infinitely worse before it had even a flicker of hope of getting better.

This was insane. Absolutely unhinged.

It was also my last resort. *He* was my last resort.

WILLA:

Did you mean it?

LINCOLN:

That I'd breed you? 1000% Just tell me the time and place and I'm there.

WILLA:

I meant about marrying me, jackass.

LINCOLN:

You know I did.

WILLA:

Why would you agree to do something like that?

LINCOLN:

Because you need help. And I promised Beau I'd look out for you while he was gone.

WILLA:

Pretty sure he didn't mean you should marry me.

LINCOLN:

Guess we'll never know.

WILLA:

I'm going to regret saying this…

LINCOLN:

But?

WILLA:

I'm in.

LINCOLN:

Knew you couldn't resist me.

WILLA:

See? I already regret it.

And you better hope I can resist strangling you, or you'll be dead before our one-week anniversary.

LINCOLN:

Ohhh...more kinks to explore. I definitely wouldn't say no to some light choking.
What about you, hellcat?

"Jesus Christ," I muttered, tossing my phone on the desk and closing my eyes. "I can't believe I'm doing this."

I was going to marry Lincoln Steele. Youngest Steele brother, obnoxious flirt, and the one man in this town I'd happily throttle before breakfast.

What could possibly go wrong?

CHAPTER FOUR

LINCOLN

THAT WAS IT. No greeting. No punctuation. Not even a threat, which pretty much counted as affection from her.

We weren't even married yet, and she was already bossing me around. Not gonna lie—I wasn't mad about it. Especially if she did all that bossing while her cheeks were flushed and her eyes were narrowed little slits and her bee-stung lips were hurling insults my way.

Good*damn*, I was hard up.

I set my phone on the counter, tossed a rag over my shoulder, and went back to restocking. Continuing on with my day like I wasn't about to meet with the most stubborn woman in the entire state of Maine to discuss our soon-to-be fake marriage.

Just a totally normal Thursday over here.

The bar was still closed for another hour, which meant we would have the place to ourselves. Willa would probably stroll in, her expression set to murderous, and bark orders like she expected everyone—me, specifically—to follow them without question. She'd no doubt pretend this entire thing wasn't a big deal. Even though I knew she'd only go through with marrying me if she'd already mapped out every other worst-case scenario.

Which made me her best-worst option.

And, well...that was better than most things she called me.

The back door slammed open like it always did when Willa graced the bar with her presence. She strode inside with an actual clipboard in hand, her mouth pinched, her brows drawn down in a scowl that said it wasn't too early to kill someone. And that someone would probably be me.

She wore what she always did—a faded T-shirt, old jeans that looked as soft as butter, and boots with mud crusted in the treads. And, as always, she made even that look hot.

Maybe it was her messy braid and how loose strands of hair framed her face—a small part of her that even she couldn't control.

Maybe it was the ever-present impatience rolling off her in waves that loudly proclaimed to everyone within a three-mile radius to get the fuck out of her way.

Maybe I just had a thing for surly, unbearably hot women who could out-stubborn a mule and yelled at me like it was a sport.

Whatever it was, this woman had been getting my dick hard with nothing but a scowl for more than a decade.

I didn't bother hiding my grin as I greeted her. Where would be the fun in that? "Morning, hellcat. You're looking exceptionally grumpy today."

She didn't break her stride, just slid her gaze to me. "Yeah, well...you're apparently breathing, so there's that."

"Ah, yes. Breathing. Truly, the highlight of my day."

She pulled two cartons of eggs from the tote slung over her shoulder and shoved them into my chest. "They're fresh. You're welcome."

"Restocking my supply after yesterday's...encounter? Nice. I'm loving these farmer's fiancé perks already."

She ignored me completely as she grabbed a stool, set her bag aside, and placed her clipboard down in front of her. "Let's get to it. I've got other shit to do today that doesn't include you."

"Probably gonna be the last time you can say that for a while..." I tipped my chin toward her papers. "You bring a prenup?"

"I brought a *plan*," she corrected. "Try to keep up."

She tapped her pen on the paper attached to the clipboard. On it was a checklist, underlined and annotated in her handwriting. Rules. Expectations. Timelines.

Jesusfuck, she was sexy.

"All right." I leaned against the counter and crossed my arms. "Lay it on me."

"Rule one..." Willa lifted her eyes to meet mine, her expression dialed to *do not fuck with me*. "No funny business."

The corners of my mouth twitched, but I cleared my throat and nodded like this was a perfectly reasonable ask. "What, exactly, is 'funny business'? Just to make sure we're both on the same page."

She held up her hand, ticking off the restrictions on her fingers. "No kissing. No touching. No flirting."

Her tone was firm, brooking no argument. But, unfortunately for her, I wasn't a man who was easily discouraged.

"Afraid I'm gonna need clarification on all three," I said. "Because unless you plan to avoid every human in town till you get this grant money, some of that is going to be unavoidable."

She narrowed her eyes on me. "For starters, I mean you can't flirt with me, jackass."

I hummed thoughtfully and rubbed a hand down my stubbled jaw. "So it's okay if *you* flirt with *me*?"

"I'm not going to flirt with you."

"Could've fooled me." My tone was low, but she heard it, her attention snapping to me. "Those jeans are doing a lot of heavy lifting today, hellcat."

She aimed the pen at me like it was a dagger. "This is exactly what I'm talking about."

I shrugged. "Not my fault you're hot. And as your *husband*, I'll be telling you that. Frequently. You want honesty in this fake marriage, don't you?"

"I don't want this fake marriage at all!" She threw up her hands in exasperation. "And you don't have to broadcast all of your thoughts to the entire world."

"Tell you what..." I braced my hands on the bar top and

leaned toward her, my gaze skating over every inch I could see. "I'll stop shouting my thoughts about how good you look when you stop being so loud in your hotness."

Her breath hitched the tiniest bit as she stared at me. Barely there, but I noticed. Also noticed when her gaze dipped to my mouth for half a second before snapping back up like she'd touched a hot stove.

And there it was.

That ever-present spark between us she pretended not to feel or even notice.

But I noticed. Every fucking day.

"All I'm saying is if the goal is for us to look like a real couple, we're going to have to do some things real couples do. Like kiss. Or, you know, *touch*. And I flirt with Mabel, so I'm sure as fuck going to flirt with my wife."

"I'm sure we can convince the gossip hounds in other ways."

I raised a brow. "Like what? Flashing them our marriage certificate anytime suspicions arise?"

"Sounds good to me."

"And when people begin whispering about how it's weird I don't kiss my wife...ever? What, then?"

"Then we'll—" She huffed. "I don't know! We'll come up with a special handshake. Or a wave."

I stared at her, barely suppressing my grin. Okay, not at all suppressing my grin. "I have a special handshake with my niece. I'm sure Emma would love to have one with you too. And the only time I wave is at one of the many parades this town hosts."

"Well, you're going to have to crack out both more often for your wife."

"Uh-huh. And you think that will satisfy the regulars here at the bar? Or Mabel? Or my mom, who will probably have baby name books checked out from the library fifteen minutes after we tell her the news?"

"*Baby name books?*" Willa nearly shrieked, the mask of horror on her face comical. "Kids aren't part of the plan! That's why we're getting married. There'll be no..." She cleared her throat and glanced away. "Procreating."

"So, breeding is only done in your books." I nodded firmly, grabbing a pen from the register and pretending to scribble a note on a napkin. "Only in books... Got it."

She exhaled a frustrated breath, her nostrils flaring. "I'm being serious, and you're being a jackass."

I grinned at how easy it was to get a rise out of her and held up my hands in surrender. "I *am* being serious. And we'll seriously need to act like we don't hate each other for the next however long this grant shit takes."

"I don't *hate* you," she mumbled, her focus on her task list as she checked off items one, two, and three.

"Careful, hellcat. That almost sounded like you said something nice to me."

She rolled her eyes. "I said I didn't hate you. Don't make it weird."

"We're planning our fake marriage, and you're suggesting we *wave* to show our affection. It's already weird," I said. "But for the record, I don't hate you either."

She slid me the world's most intense side-eye. "And yet

you worship daily at the altar of annoying the ever-loving fuck out of me."

"And yet *you're* marrying me anyway."

"I must be out of my mind," she muttered, eyes back on her notes. "Okay, time to get our stories straight."

"Nice. I've never discussed committing a felony on a first date, but I'm glad you're the one popping my cherry."

"I'm not joking. I don't want your brothers to ambush me because you forgot what lie you're supposed to be telling."

I waved off her concern. "Atlas and Declan will take this at face value—Atlas because he trusts me, and Dec because he doesn't give a fuck. Xander might be a little trickier to get things past, but we can do it. Your brother, however..."

Was absolutely going to kill me.

"We're not telling him. Not yet."

"That can only end well," I said dryly.

"Let me handle Beau. As for everyone else, we'll tell people we eloped. Spur-of-the-moment decision, which isn't totally out of character for you."

"I'll take that as a compliment."

"It wasn't one," she said flatly. "Since this is highly out of character for me, that might be harder to sell."

"I don't think we'll have an issue." I braced my forearms on the bar, leaned toward her, and flashed her my dimples. "People aren't going to have any trouble believing I charmed my way into the rest of your life."

She stared at me blankly for a long moment. "God, you are *so* annoying."

My grin widened as she shifted her attention back to her notes, checking things off as she went.

"Maine doesn't have a waiting period, so we can get married tomorrow, if that works for your schedule."

"You bringing that clipboard to our wedding?"

"Since you'll be lucky if you remember to bring pants, I'm bringing the organized approach to our shared felony."

God, she was hot when she was snippy.

"Anything else, wife?"

"*Temporary* wife," she corrected, flipping a page. "Last thing... We need to keep up the whole in-love act while we're waiting for the grant money." She let the page fall and met my eyes. "That means you cannot sleep with other women while we're in this little arrangement."

I stiffened, offended she would even suggest that. "You think I would?"

"I think this is fake. And people who aren't really married don't usually follow married rules."

"Well, I do," I said, firmer now. "I've never cheated on anyone, Willa. I sure as fuck wouldn't start with my wife."

"Yeah, but I'm not *actually* your wife."

"The papers we're signing and the rings we're exchanging say otherwise." I leaned toward her, my voice pitching low. "And this goes both ways. You need something...taken care of...while we're married, you come to me."

Her breath caught before she could hide it. A flicker of something she definitely didn't want me to see crossed her face, and she refocused her attention on her clipboard. "Don't worry about my needs. I'll be fine."

"No expiration on that offer, hellcat. You just let me know."

She froze mid-note, her pen hovering over the page as she

flicked her eyes up to me. I hadn't meant to drop my voice that low, but judging by the flush creeping up her neck, it landed anyway.

The air tightened between us—something sharp and undeniable sparking to life. Then she blinked it away with a shake of her head.

When she glanced at me again, the look she shot me could've stripped paint. Yeah. I was getting to her. Good, maybe she'd finally get a taste of what she'd been doing to me for years.

"There's really no way of telling how long we'll have to keep this up for," she said, back to all business.

I shrugged, unconcerned. "I figured it'd be a few months."

"At least. Maybe as much as a year, depending on the timeline for the grant." She looked up at me, her expression suddenly serious. "Just so we're clear, if you back out when you get bored, I'm screwed."

I met her gaze, mine unflinching. "I'm not going anywhere."

She cocked her head to the side, all the ire and frustration and exasperation replaced by suspicion. "What do you get out of this?"

Besides daily torture?

"A tax break, fresh eggs, and delicious jam. Not to mention a grumpy wife to keep me humble. You're always telling me I need more of that."

"Lincoln," she said. Quiet and direct. No more games.

I grabbed the rag from my shoulder and wiped down the

part of the bar I'd already cleaned twice. "You need help. I'm helping."

"That's still not an answer." She stared up at me, not budging an inch.

That was the Willa I knew. Strong. Steady. Sure. When things needed to get done, she did them. Usually by herself, without asking anyone for anything.

Which was why, when her brother was struggling with whether or not to join Doctors Without Borders, I'd told him to go. That she'd be fine without him here.

And I'd been spending the past three years watching her circle the drain, knowing she was breaking. But also knowing she'd never accept an ounce of outward help, so I'd had to figure out sneaky ways to do so.

This? Not so sneaky.

"Because I'm the one who told Beau to leave. And because no one should have to carry everything alone." I cleared my throat and shrugged. "And I still owe you for that time you drove me to the ER after we turned my mom's backyard into a giant slip and slide with plastic sheeting and dish soap. My knee never saw that jagged rock coming."

She was quiet for so long, I thought for sure she was just gearing up to rip me a new one. But instead, she said, "And don't forget about when I stopped you from getting a tattoo of the bar's logo on your ass."

"You swore you'd take that secret to your grave."

"Keep this deal, and I might."

I set aside all the teasing and met her gaze, steady and sure. "You know I will."

She took a deep breath, then gave me a subtle nod. We

weren't close anymore, but once upon a time, we'd been thick as thieves. For all the taunts and sneers and thinly veiled threats of murder, we could count on each other, and we knew it.

After shoving her clipboard into her bag, she hooked it over her shoulder and stood, pausing as she glanced back at me. "You really think this can work?"

Something shifted in her expression then—a flicker of uncertainty under all that toughness and grit.

"No idea," I said. "But I think we might have a better chance at success if you stop trying to claw my eyes out every second of every day."

She huffed and strolled toward the back door. "Then we're doomed because that's never going to happen, jackass."

CHAPTER FIVE

LINCOLN

Group text with Atlas, Xander, Declan, and Lincoln
11:14 a.m.

LINCOLN:

Need someone to take my shift tomorrow.

ATLAS:

No.

DECLAN:

On a Friday? Hard pass

XANDER:

Try again.

LINCOLN:

Rude.

What happened to loyalty?

To brotherly love?

To not being total dicks?

XANDER:

What's so important you need the night off?

LINCOLN:

Glad you asked.

I've been called upon for a highly classified mission.

There's a woman involved. And a lot of honey. And possibly a goat.

Can't say more. National security. You understand.

ATLAS:

You're not even trying to make this shit believable.

LINCOLN:

Fine. I'll level with you.

Mabel roped me into helping her. I have to escort her and George to a couples pole dancing class. Don't ask for details.

DECLAN:

I believe that more than the goat thing

XANDER:

Same

ATLAS:

I still smell bullshit.

LINCOLN:

Ok, ok. I agreed to be the naked model for Penelope's figure drawing class at the library. For the love of god, keep Mom occupied while I'm there.

DECLAN:

You better fucking be joking right now

LINCOLN:

I don't know what to tell you, man. Pen has good taste.

DECLAN:

I'll kill you and enjoy it

And don't fucking call her Pen

LINCOLN:

Jesus, all right. I was kidding. Unclench your asshole, Dec.

XANDER:

Still waiting for the real reason.

LINCOLN:

Fine. I promised a friend I'd commit a crime with her. Can't say what or where, but if anyone asks, I was with one of you the whole time.

DECLAN:

He's being dodgy as hell. That means it's serious.

ATLAS:

You better not be blowing off work to get laid, Linc.

LINCOLN:

I WISH it was for getting laid. I'm hard up. Like, literally. Hard as fuck all the time.

XANDER:

More than any of us wanted to know.

LINCOLN:

How about this? One of you does me a solid and I promise not to talk about my junk anymore.

XANDER:

Ever?

LINCOLN:

Be serious.

DECLAN:

You're making it so easy to say no

LINCOLN:

Come on. It's one shift. You'll barely notice I'm gone.

DECLAN:

We always notice when you're gone. Mostly because no one hits on someone's grandma.

LINCOLN:

You can't tell me Mabel doesn't like the attention.

ATLAS:

She's married, shithead.

LINCOLN:

Monogamy doesn't cancel appreciation, grandpa.

Come on.

Just say yes.

I'll owe you all.

First round of drinks on me.

XANDER:

We own the bar, dipshit. We always drink for free.

But fine. One of us will cover.

LINCOLN:

Knew I loved you fuckers for a reason.

ATLAS:

If I find out you're skipping work for a hookup, I'm putting you on solo Mom Situation duty for a month.

DECLAN:

And she's been talking about redoing her bathroom. By herself.

LINCOLN:

Already told you, my dick's been starved for attention. All thanks to that stupid bet I made with Sutton. No dating apps = no action. My dick's not going to suddenly be showered with love tomorrow. Unfortunately.

CHAPTER SIX

WILLA

I ROLLED into the parking lot of the courthouse like I was headed to my own funeral. Then, unable to move, I just sat there with both hands gripping the steering wheel. Mostly because I was pretty sure they were the only things keeping me from slipping into full-blown hysteria.

What the hell was I doing?

This wasn't some random weekday. I wasn't here to drop off forms or pay a speeding ticket. I was here to get *married*.

To *Lincoln Steele*, of all the goddamn people.

With my pulse beating loudly in my ears, I stared out the windshield and spotted him immediately. The jackass had always been able to draw the eye. Mine included, unfortunately.

Lincoln stood at the top of the steps, leaning against the railing like he was filming a cologne commercial. His arms were crossed over his annoyingly broad chest, the gray T-shirt he wore stretched to its limits. His hair was windblown and wild but somehow still irritatingly perfect, and that infuriating smirk was front and center on his smugly handsome face.

He was a fucking menace.

As soon as he spotted me, he straightened and started strolling down the steps with the kind of confident, lazy swagger that made people do a double take even when they didn't want to.

Like me. *I* didn't want to.

Didn't want to notice how he was wearing the hell out of those jeans. Or how the sun shot streaks of golden bronze through his dark hair. Or how those blue eyes danced as he watched me grip the steering wheel like my life depended on it.

I also didn't want to acknowledge the completely unwelcome warmth pooling low in my belly. It was probably thanks to the unseasonably hot June air and had absolutely nothing to do with the man strolling toward me like he was about to make me his.

Fuck me, he was about to make me *his*.

"What the hell are you *doing*?" I muttered to myself. And forgot my window was open, so Lincoln could hear every word.

He placed an arm on the roof of my car and leaned down, his sparkling eyes and those damn dimples greeting me. "I'm here to commit a felony with my future wife. How about you?"

I clenched my teeth, closed my eyes, and exhaled a long breath as I called upon every deity for patience I didn't possess when it came to this man.

Without waiting for him to move, I shoved open my door

and stepped out, shooting him a glare when he just smiled down at me.

"You're late," he said, highly amused.

"And you're unbearable. Glad we got the obvious out of the way."

"Unbearable, huh? And yet, here you are...about to marry me."

"Don't remind me." I slammed my door shut and crossed my arms, tapping an impatient foot on the cracked pavement. "I tried to track down a long-lost wealthy family member, but I came up empty. You're literally my last option."

He eyed me slowly from head to toe and back again. Not in a leering kind of way, but in an *I fucking see you* kind of way. And that was *so* much worse.

Because when he studied me like that, he undoubtedly noticed my tapping foot and my bitten-to-the-quick nails, and I was positive he could *see* my heart thrumming wildly against the side of my neck.

But instead of commenting on any of those things and calling out my obvious nerves, he just reached for my hand, turned around, and tugged me along behind him.

"What are you doing?" I asked but, for some reason, followed him without a fight.

"Taking you for a little stroll. You're practically vibrating, and I know you'll regret it if you bolt."

"I'm not so sure about that," I muttered.

"I am," he said without hesitation. "So we're just going to get some privacy for a minute."

"What do we need privacy for? Panicking?"

He tugged me to a stop once we were around the side of

the building, the brick wall rough against my shoulders. "*Practicing*."

"Practicing what?"

His gaze lowered to my lips, his voice dropping to that low register that always sounded like both a promise and a warning. "You know what."

My stomach flipped over itself like it was a gymnast at the Olympics.

And...no. *No*. Absolutely the fuck not.

I was not going to go all *swoony* for Lincoln Steele. The man who probably practiced smoldering in the mirror every day just to stay on top of his game.

With a snort, I rolled my eyes. "It figures you'd drag me back here just to get a kiss. Afraid everyone will laugh at you when your attempt to woo me fails?"

He didn't even dignify my accusation with a response, and his smug little grin only grew wider. "You don't really want our first kiss to be in front of a bunch of strangers, do you?"

"I don't want to have a first kiss at all!"

"Sorry, wife." He didn't sound sorry in the slightest, actually. "Pretty sure that's mandatory for our little joint felony."

The thought of kissing him should've sent me straight into dry-heaving territory. But for one traitorous second, I wasn't focused on keeping my lunch down. Instead, my gaze dropped to his lips, and I wondered how soft they were. What he tasted like. If he kissed like he argued—cocky, relentless, and annoyingly effective.

"C'mon," he said, just a low rumble. "I bet I could make you forget why you're nervous."

"Please." I huffed out a breath and glanced away from him to give my body a chance to regulate itself and stop this nonsense. "You couldn't make me forget my grocery list."

He took a single step closer. Not yet touching me, just hovering in that irritatingly magnetic way of his. "That sounds like a challenge."

"It's not a challenge," I snapped. "It's just a fact. There is literally nothing you could do right now to help."

He glanced down at me, his gaze focused on my mouth as he licked a slow, entrancing path across his bottom lip. "Give me the green light, Willa."

My palms were suddenly sweaty and my heartbeat tripled and my breath grew shallow as he surrounded me with all his...his...*presence.*

God. *God.*

What in the ever-loving hell was this jackass doing to me?

He'd somehow snared me. I didn't know if it was that infectious twinkle in his eyes or the confident curve of his mouth or the bulk of his body right up against mine that made me want to crawl out of my skin. Or if it was how he smelled, all ocean air and warmth and *man,* but I was dangerously close to leaning in.

God help me, I was leaning in.

"Fine," I muttered. I was going to regret this. I was *so* going to regret this. "You have the green light. But only because I love proving you wrong."

That confident curve of his mouth turned positively

lethal as he closed the scant distance between us. "Whatever you need to tell yourself, hellcat."

He towered over me, the heat from his body seeping into mine and sending a shiver skating through me. Everything in me went still. Everything except my heart, which had apparently decided now—with my nemesis close enough that I could see the specks of gold in his eyes—was the perfect time to stage a rebellion and damn near beat out of my chest.

With two fingers under my chin, Lincoln tipped my head back and stared down at me. His breaths ghosted over my skin, his thumb dragging across my lower lip as if he was trying to memorize its size and shape, and *Jesus*. My knees were already weak, and an incessant—and, quite frankly, irritating—throb was beating between my thighs like a drum.

And he hadn't even touched me yet. Not really.

I curled my hands into fists at my sides just to stop myself from gripping him in order to hold myself up. I was *fine*. Totally and completely fine. I wasn't losing my shit at his nearness. Not at all. What had me losing my shit was all this waiting.

"Would you just kiss me already, jackass?" I snapped, tired of fucking around and wanting to get this over with.

He huffed out a laugh, his warm breath sweeping across my mouth as he slid his hand around to cup the back of my neck. He gripped my hip with the other, his thumb rubbing a featherlight and maddening path over my soft belly.

The world narrowed to the minuscule space between us, to every part of my body connected with his, and suddenly, I couldn't breathe. Especially when he lowered his head toward me and pressed his lips against mine.

The kiss was soft at first. Tentative. Just a brush of skin on skin.

At least until I exhaled and melted into him, instinctually swiping my tongue against his lower lip. That simple move might as well have been a gunshot, because suddenly, it wasn't just a kiss.

It was a detonation.

Lincoln groaned into my mouth, both of his hands cupping my face as he tilted my head exactly how he wanted it. He deepened the kiss, clutching me to him as if he'd been waiting for this moment for years—for a *lifetime*. He stroked his tongue against mine, scraping his teeth softly over my lower lip before sucking it into his mouth.

And somehow—*some-fucking-how*—I'd shifted even closer, the front of his shirt now clutched in my hands like it was a lifeline and I was drowning in the middle of the ocean.

I wasn't so sure that wasn't actually happening.

How else could I explain this feeling blooming inside me —like gravity disappearing and sweeping me away all at once?

The taste of him, the feel of him... And the sounds he made—all low and rough and uncensored? As if he really, truly wanted what was happening between us and wasn't afraid to let everyone know how much he was enjoying it. It was all too much.

His reaction to this made my nipples tighten. Made my pussy throb. Both of which were only amplified when he dropped one hand to my lower back, cushioning my body from the unforgiving brick as he pressed himself against me.

His cock was thick and hard and so fucking big. *Jesus.*

When he finally pulled away minutes or hours later, I had to steady myself with a hand against the wall as I struggled to catch my breath.

My eyelids fluttered open as I took stock of everything. My lips were tingling, my body thrumming with a need I hadn't felt in far too long—maybe ever—and my mind was focused on one thing and one thing only.

Who the hell knew the jackass Lincoln Steele could kiss like that, and why the fuck had I allowed myself to find out?

This man had been on my shit list for so long, I no longer even remembered the catalyst that had sent us down the path of enemies instead of friends. Only that my disdain for him grew with every year that passed. He was my twin brother's annoying, irritating, infuriating best friend. The human equivalent of a splinter under my nail.

But my body was still lit up from the inside, all thanks to a measly kiss, and my knees were three seconds away from filing a formal complaint with whoever was in charge of this shitshow.

He stared down at me, his cheeks flushed, his pupils blown wide, his hair mussed from something. Oh my *god*, had I dragged my hands through his hair?

Yeah. Yeah, that was exactly what I'd done.

Lincoln's smile was slow, smug, and stupidly enticing. "Told you."

"That was—" I cleared the rasp from my voice and tried again. "That was average."

"Uh-huh." His grin deepened as he placed his hand on the wall beside my head and leaned down until our lips were millimeters apart. Dropping his voice to a low murmur, he said, "You always try to grind your pussy on the person giving you an '*average*' kiss?"

Before I could respond with a scathing remark—or by stabbing him with a pen—he stepped back, pulled something from his pocket, and held up two rings tied together with twine.

"Come on, wife." He grabbed my hand again to tug me along behind him and winked at me over his shoulder. "Let's go get hitched."

CHAPTER SEVEN

LINCOLN

LINCOLN:

Where are you?

WILLA:

Just because you put a ring on it doesn't mean you get to demand my location any time you want.

LINCOLN:

It's not my fault you ran out of the courthouse before the ink was dry on our marriage certificate. We didn't even get a picture.

Made me feel a bit used, actually.

WILLA:

I AM using you. That's the whole point of this.

LINCOLN:

Just so everyone's on the same page, if you want to use me while naked, I'm not opposed to that.

WILLA:

I'm not dignifying that with a response.

LINCOLN:

Fine. Answer my original question, wife.

WILLA:

Why?

LINCOLN:

Because I just stopped by your house to move in.

But apparently it's not your house at the moment?

That was an awkward piece of information for a husband to learn about his wife from Mabel's close, personal friends.

WILLA:

Omfg

What did you say?

Did you TELL them we're married?

LINCOLN:

And admit I don't know where my wife lives? Hard pass.

WILLA:

Well, what DID you say?

It's too soon to have busybodies already onto this sham!

The last people we need to know about this are Mabel's cronies!

LINCOLN:

Relax, hellcat.

They asked if I could help move a few pieces of furniture, so I did.

Shirtless.

And then I made them some iced tea because they were on the verge of passing out.

Believe me, they're not going to remember anything else.

WILLA:

Omg you're the WORST.

LINCOLN:

And yet you married me.

WILLA:

I can hear your smugness all the way over here.

LINCOLN:

Good, then it came through. Now tell me where my wife is living so I can haul my shit there.

WILLA:

Um. No.

LINCOLN:

Wtf do you mean, no?

WILLA:

I mean, there's no way in hell you're living with me.

LINCOLN:

Afraid that's not an option, snookums.

We're married, remember?

You know, that little event you attended this afternoon before bailing like you just robbed a bank?

WILLA:

I have, unfortunately, not forgotten.

LINCOLN:

Well, I hate to break this to you, but we're going to have to cohabitate unless you want this little shared felony discovered before you can even apply for the grant.

WILLA:

Obviously I don't!

LINCOLN:

Then what's the holdup? You want to move in to my apartment instead?

I just figured you'd want to be as close to the farm as possible for wrangling your chickens and glaring at berry bushes before sunrise.

WILLA:

We're not living together in your apartment.
And I'm staying in the converted silo right
now. There's no space for you and
your ego.

LINCOLN:

Don't worry, wife. We'll make it fit.

CHAPTER EIGHT

LINCOLN

FINDING out my wife wasn't residing at the home I'd only ever known as the Jameson farmhouse had been a real kick in the balls. Thankfully, getting fawned over by two women old enough to be my grandmother helped soothe my battered ego a bit.

Expecting Willa to answer the door, I'd just about fallen on my ass when Pearl—an older Black woman with silver braids piled high and a mischievous smile—and Bernice—a white woman around the same age with zero filter and the kind of side-eye that could knock down a lesser man—had actually greeted me. Apparently, they were Mabel's self-appointed watchdogs, just visiting Starlight Cove for the summer.

After five seconds in their presence, I knew they were the kind of women who didn't just gossip—they deployed it like a tactical weapon. Thank fuck I could think on my feet and bullshit with the best of them, so neither had been privy to my epic what-the-fuck moment.

If they'd caught even a whiff of confusion on my face about why they were staying in my wife's home and she wasn't, I knew they would've called in the troops and launched a three-part investigation before midnight.

So, I'd done what I did best and distracted them with sweet talk and my dimples—not to mention all the shirtless flexing while rearranging the living room.

After promising Bernice and Pearl I'd stop by next week to help them move around the patio furniture for their seniors-only speed dating event, I made my way over to the converted silo on the other side of the farm to find my wife.

With its matte black siding contrasting the old corrugated metal of the silo, the building looked different now than it had while we were kids. But the vines trailing up the trellis and the perfectly tended flower beds had Willa's fingerprints all over them. The two red rocking chairs on the porch didn't match her usual scowl, but they made sense in a way.

Stubborn. Bold. Refusing to blend in. Willa in a nutshell.

This place used to be rusted out and ugly. Purely functional grain storage for the dairy cows, back when the Jameson farm was a bigger operation than it was currently.

Willa had started restoring the silo about a year after her dad passed away—when it had become clear that running a dairy farm on top of everything else was too much. And as with everything she did, she hadn't half-assed the renovation. She'd sanded, stained, and sweated her stubborn ass through the entire process, accepting little assistance from others.

Fortunately, I hadn't let that stop me.

She'd kept saying she didn't need help. I'd kept showing up with tools and snacks. Eventually, she'd stopped threatening to bury me in the compost pile. That was basically a proposal in Willa-speak.

After pulling up the gravel driveway, I parked between Willa's beat-up old truck and the ATV she used to get around on the property. With the number of times we'd stolen that thing as kids and gotten up to absolutely no good, I was surprised one of us hadn't ended up dismembered or dead.

I grabbed my bags and guitar case from the back seat and strolled up the walkway toward the door, glancing around. The last rays of the sun cast the treetops in burnished gold, and their shadows stretched tall across the fields surrounding the silo. The trellis-framed porch was secluded enough where I could definitely get into some trouble with my wife.

If only she didn't hate me...

I knocked twice before the front door swung open, and there stood Willa. Arms crossed, scowl firmly in place as she glowered at me while I dared to breathe.

"Honey, I'm home," I said, voice far too chipper for the death glare she was giving me.

She narrowed her gaze at the duffel in one hand, my guitar case in the other, and the backpack slung over my shoulder. "I told you not to come here with your entire life."

I smiled like I hadn't caught her sharp tone. "Actually, you invited me with the whole, *hey, do you want to get married* thing. I'm just following through."

"I invited you into a *legal arrangement*. Not into my very limited square footage."

"'Fraid they go hand in hand, buttercup. And you knew I came with baggage. All the hot guys do."

Her gaze snapped to mine, her lips pursed. "That's not funny."

"Oh, come on. The truth is always funny."

Stepping inside the entryway that was smaller than my wingspan, I brushed her shoulder with mine because there wasn't space to do anything else.

Holy shit.

She hadn't been exaggerating when she'd said there wasn't room here for two of us. I wasn't sure there was room here for a squirrel, let alone a married couple.

I gave a slow spin, taking everything in and realizing I was about to get up close and extremely personal with Willa Jameson.

The whole place was one big circle consisting of maybe two hundred square feet. *Maybe.* Along the far wall sat the postage-stamp-sized kitchen with its whitewashed planks for walls, white cabinets, and warm wooden countertops curved to mirror the silo's shape. A small butcher block island doubled as an eat-in table with stools, and the reclaimed wood stairs hugging the side of the wall doubled as storage— because of course they did. Willa didn't waste space, and everything was always pulling double duty.

Hell, her pulling triple duty all by herself was her favorite way to piss me off.

There were a pair of cozy-looking armchairs and a French door that led out to the patio, and...that was it. Not even a couch.

This was her entire life, crammed into what amounted to a shed with plumbing. *Jesus.*

"Let me guess," I said, cocking a brow in her direction. "There's only one bed?"

"Rethinking your whole, *'we'll make it fit'* bullshit?" she said, sarcastically dropping her voice to mimic me.

"First of all, I don't sound like that. And second, I've never once rethought uttering that phrase."

Instead of dignifying that with a response, she just narrowed her eyes on me, turned on her heel, and stomped up the stairs. I followed, because I was a married man now, and I wasn't going to ask questions of my obviously very pissed off wife.

I valued my junk too much for that.

I also wasn't going to mention how her mad walk made her thick ass sway and jiggle in front of my face in a way that should've been outlawed. But I *was* absolutely going to be saving that imagery for future reference.

At the top of the stairs was an open loft bedroom that held a bed, a pair of small nightstands, a tiny dresser, a chair, and a door that presumably led to the bathroom. Even the domed ceiling, which made the space feel larger than it was, didn't help much.

She threw out an arm and gestured at the room. "See? This is it. Barely enough room for one person, let alone two, when the other one is *you* who takes up so much damn space."

"Been taking up this much space since junior year, pooh bear. I didn't hear you complaining then."

"I must not have been loud enough," she said flatly.

I grinned and set down my bags and guitar case. "This is gonna be great. I knew this would bring us closer."

"Closer to divorce, maybe."

"Relax. I promise not to try to seduce you while I'm here."

She scoffed and rolled her eyes. "Please. If I ever fall to your charms, it's because I've suffered a traumatic brain injury and don't know who you are."

I ran a hand along my jaw and smirked at her. "Damn, that was good. You been rehearsing that one?"

"Yeah. I practice insulting you every morning. Helps lower my blood pressure."

She turned her back on me and started shoving my bags with the toe of her boot, like maybe she could make them *and* me disappear with enough force. Meanwhile, I was trying not to recall, in great detail, the sway of her hips as she'd climbed the stairs in front of me.

Fuck.

"You mind if I shower?" I asked.

"Please do. I can smell you all the way over here."

She was a lying liar because Pearl and Bernice had both appreciatively leaned in for more than one sniff, but whatever Willa wanted to tell herself.

She obviously needed some space. I very much needed a cold shower. And this tension between us that was thick enough to slice with a butter knife needed to chill the fuck out.

I HADN'T SEEN a bathroom this small since that one tour

bus my dad's band had been forced to use when their usual one had broken down.

There was a toilet, sink, and—technically—a shower. But I had to tilt my head to the side to be able to fit under the peaked roof, and I'd lost count of how many times I'd cracked my elbows on the tile walls.

Forget trying to jerk off in here.

That meant I was going to have to get creative on just how the fuck I was going to release this tension that always simmered when Willa and I were together. Otherwise, I wasn't lasting for months here. Hell, I wasn't sure I'd last till the end of the week.

Ten minutes later, I stepped out in a pair of joggers and scrubbed a towel through my hair. Willa stood on the opposite side of the small room, glancing at something on the floor.

"You better not have wasted all the warm wa—" Her words cut off as soon as she caught sight of me, her gaze dropping to my chest, then lower to my abs, then lower still before promptly shifting to look everywhere *but* at me. "Did you forget clothes when you packed up the rest of your shit?"

"We live in a silo, wife. I didn't realize there was a dress code."

"I didn't realize you needed to be told to wear clothes."

After hanging my towel on the hook next to hers, I shot her a grin. "I figured it'd take me strolling around in my boxer briefs to hear that scandalized tone. Which I'm happy to do, by the way. I usually sleep naked, so the whole sweatpants thing is a bit much."

She narrowed her eyes on me until they were tiny slits.

My little angry goblin. "I'm going to take a shower, and if you've lost even a stitch of clothing by the time I'm done, I'm going to murder you with my bare hands."

Then, without another word, she marched past me carrying a pile of clothes and slammed the bathroom door behind her, the lock clicking into place a second later.

Goddamn, she was so easy to rile up. I smirked to myself, thinking of all the fun we were going to have being crammed together like this. Especially if she—

My thoughts came to a skidding halt and the smirk evaporated from my face when I found what she'd been working on while I'd showered.

In the small nook next to the stairs was a pallet with a blanket and a couple of throw pillows set up on the floor. It was functional, if not exactly cozy, and comically small. Obviously meant for her, not me.

Fuck. No.

Willa and her bad back would sleep on this uncomfortable pile of misery over my dead, shirtless body.

While the shower was still running and I was trying diligently not to imagine her in there, soaping up all that gorgeous skin and scowling at the thought of me in her space while she was at it, I made myself at home on the hobbit-sized pallet.

I'd follow her rules and keep my pants on. I'd even let her bark orders at me all day long. But one thing I was absolutely not going to do was allow her to sleep on the fucking floor. Not when she went through most days with more pain than the average person would have to endure in their lifetime.

Not when she was already wincing every time she bent over, which meant it was an exceptionally bad day.

Not when she needed someone to take care of *her* for once.

Unfortunately for my brand-new wife, she'd married the guy who'd been waiting longer than he'd care to admit for a shot at doing exactly that.

CHAPTER NINE

WILLA

MARRYING LINCOLN STEELE had been a bad idea. Probably the worst idea of my life, to be honest.

I'd known it from the second I'd sent him that text asking if he was serious about his proposition.

Confirmed it this afternoon after that kiss behind the courthouse.

And that gut intuition proclaiming I was an idiot had been screaming at me since I found my brand-new husband on the doorstep of my very small, very much single-occupancy home.

I wasn't sure closing myself off in the bathroom for twenty minutes was going to ease this freak-out. Hell, escaping to Istanbul probably wouldn't have helped.

Not when my nemesis was in my home. To *live* with me.

And sure as hell not when I now knew, thanks to that kiss, the sounds Lincoln made when he was turned on. Not to mention the up close and personal introduction I'd received to his not-so-little friend.

Still. I had to make this work—*had* to. I didn't have another choice.

It was either learn to suck it up and deal with the most insufferable man on the planet day in and day out...or kiss my family farm goodbye.

By the time I stepped out of the bathroom, steam billowing out behind me, my mood had downshifted from murderous to merely irritated. Which was about as much as I could ask, given the situation.

Glancing around, I made it three steps into the bedroom before I did a double take so hard I nearly gave myself whiplash. In the time I'd been in the shower, Lincoln had contorted himself onto the pallet I'd made on the floor, and the sight of him there halted me in my tracks.

He looked ridiculous—like a grizzly bear curling up on top of a hand towel. With one arm tucked behind his head, he held my book with the other, clearly making himself at home. His legs were positioned straight up on the curved wall because that was literally the only place for them to go.

The bed I'd made didn't even really fit *my* 5'9" stature, so it had no hope of holding the towering wall of smug muscle that was Lincoln Steele.

"What the hell are you doing?"

He lowered my book and glanced at me over the dog-eared pages. "Just enjoying the accommodations. It's nice and cozy down here. And you even hooked me up with some late-night reading material." He tapped his finger on the cover. "Shifters aren't usually my thing, but you really got me interested with that breeding book."

I didn't bother responding to his taunt because the last

thing I wanted to do was discuss my kinks with my husband. "That's not meant for you."

"The book? Fine. I brought my own." He gathered his duffel close and patted the side pocket where a paperback featuring a half-naked man on the cover was poking out.

I crossed my arms and narrowed my eyes. "I meant the floor bed, jackass."

"Well, it's sure as fuck not meant for you." Though his tone was light, the words were harsh—a directive he expected me to follow.

My brows flew up as I stared at the absolute audacity of this man. "Excuse me?"

"Hate the break this to you, snickerdoodle, but you have a fucked-up back. As much as you're bound and determined to pretend otherwise." He gave one firm shake of his head. "I'm not letting my wife sleep here."

I didn't know which part got under my skin more—*letting* or *wife*.

"You don't get to *let* me do anything," I said through clenched teeth. "And I've slept on worse."

"And paid for it the next day, I'm sure." He tapped the blankets that were poorly padding the floor. "This little torture mat is barely fit for a rabid raccoon. I'm not about to watch you wince your way through all the shit on your to-do list tomorrow just because you're stubborn."

My pride swelled, ready to bite back at his asinine proclamation and set him straight. Except as I squared my shoulders, my back twinged—the traitorous bastard—and it took everything in me to swallow a grimace.

He dropped his voice, his words coming out soft but firm. "That's what I thought."

God, he was *insufferable*.

"Well, you're not sleeping there either," I snapped. "It's not made for a seven-foot behemoth with an ego the size of North America."

"Think about the size of my...ego...a lot, do you, hellcat?"

"I swear to *god*, Lincoln..."

He waved me off. "I'll be fine down here."

Fine? Yeah. He'd be fine because he didn't have a back that hated his guts or nerve pain shooting down his legs every second of every day. But I also knew he'd hold this selfless act over my head for the rest of eternity. A chivalrous little martyr. He'd toss it into every conversation he could—*hey, remember that time you let me destroy my spine for your comfort?*—and he'd *enjoy* it.

The man was an absolute pain in my ass.

If I had to listen to him brag about how *heroic* he was for letting me have the bed, I'd snap and strangle him. And then I wouldn't get the damn grant, which left me right back at square one.

"Fine," I growled, stomping over to my side of the bed before tossing back the covers. "We can both sleep in the bed." I stabbed a finger in his direction. "But I swear to god, I better not wake up to your stupid boy parts poking me in the back."

I'd barely gotten the words out before he leapt to his feet and headed—still shirtless—straight for our shared doom.

"I'll do what I can," he said, that smug little grin back in place. "But fair warning—this bed's fucking tiny. And my dick is…not."

I ground my molars together and had never wished harder for lasers to burst from my eyeballs. Just incinerate the hell out of him, right on the spot. "I *will* throw you over the loft railing. It won't kill you—probably. But it would hurt."

"With your back? I don't know, wife." He shrugged those giant shoulders, completely unbothered. "Seems unlikely."

"You've heard of mom strength, right? That has nothing on fake-wife fury."

Instead of being offended or concerned about his safety, he just laughed and settled on the other side of the bed. Except there was no *other side* of this tiny double bed.

The mattress dipped under his weight, which meant *I* dipped too, shifting just close enough to feel him slip in beside me. And that was the last damn thing I needed—to be anywhere near enough to brush against him, skin on skin.

Except that was exactly what happened.

No matter how either of us moved or settled, one of us was always touching the other. Our knees bumped, my elbow brushed his forearm, his biceps ruffled my hair. And through it all, I swore I could feel every damn one of his breaths against me.

To give myself some space, I scooted over and reached for the light switch, plunging us into darkness. But that only made it worse.

Static buzzed in the minuscule space between us, hot and charged and completely maddening. Because all I could think about—all I could fucking think about—was that damn kiss at the courthouse. The one I wasn't supposed to enjoy.

The one I hadn't been able to forget.

"This gonna work, wife?" Lincoln asked, breaking the silence.

"Don't call me that." I yanked the covers toward me a little harder than necessary, which only caused him to chuckle.

"Well, in that case...good night, Mrs. Steele."

I could *hear* his smile in the darkness. "I'm not above choking you just to get you to shut up."

"*Nice.* I already told you, I'm into it if you are. But in that case, we should have a safe word. I pick grumpelstiltskin."

Squeezing my eyes shut, I turned my head, growled into my pillow, and prayed for peace as Lincoln chuckled behind me.

My restraint was desperately close to snapping. But I just had to remind myself that I could get through anything. Even him.

As long as I had some time to get used to my fake marriage to this jackass before the public got their claws into it, I'd survive.

I hoped.

CHAPTER TEN

WILLA

IF I HAD any self-preservation instincts left, I would've faked a tractor emergency and stayed on the damn farm. But I couldn't do that to Chloe or Emma or the Little Crafters Camp I'd been contracted to provide supplies for.

So instead of bailing, I rolled up to Xander Steele's house at dusk. I had a crate full of mason jars and wildflowers on the bench seat next to me, fresh sweat clinging to my spine, and truly unfortunate smears of dirt right across my boobs *and* my thigh that I hadn't noticed until it was way too late to do anything about.

But why should I anyway? It wasn't like I *cared*...

Except that lie had been a lot easier to tell myself before I'd woken up this morning next to my husband, my black silicone wedding band a stark reminder of what we'd done. Plus, Lincoln had been *right there*, looking all sweet and rumpled and soft around the edges. Like a smug fucking lion, peaceful in sleep but dangerous all the same.

My face had been inches from his as he'd slept soundly

next to me, his large palm cupping my outer thigh and damn near throwing me straight into cardiac arrest. Not just from the feel of it against my skin, but from the sight of his matching wedding band on display.

With my common sense on sabbatical, I'd allowed myself to study his face, admiring his thick eyelashes and those full lips. And then I'd noticed just how shadowed his jaw had gotten overnight and wondered what that scruff would feel like on my inner thighs.

On. My. *Inner. Thighs.*

So basically, I was fucked.

Fucked and about to walk into *his niece's* birthday party at *his brother's* house and pretend like everything was fine. Totally *fine.* And I definitely hadn't married the man I took great pleasure in cussing out on the daily but whom I now apparently fantasized about eating me out.

After throwing the truck into park, I shoved open the door, slid out, and grabbed the crate of supplies for the crafting camp. Once I had everything hefted and settled in my arms, I shut the door with my boot and headed toward my doom.

The party was in the winding-down stage, the music just soft background noise as the murmur of adult conversation and the sudden crack of laughter floated over to me. Lincoln's entire family sat around the balloon- and streamer-filled yard, the tired star of the show halfway comatose. Lincoln's niece Emma slumped in a chair with a homemade sign that read, *Birthday Princess.*

Okay. This was fine. There wasn't a lot of commotion to

distract them, but I could handle this. I was going to get in, drop off the supplies, and get out. Easy peasy.

Or it would have been if it weren't for my pain-in-the-ass fake husband who couldn't leave well enough alone.

I hadn't even taken three steps toward the garage when Lincoln came storming over, his brows drawn down as he eyed me.

"Are you hauling that by yourself?" he said, sounding as close to angry as he ever got.

I didn't even get a chance to answer before he plucked the crate from my hands like I was some kind of damsel in distress.

"You see anyone else with me?" I braced my hands on my hips and glared at him. "Yes, I hauled it myself, jackass. I'm not made of glass, you know."

He clenched his jaw and pressed his mouth into a thin line like *I* was the problem here. "No, you're made of stubborn. And you're going to hurt your back again if you keep trying to do this shit on your own."

Oh, he had a lot of nerve.

"Been doing a lot of shit on my own for a lot of years, Lincoln." I crossed my arms and lifted a single shoulder in a shrug. "Besides, fucking up my back wouldn't be the worst way to get out of mowing the lawn."

That earned me a deeper scowl. "Real funny, wife."

I froze, the word landing as subtly as a bucket of ice water to the face. Immediately, I darted my gaze around the backyard, checking for witnesses to his little slip. He'd better hope no one noticed.

I stepped closer to him, pinching his side hard enough to make him jerk. "It's not even real," I hissed.

He just shrugged, completely unrepentant, and strode toward the empty picnic table near the garage. "Don't care."

"How about I *make* you care with my foot up your ass?" I whisper-yelled as I stalked after him.

After setting the crate on the table, he turned to face me, his arms crossed and jaw tight. "My *wife*—real or not—isn't going to haul this shit by herself while I sit on my ass and watch."

"Oh my *god*, you are insufferable! I'm not going to break. I can carry a crate weighing all of ten pounds. I hauled five weighing triple that earlier today."

"Did you?" he said in a way that had my hackles rising. "Noted. I'll adjust my schedule at the bar so I can be at the farm to help when it's hauling shit time."

I wouldn't have been surprised if I looked like an actual cartoon character with steam pouring out of my ears. "I don't *need* you to do that. That's my entire point."

"And my entire point is I'm your husband now, and it's part of the job."

I gripped him by the arm and tugged him around the side of the garage, away from any prying eyes or ears. "Would you stop throwing that around! We said we were going to wait. Remember?"

He shrugged like he wasn't in the process of blowing up our plan and making things even more difficult for everyone involved. "I figured there was no time like the present."

"You're not even a little bit sorry about this!"

"You're right. I'm not." He stepped closer until our shoes

touched, his heat seeped into my body, and I was reminded—again—about that kiss that practically melted my brain. "But if you hadn't tried hauling this shit on your own in the first place, we wouldn't be dealing with the fallout. So maybe let that be a reminder for next time."

Fuck me, I was going to lose my mind before the grant had any hope of helping the farm.

I clenched my teeth and my fists, resisting the urge to sock him right in his obnoxiously defined abs. Instead of doing just that, I spun around and stormed off so I wouldn't make a scene, intent on a quick and silent exit.

Spoiler alert: that did not happen.

"Willa!" Chloe called, stepping in my path with a bright smile, her long blond hair pulled up in a messy bun and her cheeks dusted with pink glitter. "Thanks for dropping all that off. I know Emma and her friends are going to have a great time with their crafts tomorrow."

I forced my shoulders to relax and smiled tightly. "No problem. Thanks for ordering them from me."

She laughed, the sound light and airy. "Like I'd do anything else." Then she leaned in and dropped her voice to a conspiratorial whisper. "And like Lincoln would *allow* anything else. He practically held the phone to my ear while I called and placed the order just to make sure it got done."

I froze, my smile faltering enough that I hoped it didn't betray me. He hadn't said a word…hadn't even sent a smirk or a smug grin in my direction. He'd just made sure I'd gotten the business without any fanfare.

Chloe moved on, talking about the projects they were planning to do at camp, but I just stood there. Trying not to let Lincoln's small act of kindness lodge itself somewhere dangerous—like under my ribs. Too damn close to my heart.

When I was able to step away from Chloe, I tried—*again*—to leave. I even made it two steps past where everyone was gathered before Sutton's voice rang out and stopped me in my tracks.

"Um...hello?" she asked, her head cocked to the side, loose brown waves just kissing her shoulders.

I lifted a hand in greeting and forced a smile, hoping that was enough. I should've known better.

Laurel—Sutton's sardonic teenage daughter and mini-me—snorted and raised a brow. "You think we're all just gonna ignore the whole *wife* thing?"

Sutton leaned back into the vast expanse of Atlas's chest and tipped her head toward her daughter. "Lolo has a point."

With a smile in my direction, Chloe settled on Xander's lap. "Were you planning on saying anything, orrr...?"

And then, as if he'd been waiting for his cue to arrive, my jackass husband strolled over, wrapped an arm around my waist, and tucked me into his side. "I *did* say something. Everyone heard when I called her my wife, right?"

Silence settled for long moments as I shifted on my feet, my pulse speeding into a gallop. I wanted to pull his armpit hairs for this bullshit. But instead, I just stood there, afraid any small reaction from me would only make things worse.

Finally, Declan said, "I heard it. I just want to know how you managed to trick her into it."

"No tricking involved," Lincoln said smugly. "My little hellcat couldn't *wait*."

Forget pulling his armpit hairs. I was going to shave off his eyebrows after he fell asleep tonight.

"Everything okay?" Atlas asked, eyes intent and mildly suspicious.

"Better than okay." Lincoln grinned and hugged me tight, pressing a kiss against my temple to really lay it on thick. "I've been enjoying the hell out of her being my wife."

His words rang with such sincerity, I had no doubt everyone could hear the truth in them. But only I knew what he'd actually enjoyed about my being his wife was irritating the ever-loving shit out of me.

"I didn't want to get my hopes up..." Holly, Lincoln's mom, stood and clasped her hands, a bright smile on her face. "But Mabel mentioned something last night at book club!"

"*Mabel?*" I asked, eyes wide, because how in the actual hell?

Lincoln and I had specifically traveled to another town so we wouldn't raise any suspicions in Starlight Cove. Not until we were ready to spill the details. And that wily old woman had apparently known *hours* after Lincoln and I had said I do?

"Oh, you know her..." Holly waved a hand through the air as she strode toward us. "Once a journalist, always a journalist."

"I think you mean the walking leak," Xander said dryly.

"I'm just so happy!" Holly pulled me from Lincoln's hold and wrapped her arms around me. Squeezing me tight, she enveloped me in her familiar scent—the one I'd long associated with the only true motherly presence in my life. "I've been waiting for this day for a long time."

Waiting for one of her fully grown sons to finally find a wife? I didn't blame her. Though, she'd probably assumed it would happen first with Atlas or Xander since they were both in committed relationships. But here I was, swooping in out of the blue and throwing a wrench into things.

She held me at arm's length, her smile as bright as the sun. "We have to throw a party!"

I stiffened, my face probably resembling that of a deer caught in headlights. "Oh, that's really not necessary."

"Nonsense! I *want* to. You don't worry about a thing. I'll take care of it all!"

Could she take care of me sinking into the earth? Because that would be the only acceptable outcome for this little party.

I wasn't what you'd call *social*. I didn't enjoy being around a ton of people, and I absolutely hated being the focus of all those people. Not to mention having to act like a happy little wife to my fake husband.

Before I could start sweating, Lincoln slipped his arm around my waist again and tucked me back into his side. He slid his hand into the front pocket of my overall shorts like that was *totally normal* behavior and not seventh circle of hell territory.

"You throw an awesome party, Mom," he said, his thumb rubbing a maddening path up and down the soft curve of my stomach. "But if I know my wife—and I do—" he lowered his head, dragging his nose up the column of my neck before placing a kiss below my ear "—she'll hate having a party where she's the center of attention."

As if that chaste-but-actually-quite-indecent kiss wasn't

enough, Lincoln glanced down at me with a soft smile. This wasn't the charmer schmoozing his way through the night, and this wasn't the jackass goading me just to see how much I could take before I snapped.

No, this was infinitely worse.

This was Lincoln Steele—my fake husband and apparent protector—reading my cues. Like he knew me. Like he *got* me.

And that was absolutely terrifying.

"And let's face it," he continued. "You put Willa in any room, and she'll *definitely* be the center of attention."

A chorus of awws rose from the table, but I couldn't drag my gaze away from Lincoln's. Just what the hell was he playing at here? This *had* to be a trick or a con or a...I didn't know.

What it absolutely could *not* be was real.

CHAPTER ELEVEN

LINCOLN

WILLA STOMPED into the silo like she was trying to wake the dead. Or pretending like she was smashing my skull in. Either was plausible.

After I'd gotten my mom to agree not to throw any parties, we'd said our goodbyes, and I'd hitched a ride with Willa since I hadn't driven my car over to Xander's.

The entire drive back to the farm had been filled with heavy silence. The kind where I'd known something was churning through her mind—probably all the different ways she could kill me in my sleep.

And that was only confirmed as she paced around our small space like a bull in a pen.

I leaned against the island, hands tucked in my pockets as I watched her vibrate with irritation. I'd be lying if I said it wasn't kind of hot. Then again, *everything* about Willa Jameson was kind of hot. It was why I'd spent the vast majority of the past hour thinking about that dirt smeared on her thigh and wondering just how far up the smudge went.

"You wanna talk about what has you in a tizzy?" I asked.

She whirled on me, her glare hot enough that I half expected to find myself suddenly a pile of ash on the floor. "You called me your *wife* in front of your *entire family!*"

"So what? You *are* my wife."

Her stormy expression faltered for half a heartbeat, and something I couldn't quite name flickered across her face—as startling as lightning and gone just as fast.

If I didn't know better, I'd swear a part of her *liked* hearing when I called her that.

"This marriage is a means to an end. That's it," she said, her voice clipped. "We're doing this for one reason and one reason only."

"So you can be my arm candy?"

Her nostrils flared as she took a deep breath. "For the *grant*, jackass. I'm heading to the library tomorrow to work on it."

I slowly walked around the island toward her. "You know what we should be working on?"

She narrowed her eyes at my approach. "I swear to god, if you tell me—"

"Your resistance to physical affection."

Her mouth dropped open. "Excuse me?"

"Don't think I didn't notice how you jerked away from me at the party."

"You're the one who came in for a kiss without warning!"

"Oh." I cocked my head, not even trying to tamp down my smirk. "You mean like most married people do?"

She looked at me like she was mentally drafting my

obituary, but I didn't budge. She knew I was right, and that was confirmed when her shoulders sagged a moment later.

"I see your point," she said, though conceding to me was obviously painful for her. "But I can't help it. I'm allergic to jackasses."

"Maybe not the best idea to marry the biggest one in town then, huh?"

"Now you tell me," she said dryly.

"We've gotta figure out something because we're going to be in front of a lot of people who expect us to act like newlyweds."

She crossed her arms over her chest. "That's going to be a challenge, don't you think?"

My gaze dropped to her lips, remembering exactly how soft they'd been. Remembering exactly what she'd tasted like. Exactly how hot her pussy had been as she'd practically climbed me to get closer.

Fuck.

"Nope," I said, my voice coming out thick. "Kissing you is the easiest thing I've ever done."

For a heartbeat, she didn't move, didn't even blink. Then her mouth parted—just slightly—before she shut it again and turned her back on me. "We're not talking about just once. You're going to have to kiss me over and over and over."

My dick twitched at that nice little reminder. *Jesus.* If I didn't know better, I'd think she was intentionally doing this just to fuck with me. I had no idea when or how I was going to jerk off in this tiny sardine can, and she probably reveled in watching me squirm. The evil little minion.

"You know what we need to do to make you more comfortable with it, right?"

She eyed me warily. "What?"

"Practice."

"Practice," she repeated flatly.

"Yep. Like exposure therapy." A grin spread slow and wicked across my mouth as my gaze dropped to her lips. "But with a little tongue action."

"Absolutely not."

"Absolutely *yes*." I stepped close enough that the scent of her shampoo invaded my senses, and I had to stop myself from inhaling deeply. Keeping my sanity intact was challenge enough without becoming a hair-sniffing pervert. "The more we do it, the easier it'll be. And hopefully soon, you'll be able to kiss me without flinching."

Silence reigned for several tense moments. I was a little worried she'd knee me in the balls and storm up to bed.

"Fine," she said, shocking the hell out of me. Then she jabbed a finger into my chest. "But if we do this, this isn't going *anywhere*. None of your charmer bullshit, got it?"

I raised my hand. "Scout's honor."

"I've known you for twenty-five years, jackass. You've never been a scout."

"Fine, then. Charmer's honor. Practice only. Nothing else." I lowered my face until we were eye level, one side of my mouth ticking up. "At least until you beg me otherwise."

"So, when hell's frozen over, then?" Her words were harsh, but her voice wasn't as steady and sure as it usually was.

She was nervous—something strong, unflappable Willa rarely was.

I softened my voice and asked, "Ready?"

"Not even a little bit."

But she didn't move away. Instead, she lifted her chin, her eyes flashing in defiance, and those full, pouty lips of hers set in a firm line, daring me to come closer.

So I did.

I lifted a hand to cup her neck, my thumb brushing across the soft curve of her jaw. "I'm going to kiss you now, wife."

"And I'm going to hate every second of it," she murmured, her gaze tracking my movements as I lowered my face, inching closer to hers.

"We'll see about that..."

Her eyelids fluttered shut at the first brush of our lips together, and she sighed into my mouth. As if she hadn't been expecting the softness of it. As if she hadn't been expecting to like it either.

It was taking everything in me not to cup her ass and haul her up against me. Pin her to the countertop and lick my way inside. Remind myself exactly what she tasted like.

But she needed slow, so that was exactly what I was going to give her.

I dragged my mouth against hers, back and forth, so fucking desperate to taste her but holding myself back. Our lips met again and again, brief and soft.

When she parted her mouth on a shaky exhale, her tongue tentatively brushing against my bottom lip, I took the invitation and deepened the kiss. On a quiet groan, I licked into her mouth in slow, deep strokes, savoring the way her breath hitched every time I pulled back.

She was intoxicating—better than any high, better than any fantasy. And there had been a *lot* of fantasies over the years. But this was real. *She* was real, and she was kissing me like she couldn't get enough.

That thought only made me want her more.

I wrapped her braid in my fist and tugged, tipping her head exactly how I wanted it. This time, she didn't even try to hold back her moan, the rough sound going straight to my dick. She fisted my shirt, gripping it tightly like she didn't know whether she wanted to tug me closer or shove me away.

Our once-soft kiss wasn't tentative anymore. It was hungry. Messy. Desperate.

There wasn't a breath of space between us, but, still, I needed more. Needed her closer. Needed her naked and writhing beneath me, moaning my name as she came around my cock.

Fuck me.

Without breaking the kiss, I reached down and cupped her ass, lifting her easily onto the island before stepping between her spread thighs. She felt so fucking good, everywhere. And she tasted as delicious as I remembered—all sweet and tart.

I had to stop myself from grinding against her hot little pussy. From taking this further than she wanted to.

But it was clear from how desperately she kissed me back just how much she'd needed this and only this. She deserved a kiss that unraveled her. That made her forget every worry and obligation and just fall into pure pleasure.

It'd been a long time since I'd made out with someone without the intention of more. But I found I didn't need that.

Not with Willa.

Just kissing her was better than anything else I'd ever done—sex included. It was so fucking good, I never wanted it to end. And from the way she'd locked her ankles at the base of my spine and began rocking her hips against me, she felt it too.

But I'd made her a promise.

And I knew if we didn't stop right now, I'd have her clothes off in two minutes flat and her spread out on this island while I feasted on her cunt.

As much as it pained me to do so, I slowed the kiss and unhooked her legs from around my waist. Until, finally, I pulled away, still panting and hard as a fucking rock.

Unfortunately, even stepping back didn't help my predicament. Not when I got an eyeful of my hot-as-sin wife. Chest heaving, lips kiss-swollen, pupils blown wide, and those thick thighs spread and just waiting for me to settle between them again.

"Day one practice, complete," I said, gravel coating my throat. "Same time tomorrow, wife."

For a second, she just sat there. Dazed and flushed, her eyes wide with something she clearly hadn't intended to feel. Then those walls she loved so much slammed back into place, and she aimed a scowl at me. "That's assuming I don't murder you before morning."

She slid off the island and stomped her way upstairs, as if she could outrun what had just happened between us.

I let her go and gave her the space. Because fuck knew I'd

need a solid fifteen minutes to talk my dick down. Especially when I kept thinking about doing this all over again tomorrow.

Practice was supposed to make things easier. Instead, it had lit a fuse I wasn't sure we'd be able to extinguish.

CHAPTER TWELVE

WILLA

Group text with Chloe, Sutton, and Willa
8:47 p.m.

SUTTON:

Um. Wtf?

CHLOE:

SERIOUSLY. WTF???

WILLA:

Wtf what?

SUTTON:

Don't play dumb with us, babe

WILLA:

I'm not playing anything. I don't know what you two are wtf-ing about.

CHLOE:

Oh idk. Maybe the fact that on Monday you told me what a pain in the ass Lincoln is and NOW YOU'RE MARRIED TO THAT PAIN IN THE ASS?

WILLA:

Pretty sure every woman alive who's married to a man could say the same.

SUTTON:

I mean…you're not wrong.

CHLOE:

BUT STILL

SUTTON:

WHEN did this happen??

CHLOE:

HOW did this happen??

SUTTON:

And why tf didn't you tell us??

WILLA:

You're going to have to be more specific. What *this* are we referring to?

SUTTON:

You know exactly which one, you evasive little shit.

WILLA:

Idk what to tell you. I wasn't married to Lincoln on Monday and now I am.

CHLOE:

WE ALREADY KNEW THAT!!!

YOU'RE GIVING US NOTHING!

SUTTON:

Idk wtf is going on, but blink twice if you're being held hostage by his dimples.

WILLA:

I'm fine. Everything's fine. Totally fine.

SUTTON:

That's too much fine for it to actually be fine.

CHLOE:

We need a night filled with tequila to get the whole sordid story.

SUTTON:

I'm free tonight

CHLOE:

Same

WILLA:

Can't, sorry. Berry season really keeps me busy. But soon.

SUTTON:

I hope you know we're holding you to that.

CHAPTER THIRTEEN

WILLA

WHOEVER DECIDED library chairs should be made of wood clearly had a vendetta against bookworms. These things were about as comfortable as sitting on a pile of rocks, and my back had been screaming as much after only ten minutes.

Wincing, I shifted and glanced down at the grant paperwork spread across the table. This was taking far longer than I'd anticipated. It didn't help that the Wi-Fi stuttered along at the speed of molasses, my laptop fan wheezed like a dying cow, and every time I tried to focus, all I saw was Lincoln Steele's mouth.

Not the mouth that cracked jokes across the bar or the mouth that had been teasing and taunting me for decades. No. Instead, I saw the mouth that had kissed me last night like it had a lifetime of catching up to do.

Practice. It was supposed to be practice.

But somehow, my body hadn't gotten that message. Worse, it had leaned into him like a greedy, reckless idiot.

And look where that had gotten me—in the library, inching up on hour two, with not much to show for my time here except explicit fantasies about my fake husband's tongue.

"Get it together, Willa," I muttered, shifting in my seat and trying to alleviate some of the nerve pain running down my legs.

Since my once-quiet house was now also the home of the loudest man in existence who could scream without saying a word, I'd figured the library was the best escape. The peace, the quiet hum of turning pages and shifting papers, the order of it all, should've grounded me.

But the silence only pressed in until all I could hear was my own heartbeat and recall exactly how easily Lincoln had made it race with a simple kiss.

True, it was a kiss that had been better than even the best sex of my life, but still. It was *just* a kiss.

I huffed out a breath and rolled my eyes. I should've known just a kiss with Lincoln would've been the beginning of the end for my sanity.

Shaking off the memory, I shuffled through the papers spread out around me until a small paperback slid across the table toward me. *Plowed by His Seeder*, its cover featuring a well-built shirtless man wearing muddy jeans that accentuated his very large, um, *seeder*.

Brows raised, I glanced up to find Penelope shifting on her feet. Her pale pink cardigan was buttoned all the way up, her matching glasses perfectly in place. From the outside, she looked like your average prim, proper librarian. But I'd officially met her in front of a display of ten-inch tentacle dildos at Wicked Little Things, and she'd just dropped a book so filthy, I didn't think the library even carried that level of smut.

"Good morning to you too, Pen. New favorite?" I asked, tipping my head toward the book.

She cleared her throat and ran a hand down her skirt. "Lots of, um...readers seem to like this one. Thought it might help you relax at the end of the day. You look like you could use a bit of that."

I huffed out a laugh and leaned back, wincing when fire shot down my leg. "That obvious?"

"Maybe not to most people." She lifted a single shoulder in a shrug and smiled softly. "But I'm observant."

Of course she was. The woman noticed everything—observation was practically her kink.

I flipped the book over and scanned the back, my brows lifting as several words stood out—*fertile*, *harvest*, and *massive seeder*, to name a few. "Thanks for this. Sounds like it'll pair nicely with a huge tentacle peen."

A soft squeak came from Penelope, and crimson stained her cheeks. "Oh, um...maybe."

"Sorry, I have no filter. I know it's a lot different to talk about alien dicks when we're seated in front of a display at Wicked Little Things than it is chatting while you're at work."

"No, it's okay." Though the increased reddening of her cheeks, ears, and chest indicated it very much *wasn't*. "But I should get back to it. I'll see you later."

"Sure. And, Pen? Thanks for this," I said, holding up the book.

She gave me a subtle nod before scurrying off to the

checkout counter. I opened the book and flipped through it, my brows lifting the more pages I scanned.

This wasn't just any library book. This was a fully annotated Penelope original, complete with color-coded tabs and a heart-shaped sticky note marking one of the hottest scenes I'd ever read.

Well, damn. Apparently those buttoned-up cardigans and innocent blush were hiding something a little bit naughty under the surface.

I tucked the book into my bag because I was *definitely* going to be rereading that scene later. Just to really give it the time it deserved. For academic purposes, obviously.

Blowing out a deep sigh, I nudged my laptop back into place and tried to refocus. The form in front of me stared back with silent judgment. I glared at the line labeled Family Details and swallowed hard. Shockingly, there wasn't a checkbox for *fake husband, real tension, zero clue what the fuck I'm doing.*

This grant wasn't only about saving the farm. It was about proving—to myself, to my brother, to my fake husband—that I could do this. That I was still the version of me who could carry every burden without flinching.

Except sitting here, my back screaming, my brain fried, and my skin still tingling from Lincoln's touch, I felt less like a rock and more like a cracked pane of glass, one wrong move away from completely shattering.

"Fuel delivery," a warm voice interrupted my spiral.

I glanced up to find Holly standing next to me, a paper bag in one hand and a coffee cup in the other.

"You've been buried back here so long, I thought you

could use a little something," she said, placing the items on the table with a smile.

I scanned the writing on the side of the to-go cup—extra cream, two sugars, dash of cinnamon, exactly how I liked it—and peeked inside the bag to find a blueberry Danish. My favorite, from the bakery I limited myself to once a month because if I didn't, I'd replace my entire food supply with flaky pastries.

Suddenly, my throat felt too thick and my chest felt too tight and I didn't know where to put all this emotion. Which only felt stupid because what the hell was I getting all worked up about? It was coffee and a pastry, not a million dollars.

But it was *my* coffee and *my* pastry, and it was coming from someone who so easily exuded motherly comfort to someone who wasn't even hers. And considering my mom's version of comfort was calling me a couple times a year from her perch in Florida to bitch about her latest woes, this was altogether new for me. And completely unexpected.

After clearing my throat several times, I murmured, "Thank you. You didn't have to do this."

Holly waved away my words. "I *wanted* to. And all it took was a quick text to your husband to find out your favorites."

My *fake* husband... I'd been shocked to learn he knew my coffee order, but this? He also apparently knew which bakery was my favorite and the Danish I couldn't get enough of?

When the hell had that happened, and why did it make me feel all warm and melty inside?

"Besides, I'm just so happy you're family now." She

squeezed my shoulder, her sincerity bleeding through. "You and your brother have always felt like you were, but this just cements it as fact."

Her words and the love shining in her eyes hit harder than I was prepared for. Guilt settled on my shoulders, heavy and unrelenting.

Because I *wasn't* actually family.

This whole thing was all a ruse. Nothing more than a lie. And I hadn't taken into consideration just how many others would be affected by our little farce.

Before I could spiral down the path of Nothing Good This Way Lane, Holly straightened and smiled at someone over my shoulder.

"Hi, honey!"

I glanced over to find Declan headed our way, looking pissed off at the world for existing. Tattoos ran up both of his arms, disappearing beneath the black T-shirt wrapped tightly around his biceps, and his scowl screamed *Don't talk to me. Don't even* look *at me.*

Holly obviously wasn't deterred because she gave him a quick hug, and my brows flew up when he bent to press a kiss against her cheek. Apparently Declan Steele had a soft side for his mom. That wasn't exactly how I remembered him in high school. Then again, neither was Lincoln.

The fact that the Steele brothers all seemed to have different sides than I recalled was kind of dangerous, actually.

"Hey," he said. "Came by to grab your car keys."

"I don't really think all this is necessary," Holly said,

waving a hand through the air. "It's only making that screechy-grinding noise once in a while."

Declan pinned her with a stare that would've had most people wetting themselves, but not his mother. "*Once* is too often for anything you describe as 'screechy-grinding,' Mom. Once in a while is *way* too fucking often. Hand 'em over."

Holly blew out an aggrieved sigh and glanced around, her smile brightening when she caught sight of something. "Ah! Penelope? Can you please grab my keys from behind the counter for Declan? I'm just in the middle of helping Willa over here."

That was news to me, but I wasn't about to interrupt to contradict her. Not when Penelope's whole body jolted and Declan stiffened like he was headed to face a firing squad.

"Um, sure..." Penelope fumbled a stack of books onto the cart as she glanced at Declan, her brows furrowing all while crimson stained her cheeks. Then she spun on her heel and headed to the checkout counter, not waiting for Declan to follow.

But, to my surprise, he did.

Strode straight toward her, his gait all confident swagger and don't fuck with me vibes. They didn't say a single word to each other—barely even *looked* at each other—but the tension between them was thick enough to bottle. Even after Declan strolled out the way he'd come, that tension didn't wane. Just hung in the air like it was waiting for ignition.

"Okay...what was *that*?" I asked, brows raised as I stared at Penelope.

She was trying to get back to work, but it was clear with the number of times she'd fumbled the books that her mind was elsewhere. My money was on a certain tattooed bad boy she could barely look at.

"Nothing," Holly said, amusement heavy in her tone. "*Yet*."

———

MY BACK WAS KILLING me and my left leg had gone numb a while ago, but I'd finally submitted the application for the grant.

Now, all I could do was wait.

Holly had left me to it about an hour ago and now sat perched on a stool nearby. Penelope had retreated into the stacks, no longer on high alert for a Steele brother to come swooping in.

Apparently, *I* was the one who should've been on high alert for that.

I was gathering up my things when the front door to the library opened, and the air shifted.

I glanced up to find Lincoln striding across the space in a worn T-shirt that molded to his chest, jeans that should've been illegal, and a grin tilted just enough to make my pulse skip. Especially when his eyes landed on me.

I froze as I stuffed papers into my bag, my entire body going stiff at his approach.

If he noticed my reaction, he hid it well. He didn't break stride as he headed toward me. Didn't hesitate when he reached me. Didn't pause for even a moment as he placed one hand on the table, the other on the back of my chair, and leaned down to kiss me.

Right on the mouth.

It wasn't lewd or graphic—nothing like our make-out session last night. No, this kiss was warm and steady. Comforting in a way it absolutely should not have been. Our lips met and held like we'd been kissing each other for years instead of exactly three times.

I sat frozen in my seat, but behind my mask, the world shifted. My pulse leapt into a gallop as I tried with everything in me not to melt into a puddle on the floor right there at his feet.

And then just as quick as he claimed me, he pulled back, that smug grin already in place and his eyes twinkling. "Knew I'd find you here, wife."

I blinked at him, slow and dazed, as my body tried to reboot itself. "What the hell was that?"

"A kiss." He cocked a brow. "Was that not obvious? Maybe I should do it again..."

Glaring up at him, I slammed my hand against his chest as he bent toward me. "You can't just walk into a public library and...and...*maul* someone in front of the Pride Month display!"

He raised a brow, his lips quirked in an amused smirk. "'Maul'? That's a pretty strong word for the way you leaned into it."

"I did *not*—"

"You did," he said, his grin widening. "Pretty enthusiastically too."

"You're *delusional*."

"Maybe. But I'm *your* delusional husband. And public displays of affection are part of the job requirement, remember?" His gaze dropped to my mouth as he licked a slow, mesmerizing path along his lower lip. "That's what all the practicing is for."

I ignored the swoop of my belly and the heat blooming in my cheeks. "The only thing you're practicing is how fast you can make me want to commit a felony in broad daylight."

"Well, we've already done it once—what's one more?"

"Lincoln," I hissed, darting a glance around to make sure no one heard him. "Jesus, you're like a child who can't keep a secret."

Even the glare I sent his way didn't deter his smile.

He just braced his ass against the table, crossing his ankles as he met my gaze. "It's a good thing you're hot when you're mad since you're pissed off at me ninety-nine percent of the time."

"Believe me when I say, you deserve it ninety-nine percent of the time."

"And the other one percent?"

I opened my mouth to respond, but nothing came out. I was blaming his impromptu visit and the short-circuiting of my brain for why I didn't have a comeback ready. That, of course, only made his grin widen.

Before he could piss me off more, Lincoln stood to his full height and, casual as ever, glanced to Holly. "You have that stack of romances for me, Mom?"

Holly split a grin between Lincoln and me before nodding and sliding off her stool. "Of course I do."

I blinked, certain I'd slipped into some kind of alternate reality. Because in what universe did a man casually source his smut from his mother? Of course the answer to that was *this* universe because Lincoln Steele existed in it, and that was totally on-brand for him.

"I just want to make sure I have this right," I said, watching Holly retrieve a stack of books from behind the counter before making her way toward us. "Your mom is your smut dealer?"

"Hell yeah, she is." He shrugged like it wasn't a big deal. "Head Librarians know their shit, wife. Why fuck around when I can go straight to the best source?"

Before I could respond to that, Holly dropped a stack of books on the table between us.

"Here you go, you two." She grinned, her eyes dancing as she shot us a wink. "Some light reading for the newlyweds."

"You're the best, Mom." He rested a hand on the back of my chair, close enough that his knuckles brushed my shoulder. "Can't wait to get home and dive into them. How about you, wife?"

He looked directly at me as he said it, the last word landing with all the subtlety of a rooster at sunrise. He'd said the words slow and intentional. Like he knew exactly what he was doing and using everything in his arsenal just to unravel me.

The electricity between us hummed so vibrantly, I didn't even realize Holly had left us until I heard her laughing with a silver fox at the checkout counter.

I shook myself out of whatever daze Lincoln had managed to put me in, hoping like hell he couldn't actually hear the rapid beat of my heart. "Stop saying wife like that."

"Like what?" he asked, his eyes scanning my face.

"Like you mean it."

He didn't deny it. In fact, he didn't say anything at all.

Instead, he gathered up my things, tucked them into my bag, and hefted it over his shoulder. Then he held out a hand for me.

"C'mon, hellcat. We're gonna get you some lunch. And then it's time for more practice."

CHAPTER FOURTEEN

WILLA

LINCOLN:

A vendor just showed up, and I'm not sure when I'll be done with them. If you get here while I'm still busy, grab Brooks to help you haul in the order.

WILLA:

Or how about I just do it myself?

LINCOLN:

Or how about you stop being a stubborn shit for one goddamn morning and let the able-bodied 22 yo kid do it?

WILLA:

You're a pain in my ass

LINCOLN:

Better than a pain in your back

IF LINCOLN SENT me one more text like he was the director of my day, I was going to stab him with a fork while he was sleeping. He could take his overprotective bossiness and shove it up his ass. Honestly, who did he think he was? My *keeper*?

I'd been living the chronic pain life for six years. I wasn't new to this. And in that time, not a single day had gone by when something didn't ache, pinch, stab, or radiate down my legs like hellfire. If I waited for a pain-free window to do things, I'd be rotting in the silo, getting absolutely nothing done, all while being buried under a mountain of unpaid bills.

So, no. I wasn't going to sit around with a heating pad waiting for Prince Charming with giant biceps, annoying dimples, and a rescue complex to show up.

I was going to do what I always did and get shit done.

I backed up my truck to the delivery door at One Night Stan's, already mentally organizing the crates of honey, syrups, and eggs by drop point. The bar was the first of many deliveries today, and I had it timed down to the minute. Which meant I wasn't going to wait around to grab someone to help.

Except I hadn't even turned off the ignition before Brooks came bounding out the back door.

"Morning, Willa," he called with a wave, already popping open the tailgate and pulling crates from the truck bed.

I opened my mouth to tell him to slow his roll, but he was already halfway to the door carrying three crates, so fine. *Fine.* If he was gonna be eager, I wasn't going to stop him. I still needed to make sure the back storage shelves were cleared and ready for the delivery anyway.

Inside the bar, the early morning quiet was almost eerie. No music, no crowd, no obnoxious husband. Just the gentle clink of glass as I checked the storage shelves, taking note of what they'd gone through and mentally adjusting for the next order.

By the time I turned around to head back outside, I expected six crates to be waiting by the door. What I did not expect was *all* of them.

Like, literally, all of them. Every single last one from the truck bed was stacked three high along the back wall.

Shit.

That wasn't just One Night Stan's order. That was *everyone's* order. The bar. The bakery. The café. The resort diner. Even the extra crates that were supposed to be dropped at Starlight Cove Resort for an event they were hosting this weekend.

I blinked, hoping maybe I was hallucinating from lack of caffeine. I wasn't.

"Goddammit," I muttered and rubbed at the tension setting up shop between my brows.

I glanced around, finding the culprit of this mayhem standing at a table near the front of the bar, earbuds in, head bopping to some beat only he could hear. Brooks moved to the rhythm as he set up the chairs and wiped down tables. Blissfully unaware of the chaos he'd just caused.

I dragged a hand down my face, exhaling hard.

Of course. Of *course* this was what happened the one time I let someone help.

Now, instead of staying on schedule and knocking out the rest of my deliveries on time, I was stuck hauling three-quarters of the inventory back to the truck, reorganizing everything in reverse order, and losing time I didn't have to give.

Twenty minutes later, I hoisted the final fuck-up crate into the truck with a grunt and turned toward the back door, only to come face-to-face with Lincoln.

His grin dropped the second he slid his gaze over me, clocking the crate I'd just shoved into the back of the truck. "Um, I gave express instructions that you weren't supposed to unload the truck."

"I didn't unload it," I said with an eye roll. "I'm *reloading* it."

"Why the fuck are you doing that?"

"Because your helper helped a little too much," I said, hands on my hips. "And now I need to get the orders reorganized and ready for the rest of my deliveries."

"If Brooks fucked up, then you tell him he fucked up and get him to unfuck his fuckup."

"Or I just do it myself and make sure it gets done right. Like I should've done in the first place. Besides, it was just a little bit of hauling."

His jaw ticked, drawing my attention to the thick layer of stubble he hadn't shaved off this morning. "Right. I didn't realize a *little bit* of hauling was okay for your back."

"Well, it is."

Lincoln didn't respond. Instead, he just stared. Not in a way that made heat lick over my skin like it had been doing, but in a way that made me feel cracked open and vulnerable.

Like he saw more than I wanted him to, adding up everything from the slight pinch between my brows to the stiff way I was moving and coming to the conclusion I was in pain.

News flash: I was always in pain.

"Uh-huh," he said flatly. "And how's your back doing now that you've done all this unfucking?"

"It's fine."

"Right."

I took a deep inhale, praying for patience I knew wouldn't come. No amount of breathing exercises could ease the constant friction between Lincoln and me.

"I'm *fine*," I bit out. "I've done these deliveries every week for *years*. And I haven't had Brooks with me to help with a single fucking one of them. I've handled it, and I've handled it fine. The deliveries get done and done right, and guess what? That all happens thanks to this one-woman show. So maybe stop acting like I need rescuing every time I lift something heavier than a coffee cup, and—are you even *listening* to me?"

Instead of responding, he turned around and strode back inside, walked behind the bar, and grabbed a piece of paper and a thick black Sharpie like I hadn't said a word. Then he started scrawling something so aggressively I was surprised the marker tip didn't snap off.

"Are you seriously writing a to-do list right now? What the *fuck*?"

It was only then that he met my gaze as he capped the marker, then tore off a piece of painter's tape. With his eyes still locked on mine, he slapped the paper to the back wall, rubbing his finger over the tape to make sure it stuck.

"I wasn't writing a to-do list," he said.

"Well, you sure as hell weren't listening to me."

"Oh, I was listening. I just don't believe the parts where you insist you're fine."

I shifted my gaze to the sign he'd taped to the wall. In thick black marker and underlined three extremely aggressive times, it read:

WILLA LIFTING BAN
IN EFFECT UNTIL FOREVER

"Oh my god," I seethed. "You're not serious."

"I'm *very* serious, wife." He crossed his obnoxiously muscled arms over his obnoxiously broad chest, standing guard next to the sign as if just daring me to rip the thing down.

"This is fucking ridiculous," I said. "*You're* fucking ridiculous. And I can't stand around arguing with you all day. I've still got deliveries to make, and I'm now almost half an hour behind."

He glanced out the open back door and to the truck bed with all the crates stacked inside. His mouth pinched into a firm line, his jaw ticking once. "I don't like that you're doing these by yourself."

"And I don't like that I married a jackass," I shot back, stalking out the back door. "Guess we'll both have to figure out how to go on with our days."

CHAPTER FIFTEEN

LINCOLN

Group text with Atlas, Xander, Declan, and Lincoln
9:57 a.m.

LINCOLN:

Need someone to cover my shift today.

ATLAS:

Again?

DECLAN:

Today as in right now?

XANDER:

This is becoming a habit, man.

LINCOLN:

So is pretending I can win an argument with my wife.

XANDER:

Not even remotely the point. Who else is on shift?

LINCOLN:

Just me and Brooks.

DECLAN:

Oh cool, the guy who set off the alarm three times in one day. I'm sure that'll be fine.

XANDER:

He's a solid pour, but that kid's scattered as fuck.

LINCOLN:

It's Monday. Mondays are graveyard slow.

I just need a warm body with enough brain cells to keep the lights on and not pour vodka into the fry oil.

ATLAS:

Can't. Training camp runs until 4.

DECLAN:

I've got back to backs all day.

XANDER:

I'm at the firehouse till 8 AM tomorrow.

Tell me again why you need to bail mid-shift?

LINCOLN:

Because I have a thing.

ATLAS:

What kind of thing?

LINCOLN:

Nothing bad. I just need the time.

DECLAN:

So vague. So very vague.

XANDER:

Do we need to be concerned or just
incredibly fucking annoyed?

ATLAS:

Just call Tasha and see if she can come in.

LINCOLN:

On her day off? Dick move.

DECLAN:

You texted all of us on OUR days off

LINCOLN:

Yeah, because this is YOUR bar. We don't
pay Tash enough to be on call for our
bullshit.

DECLAN:

So you admit this is bullshit

LINCOLN:

It's not bullshit. It's Willa.

ATLAS:

What's going on?

LINCOLN:

She's got deliveries today, and her back's acting up.

XANDER:

She's doing them by herself? Why??

LINCOLN:

Because she's stubborn as a fucking mule.

ATLAS:

Text Laurel. See if she can help.

LINCOLN:

Run the bar??

DECLAN:

Pretty sure he means help Willa with deliveries, dipshit

LINCOLN:

Genius move

WILLA:

You want to tell me why tf Laurel showed up as soon as I pulled up to the bakery and started hauling shit like she's being paid for it?

LINCOLN:

Because she's being paid for it.

WILLA:

Wtf, jackass? Are you serious right now?

LINCOLN:

Dead serious. That girl negotiates like a mob boss.

WILLA:

I don't have the cash flow to pay another employee! That's the entire reason I'm in this nightmare marriage in the first place.

LINCOLN:

Don't worry about it, wife.

WILLA:

Don't worry about it? DON'T WORRY ABOUT IT? This is MY business.

LINCOLN:

And you're MY wife. Just making sure you don't break before I can return you.

WILLA:

You are the fucking worst.

LINCOLN:

And yet.

Here we are.

Legally wed.

Full tax benefits.

WILLA:

I'm going to tie you to the bed and smother you in your sleep

LINCOLN:

Kinky. Text it slower next time.

CHAPTER SIXTEEN

LINCOLN

THE FOLLOWING WEEK, I was in the middle of gathering eggs from the chicken coop when a crash sounded through the open windows of the silo. Then a bitten-off string of colorful curses came from Willa—words so foul, even Mabel would've blushed.

I didn't hesitate. Just dropped the basket and ran toward the house. That wasn't just *any* string of curse words. That was Willa breaking and trying like hell to pretend everything was fine because that was her default setting.

I burst through the door at full speed, my gaze darting around the scene in front of me. Willa stood hunched against the counter, white-knuckling the edge like it was the only thing holding her up. A crumpled crate of broken jam jars lay in a mess at her feet—shards of glass everywhere, along with red streaks I hoped to hell were jam.

But that wasn't what stopped me cold.

It was her face. Her mouth was pressed in a thin line, her

cheeks flushed and tightness bracketing her eyes—a pinched expression screaming only one thing. Pain.

She glanced up, caught me in the doorway, and attempted to wipe her expression clear. "I'm fine."

No. *Fuck* no.

I was done playing this game with her, and I was mad as hell she was still trying to bullshit me.

"You're not," I said, striding toward her.

"Lincoln, I said—"

"Don't care." I stepped over the glass and scooped her into my arms before she could flinch away from me.

She gasped, her eyes going wide as she placed a hand on my chest. "This is insane. I'm—"

"Fine? Yeah, I've heard the line before," I muttered, adjusting her in my arms to take any pressure off her lower back. "Try something new."

"This is overkill, even for you," she hissed as I headed for the stairs. "You're being ridiculous."

I didn't answer right away. Couldn't. Not when I was so focused on the way she was shifting in my grip—not from pain but from sheer resistance. Like accepting help was some kind of mortal sin in her world.

I gritted my teeth and tightened my hold. "You're gonna hurt yourself worse by trying to prove a point. You really wanna be down for a week instead of just tonight?"

She opened her mouth to argue, but nothing came out.

"Yeah," I muttered. "Thought so."

Once we were upstairs, I strode straight to the bed and laid her down as gently as possible. She grimaced as soon as her spine met gravity, and I had to fight the overwhelming urge to punch a wall. I fucking knew I shouldn't have listened to her all the times she said she was fine and she could handle everything. That she didn't need my help.

Stubbornness was going to be her—and my—downfall.

"Lincoln—"

"I'll be right back."

She started to sit up, but I sent her a look that froze her in place.

"That wasn't an invitation for you to move, wife. Just sit your sweet ass right there until I come back."

The scowl she shot me was one for the record books, but, for once, she didn't argue. That, in itself, screamed volumes.

I stalked downstairs, not bothering to tread lightly. Because yeah—I was pissed and had reached my limits with this entire situation. I wasn't mad at *her*—not really. I was mad at the fact that she was obviously in daily agony and still trying to pretend she didn't need anything from anyone, least of all me. Worse, she acted like I was somehow inconveniencing her by giving a damn about my wife.

While her microwavable heating pad was warming up, I grabbed a water bottle and found her stash of pot gummies she kept in the pantry next to the dried lavender. I wasn't wasting time with over-the-counter painkillers because they wouldn't do shit when her back was this bad. She needed the good stuff.

When I made it back upstairs, she was exactly where I'd left her, and that told me everything I needed to know.

She was hurting. Badly.

After setting everything on the nightstand, I got to work. I grabbed some extra pillows from under the bed and adjusted them how she liked—two behind her back, two beneath her knees, and one under each arm...a perfect little cocoon. Once she was situated as comfortably as she could be, I helped her sit up and slid the warmed heating pad between her back and the pillows.

"This is ridiculous," she muttered. "I can—"

"Just sit your ass there and let me help."

She snapped her mouth shut and huffed out an irritated breath but allowed me to do as I'd asked.

I grabbed a gummy and held it out to her. "Take this."

"You're overreacting."

"You're *under*reacting. Now, take it."

Without a word, she snatched the gummy from my hand, popped it into her mouth, and chewed before washing it down with water.

"I hate this," she muttered, avoiding my eyes. "Being weak."

"You're *not* weak," I said, sharper than I should have, considering the amount of pain she was in. But *fuck.* "You're anything but weak, hellcat. You deal with unimaginable pain every day and just go about your life as usual. What you *are*, though, is so goddamn stubborn that you'd rather crawl across broken glass than admit you need help."

She snapped her gaze to me, eyes wide and lips parted as she blinked at me and my rising ire in surprise. "Um...where's *this* coming from?"

"Fuck if I know." I sat on the edge of the bed, careful not

to jostle her, and braced my elbows on my knees. "I'm just... tired, Willa."

"Of what?" she asked, her expression wary and guarded like she thought I was tired of *her*.

"Don't do that shit—I can see it written across your face that you think my helping you for all of five fucking minutes is reason enough for me to be sick of it. When actually, I'm tired of watching you destroy yourself just to prove some bullshit point no one ever asked you to make. And I'm tired of wanting to help you but getting shut down every fucking time like I'm offering you poison instead of a fucking heating pad."

My voice grew louder with each word as I finally released this frustration that had been bottling up inside for weeks, months... Years.

She stared at me in shock, her mouth opening and closing several times before she finally cleared her throat. "You're... mad."

"Yeah, I'm fucking mad."

"But you're *never* mad."

I huffed out a bitter laugh. "Yeah, well. I've never had a wife who's hell-bent on not allowing herself to need anyone, and it's pissing me off."

Her breath caught, and for a second, I worried I'd said too much. Pushed her too far. But, fuck. It was true.

From the sidelines, I'd been watching her suffer for years. But having an up close and personal viewing of it since being married was an entirely different beast. And it had only been *two weeks*.

She wasn't *thriving* on her own. She was barely surviving.

And I wasn't going to stand by and watch her struggle alone anymore.

I didn't care if this marriage wasn't real to her, or if we'd only entered it with the end already in mind. I was here, and I was hers—for now anyway. And I was going to act like it.

After a beat, I stood, strode around the bed to my side, and climbed in next to her. I didn't say a word. Just stretched out, one arm tucked behind my head and the other reaching for her. I ran my fingertips gently over the inside of her forearm. Featherlight and soothing.

It took a while, but eventually, she started to soften under my touch. Her breathing slowed as she unclenched her jaw and unfurled her fingers, her whole body seeming to finally exhale.

"Most people would've gone straight for my back and tried to massage the hell out of it," she murmured into the quiet space.

"I'm not most people."

The added stimulation in that area would only make her pain flare brighter, which I knew because of something she'd mentioned years ago. But I was hoping if I could distract her mind with gentle, soft movements and get her nervous system to calm down, even a little, she'd be able to find a sliver of peace.

She slid me a look out of the corner of her eye. "How'd you know?"

I lifted a single shoulder. "I pay attention."

Her expression softened. Like maybe she was allowing herself the briefest moment to admit she didn't hate being taken care of and didn't hate that I was the one doing the caring.

Silence fell again as I continued running soft fingertips over her skin and she continued letting me. It was more than I'd hoped for, so I was going to take it and do it for as long as she'd allow.

"If I weren't renting out the farmhouse, I'd soak for an hour in that big claw-foot tub," she murmured, her voice wistful. "I even thought about asking Jeff to build me something on the porch over here. An outdoor soaking tub of some kind."

Excuse the fuck out of me?

I slowly turned my head toward her. "You thought about asking *Jeff* to do this for you?"

"Jeff...the handyman?" she asked, clearly confused. "Yeah, why?"

"Nothing. Whatever." My voice came out harsher than I meant it to. "I can be handy too."

She huffed out a laugh, her eyes already closing again. "It's no big deal. Just an idea..."

I didn't say anything in response, but I clenched my jaw hard enough that it popped. *Jeff.* She was gonna ask Jeff. Like I didn't have two perfectly good hands, a YouTube app, and a possibly unhealthy obsession with making her life easier.

If she needed something, her husband sure as shit would take care of it for her, not fucking Jeff.

Willa shifted, wincing before she could hide it, and I was immediately on alert.

"What do you need? Another gummy?"

"You trying to get me high as fuck? I'm not making out with you again."

"Right *now*, you mean." I grinned as she rolled her eyes. "And I'm just trying to get you comfortable. How can I do that?"

She adjusted herself again, her face pinching in pain before she settled against the bed and the lines bracketing her mouth finally relaxed. She closed her eyes and blew out a long, steady breath. "Distract me, please."

Somehow, I didn't think she meant with another day of practice.

"How about a little educational reading?" I reached over to the nightstand and grabbed the book she'd been reading every night before bed—the one she'd gotten from Penelope. *Plowed by His Seeder*. "Farmer boys do it for you now, wife?"

"I don't need any commentary from you," she said dryly. "Just read, Linc."

So that was exactly what I did.

I flipped to the page where she'd left off and read the words aloud. This chapter started innocent enough with the two characters dancing around each other. But I wasn't even three pages in before he was stripping her in the barn loft and bending her over a hay bale.

Willa's cheeks flushed a deep pink and her breathing quickened, but she didn't ask me to stop. She just lay there with her eyes shut, her body as close to comfortable as possible, and listened to me.

Somewhere between the farmer eating out the milkmaid and him plowing her with his *seeder*, Willa drifted off, her head falling softly to my shoulder. I closed the book and set it aside. Then, as gently as I could, I lifted my arm and tucked her into my side, allowing her to settle against me.

I bent my head and took a deep inhale, closing my eyes as I realized I'd become the hair-sniffing pervert I'd been trying to avoid. But right now, with Willa in my arms, her body relaxed enough to rest against me, I didn't care.

CHAPTER SEVENTEEN

LINCOLN

THE BAR always felt different before opening. There wasn't the low thrum of music or the steady hum of voices. No clatter of glasses, no rowdy laughter, no chaos. Just the sunlight filtering through the tall front windows, shining a spotlight on the four of us.

Like we'd done a hundred times before, my brothers and I had all claimed our usual spots. Atlas sat at the end of the bar, coffee cup in front of him. Xander was a couple stools down, the ledger spread out as he pored over it. Declan reclined in his high-backed stool, his booted feet kicked up on a chair as he demolished a donut. I stood behind the bar, towel slung over my shoulder, arms crossed as I leaned back against the counter.

Our little family ritual—the Steele version of church.

And today, I had something to confess.

I'd been putting this off for far too long. Shoving it aside and figuring it could wait for another day. At least while I'd been the only one suffering.

But after the past couple weeks of watching my wife work herself to the bone while stubbornly refusing to ask for help, and then witnessing one of her severe pain flares in action, I'd hit my breaking point. Whether she asked for my help or not, I wasn't going to leave her to handle shit on her own anymore.

I cleared my throat. "We need to talk about the bar."

All three of them lifted their gazes to mine, their unspoken questions hanging in the air.

Finally, Declan broke the silence. "What? Mabel finally talk you into hosting strip karaoke?"

I huffed out a laugh and shook my head. "Not quite. Though she tried. Twice."

"What is it?" Xander asked, getting straight to the point.

I took a deep breath and glanced to each of them in turn. "We need to make some changes around here."

Atlas's gaze was steady on me, as unflinching as always. "What kinds of changes?"

"The same thing I've been talking about for a year." I blew out a deep exhale. "I can't keep devoting all my time here. Not anymore."

"Because of the farm?" Xander asked.

"Because of Willa," I corrected. "She's too fucking stubborn to admit that she can't do it all on her own. And god fucking forbid she *ask* for help. She could be on her literal deathbed and still be trying to do it all on her own. She's drowning—"

"And you're not about to let your wife sink," Atlas interrupted as he settled back in his stool, arms crossed.

I shook my head. "Not if I can do something to stop it."

"Okay, well..." Xander split a glance between Atlas and Declan before turning back to me. "What does this look like? Lay it on us."

I braced my hands on the counter and met each of their unwavering stares. "I want to promote Tasha to manager. She's already been working that role for months when one of us isn't here. She deserves the title and the raise that comes with it. And I deserve a break."

I held my breath, waiting for their arguments. Atlas would raise concerns about promoting someone who wasn't in the family, Xander would pull out the books and say we didn't have enough cash flow, and Declan would throw a wrench in the whole thing with some kind of bullshit.

Instead, silence descended. Long enough that I damn near choked on it.

Finally, Atlas grunted. "She in today?"

That...wasn't what I expected.

I cleared my throat. "Yeah. After lunch."

"Sounds like a good time to do it," Xander said, taking a sip of his coffee like we were talking about the weather and not changing the structure of our family business. "You think her wife is gonna be okay with her taking on this responsibility? I don't want Robyn on my ass."

"Um. Yeah..." I said slowly, still waiting for the other shoe to drop. "Tash mentioned they're saving to buy a house, so this'll be welcome."

Declan raised a brow. "This mean we all get fewer shifts?"

"No, dumbass." I reached to smack him upside the head, but he dodged me with a low chuckle. "Just me. I don't see any of you fuckers pulling sixty-hour weeks behind the bar."

Dec shrugged and shoved the rest of his donut into his mouth. "Fair enough."

"Wait...that's it?" I asked.

The corner of Atlas's mouth twitched—Brick Wall's version of a beaming smile. "Seems like you were waiting for a fight."

"Maybe because that's all I've gotten every other time I've brought this up?"

Atlas lifted one giant shoulder. "Well, you're not going to get one this time."

"Seriously?"

The three of them exchanged a glance so quick, I would've missed it if I'd blinked.

Xander dipped his chin in a nod. "Seriously."

"I've been trying to get you three to agree with this for a fucking year," I said, eyeing each of them. "And now you're all just suddenly good with it?"

"Yeah, well, you *suddenly* got yourself a wife." Xander shared a look with Atlas and shrugged. "Things change."

His meaning was crystal clear when Atlas grunted his agreement—they'd both had their lives shifted dramatically in the past year. First Atlas when Sutton and Laurel had moved in to town, right in his backyard. And then Xander when he had not one but two bombshells land in his lap—his four-year-old daughter he hadn't known about and the supposed-to-be-temporary nanny who'd made the three of them a family.

"You've been holding this place together on your own for

years, Linc." Atlas braced his forearms on the bar top and leaned forward, leveling me with a steady gaze. "About fucking time you get a break if you want one."

For a second, I couldn't speak. Which, for me, was saying something. I could only stare at them, my throat tightening without my permission.

Finally, my voice coming out rough, I said, "You all feeling okay? Is someone dying? Because this level of emotional maturity from the Steele men is...unsettling, to say the least."

Atlas snorted, Xander flipped me off, and something in my chest eased for the first time in a while.

I turned to Declan, who'd been uncharacteristically quiet. "What about you?"

He tipped his chair back, his arms crossed, expression completely unreadable. "You're the one who's been stuck here."

"I haven't been *stuck* here. I love this place." I ran my hand over the worn, scuffed wood of the bar. "Always have."

"But you love something else more right now," Atlas said, his voice steady and sure. "And she needs you."

His words hit me harder than I expected, that four-letter word in regard to Willa landing like a bomb. But that was exactly what everyone was supposed to think—that I was head over heels in love with my wife and putting her first.

I was playing my role well, apparently.

"Yeah. She does."

"How bad is it, really?" Atlas asked. "With the farm."

My jaw tightened as I recalled exactly how hard Willa was working, day in and day out. And she was mostly on her own because the only workers she could afford were high schoolers who weren't exactly known for their reliability.

"Bad," I said. "She's been holding it together with sheer will alone, but she's paying for it. I wouldn't be surprised if the whole thing crumbled with one missed step."

Xander's brow furrowed. "And she won't ask for help?"

"Fuck no." I shook my head, jaw flexing as I thought of just how much pain she'd been in the other day. So much so, she'd taken it easy yesterday, and that had been all I needed to know. "She'd rather break her back than admit she can't do it alone. And I'm afraid she's actually going to."

Atlas folded his hands together and leaned forward. "Laurel needs a fuck-ton of service hours before graduation. Helping a local business would count. She'd be a shitshow with anything public-facing, but you know she's a good kid. And she'd show up when she's supposed to and work hard. As long as Willa wouldn't have a problem with a surly, sarcastic teenager who says 'fuck' too much."

I pictured Laurel stomping through the fields, eyes rolling as she and Willa bitched and bonded over the idiots they didn't have time for. "She's going to kill one of us for this."

"Which *she* are you talking about?" Xander asked.

I cringed, thinking of how my wife was going to respond to this. "Both of them."

"I can't wait to watch," Declan said, popping another donut into his mouth.

"Separately, I think we can probably take either of them." Atlas ran a hand over his beard, brow furrowed. "If they team up, though, we're fucked."

Snorts and murmurs of agreement went up all around

because that much was definitely true—those two together would be a tornado of hellfire.

"We can help too, you know," Xander said. "Dec might need any instruction spelled out in crayon so he can catch on—"

"Oh, fuck you." Declan kicked Xander's chair, but there was a smirk curving his lips.

Xander's mouth twitched before he turned serious again. "I'm just saying, we can step in. No one in the family drowns on our watch."

I glanced at each of my brothers—Atlas, always steady. Xander, thorough and thoughtful. Declan, perpetually pretending not to care but paying attention more than anyone realized.

In the face of their unwavering support, I realized just how fiercely I'd been preparing for a pushback that never came. They weren't just fine with me stepping back. They were ready to step up to help to make sure everything was handled. Because that was what family did.

And, whether this marriage was real or not, Willa was now included in that.

CHAPTER EIGHTEEN

LINCOLN

I NEVER THOUGHT I'd be happily spending my mornings elbow-deep in the chicken coop, but here we were. Turned out, I liked helping my wife. Liked knowing that my helping was easing her day just a bit. Even if everything I did pissed her off.

It was worth her irritation knowing she'd get a break.

I'd just gathered the last of today's eggs when my phone buzzed in my pocket. Probably a Mom Situation or some kind of minor catastrophe at the bar. I wiped my hands on my sweatpants and pulled out my phone, doing a double take at the incoming call.

Beau's name flashed on the screen along with a picture of the three of us standing in front of a tractor when we were about ten years old.

"Fuck." I stared at the screen for a solid three seconds before accepting my fate and hitting answer.

"Hey, man," I said, keeping my tone light.

No idea what this could be about. Definitely not me marrying your sister in secret or anything.

My best friend didn't bother with pleasantries. "Any reason Mabel's shopping for a wedding gift on my behalf?"

Closing my eyes, I dropped my head back on my shoulders and let out a silent groan toward the sky. Fuck me, that meddling old woman was on my shit list.

I cleared my throat and played dumb. "When it comes to Mabel, really anything's possible."

"Cut the shit, Linc," he said, his voice clipped. "You want to tell me why the hell I'm hearing about a courthouse wedding from someone who isn't my twin or my best fucking friend?"

I cringed and scrubbed a hand down my face, knowing I deserved every ounce of his righteous fury. "Okay, to be fair, it was a very small wedding. Just me, Willa, the judge, and an intern who looked high as fuck."

The silence on the other end of the line practically roared, and I'd never been more thankful that he was half a world away than I was right now.

I grinned, brittle and fake. "I figured you'd appreciate not having to rent a tux or give a toast. I thought I was doing you a favor."

It was quiet for several long moments before his voice came through, low and lethal. "You better not be taking advantage of her."

I jerked back like he'd punched me. "What the fuck, man? You think I'd do that to her?"

"What I think is you've been into her for years, and now,

suddenly, you're *married*? When she does nothing but bitch and moan about you whenever we talk?"

I forced out a laugh. "This might be awkward for you to hear, but that's her version of foreplay."

Unfortunately, he didn't bite at my taunt. He always was like a dog with a bone when he got his mind set on something.

"I don't buy it," he said. "You and I both know she's not the impulsive type. So if she married you this quickly, there has to be a reason for it. And it ain't love."

His words hit harder than they should have, considering that was true. This wasn't about love. Just two not-quite-friends-but-not-quite-enemies partnering up to get shit done.

"That's exactly what I've been missing since you've been gone," I said, keeping my tone light. "You telling me how unlovable I am before noon."

"Don't fuck with her," he said, his tone devoid of any humor. "I mean it, Linc. If you hurt her, you and I are going to have a real fucking problem."

I blew out a breath, trying to keep my voice easy. "Noted. And hey, I'll tell your sister you said hi."

He hung up without another word—not that I blamed him since that was a dick move on my part. I stared at the screen longer than I should've, my thumb hovering over the end call button that had already gone dark.

The worst part of that conversation was he hadn't been wrong. Willa hadn't come to me for love. She'd come to me because she'd been backed into a corner. I'd said yes because she needed help.

And, well, because it was her. Simple as that.

For a long time, I'd seen the cracks forming around her foundation, the pressure getting to be too much for her to handle. And I thought that maybe I could ease some of that burden just a bit. If she got to save her legacy in the process? That was a win all around.

That was all this was. Had to be. Because I wasn't ready to gamble away my relationship with my best friend on a maybe or what-if with the girl who'd been my teenage—and adult—fantasy.

I jammed the phone back into my pocket and headed toward the silo. Willa was absolutely going to freak out when I told her this, but she needed to know her brother was asking questions.

It didn't matter whether this thing between us was fake, real, or something in between. I wasn't going to let her dream go up in smoke because we hadn't kept Beau in the loop.

CHAPTER NINETEEN

WILLA

I COULD TELL something was off the second Lincoln stepped inside.

He wasn't whistling like he usually did when he came back from the coop, wasn't cracking a joke, wasn't smirking at me like he had a secret. Instead, he just shut the door behind himself and stood against it, his eyes locked on mine.

"What?" I asked, stomach already in knots for some unknown reason.

He blew out a heavy sigh and ran a hand through his hair. "Just got off the phone with your brother."

I stilled, my breath caught in my throat as a wave of heat washed over me before everything went cold.

"Shit. *Shit*." I tried to get a read on Lincoln's expression, but for once, it was locked up tight. "What did he say?"

"That he heard about our marriage from Mabel," he said evenly. "Wasn't thrilled."

I exhaled a shaky breath and bit my thumbnail. "Okay.

Okay. That's fine. Totally fine, right? Him knowing right now isn't the end of the world."

But it *could* be. If Beau pushed or if the wrong person overheard something... If, somehow, the grant board got wind of Lincoln's and my not-so-holy union before we even had the opportunity to advance in the process.

"You're right," Lincoln said evenly. "It's not the end of the world."

Except I didn't quite believe him.

I grabbed a rag and started wiping down the already clean counter, like maybe if I scrubbed hard enough, I could rewind time. "We just need to keep things quiet for a bit longer. The final round is an in-person interview, and if we make it that far—"

"We will," he said, his voice a hell of a lot surer than I felt.

"If we do, I'll talk to him after. Or you will. We both can —it doesn't matter. We're just going to have to avoid him until then."

Lincoln stared at me for a long moment, his gaze assessing. "If that's what you want."

I breathed out a hysterical laugh. "Oh, it's definitely not what I want. But I don't see us having another choice."

As if connecting with Beau so infrequently since he'd been away wasn't bad enough. Now, I had this huge secret I couldn't share driving an even bigger wedge between us.

I started pacing again, too many thoughts flying through my head to contain my movement. "I should clean out the cupboards. Or maybe reorganize the pantry. Actually, I'll do the spices. I've been meaning to—"

"Willa." Lincoln's voice was quiet. Firm.

I froze with a jar of coriander in my hand and glanced at him.

He strode toward me slowly, like he had all the time in the world. Like I wasn't over here freaking the fuck out. "You're spiraling."

"I'm not," I lied.

He just grinned, soft and sure. Like he knew me. Knew what I needed and was ready to give it to me. I glanced away from him, staring at the jars in front of me instead.

"Look at me, wife."

I definitely could not do that. Not when he had this... this...*way* about him, all magnetic and charming. And not when I was already at my breaking point, afraid of what I might do if it all came crumbling down.

So instead, I focused on the curve of his collarbone where it peeked out from the tattered neckline of his favorite T-shirt. Smooth, golden skin, all firm and strong and—*god*. Looking there had been a giant mistake. Forget forearm porn. This man had *collarbone* porn, and I was sure he could charge admission to the show.

He grabbed the jars from my hands and set them on the counter before stepping into me. So close, my breasts brushed his chest with every inhale.

Wrapping an arm around me, he settled his hand gently on my lower back, his fingers brushing the curve of my ass. "How about some practice?" he asked, his voice low. "I've heard it's good for grounding."

I huffed out an incredulous laugh and shook my head. "You think your mouth is enough to fix my freak-out?"

His grin was slow and wicked, and I felt it straight to my toes. "You tell me."

My gaze dropped to his lips, and every response I could've given him died in my throat. The rebuttals evaporated into thin air when he leaned down, his breath skimming my cheek. Floated away as he trailed his hand up, slipping his fingertips under the hem of my shirt. Just disappeared completely when he placed a soft, tentative kiss on the corner of my mouth.

"Just relax, hellcat," he murmured against my lips. "Let me take care of you."

I was so tired of fighting—of holding everything up—that for once, I just...didn't. I didn't put up a fight. Didn't add any friction solely for the sake of being contrary. I needed to be swept away—to forget about the shitshow that was my life.

And I was going to let Lincoln do just that.

The first kiss was gentle. Teasing. The second was a promise of what was to come. And the third? Well, it had no business in a fake marriage. Not when every moment of it felt like Lincoln was pouring all of his focus into learning the shape of my mouth and memorizing the exact tenor of my moans.

This practice session may have started sweet, but it quickly shifted into something more. Into Lincoln taking... *claiming*. Stealing my breath like it belonged to him and kissing me like he was starved for my taste.

I gasped when he bit my bottom lip, moaned when he brushed his tongue against it to soothe the sting. He gripped my hips tightly, like he knew one of us was about to lose control.

I just had no idea it would be me.

CHAPTER TWENTY

WILLA

AFTER LINCOLN SLANTED his mouth against mine, deepening the kiss enough to make my clit throb, I snapped, suddenly, overwhelmingly needing *more*.

I gripped his shoulders, hooking a leg over his hip like I could climb right up his body. Like maybe being closer would settle this hum burning under my skin.

"Jesus, Willa." He anchored a hand beneath my thigh and held me there. "Your back..."

"Is fine," I murmured against his mouth, my hands tight around his neck. "Just don't stop."

He didn't. Instead, he groaned and lifted me like I weighed nothing. Like carrying me, *handling* me, was second nature for him.

And through it all, he didn't let up. His kisses were intoxicating in a way I was tired of fighting. Really, what was the big deal if I liked kissing my fake husband? What was so bad about wanting to grind my pussy against him? About satisfying this need inside me that I couldn't ever achieve with anyone else?

With my ass cupped in his hands, he walked over and sank down into one of the armchairs. He leaned back, his thighs spread, his body a solid wall of muscle beneath me. I settled on top of him, my legs straddling his, and whimpered when the head of his cock brushed against my clit just right.

"*Willa*," he growled, rough and needy. He clenched his hands against my hips, whether to hold me still or guide me over him, I didn't know. "You said just kissing. Nothing more."

I froze for half a second, the pounding of my heart and my clit overriding common sense. Overriding every ounce of self-preservation I had. "I changed my mind."

He stared at me for long moments, his gaze sweeping over me in a way that felt filthier than anyone's touch ever had. Finally, he swore under his breath and lifted his hands from my body to settle them on the arms of the chair instead. His eyes were heavy lidded, his pupils blown wide as he stared at me.

"You made me promise, hellcat. Made me swear I couldn't charm your panties off."

"You're not charming me," I said, desperate now. I didn't think I'd ever felt so hot...so *needy*...in my entire life. "Just touch me."

"That's what you want?"

"I just told you it was. Don't make me beg for it."

"You want my hands on you? You want my mouth? Want me to flip you over and fuck that attitude you love to give me so damn much straight out of you?"

I couldn't hope to hold back a whimper or my frantic nod as I envisioned each of those scenarios. Who the hell *was* this man? And why the hell did I like him so much?

Lincoln leaned in, close enough that he caught my bottom lip with his teeth and tugged. "Tough shit. You already set the rules, Willa. And now we're gonna play by them."

Groaning, I closed my eyes, gripping his shoulders tightly as I rocked over him again, my entire body shaking with need.

"You're being a jackass," I said a lot breathier than I intended.

"And you're being a brat. I gave you a promise, and I'm going to keep it."

"I hate you for this," I said, though it came out sounding a hell of a lot like, *make me come.*

"I tell you what, wife." He leaned back, arms spread, looking like a damn king, all cocky and sure, and I hated how much I loved it.

"What?"

He glanced between us, his jaw ticking. His attention was locked on where I was grinding against him, my shorts already dark with my arousal. "If you still want it when the front of my sweats aren't wet from your sweet little pussy, I'll give it to you. Whatever you want, whenever you want it. But right now, you're gonna take what you need from me."

It was so goddamn tempting. Especially when I felt like I was burning up from the inside out. Like I was finally on the precipice of something that had always been just out of reach.

But I couldn't...could I?

This was Lincoln, the man who'd been a burr in my side for more than a decade. The pain in the ass I usually couldn't get away from fast enough. I shifted in his lap, ready to climb off and scurry my way upstairs because this was absolute madness. But his cock settled right between my pussy lips, and I gasped as he dropped his head back on a groan.

Then I swore I felt him *jerk* against me, and all I could do was stare.

Somehow, I'd reduced Lincoln Steele to this—his entire body straining like he was seconds from coming undone—just by sitting in his lap. And that feeling was intoxicating as hell.

Without any input from my brain, my hips rolled over him again. Intentional this time, a slow drag against his cock, and I shuddered out a moan. God, this felt so damn good. The lace of my panties rubbed a tantalizing abrasion against my swollen clit, so I did it again.

And again.

And again.

And then I stopped pretending to hold myself back. I let myself go. Allowed myself just to feel and began rocking against him in earnest.

"Jesus Christ, look at you." He stared down between us, his voice dropping to a harsh whisper. "So wet, I can feel you through the fabric. You're so fucking desperate for it, aren't you, wife? You can't help but use me to make that perfect cunt come."

"*God,*" I choked out, collapsing against his chest. No longer caring what this looked like, what I sounded like, or what he was getting out of it.

For once, I only focused on how I felt.

"That's it," he said, low and encouraging. Like he was getting off on my pleasure alone. "Just like that. Rub that needy little clit on my cock. Make yourself feel good, hellcat."

Something between a moan and a sob slipped out of my mouth as I pressed down harder, rolled my hips faster, gripped his shoulders tighter.

"There you go. Fuck, that's my girl. So goddamn sweet when you ride me like this—like you fucking *own* me. So gorgeous when you stop pretending you don't want this."

That was exactly what I was doing. All the pretenses were gone now. And the only thing left was this need I couldn't hope to hide.

"I want you to touch me so bad." I dug my fingers into his shoulders, my forehead pressed to his as I rocked over him.

He let out a long, low curse, his hands tightening on the chair. But still, he didn't move them. "I do too, baby. So fucking bad. Want to fill my hands with your perfect tits. Want to suck on your clit until you forget your own name. Want to swallow every bit of your come."

"Fuck," I whispered on a shudder, a buzz skating through my body at the combination of the feelings coursing through me and his words.

My sexual experiences were few and lackluster, to say the least. I'd definitely never been spoken to like this before. And I'd had no idea just how much I'd *love* it. Love how wild and free and *wanted* it made me feel.

"I bet you taste so fucking sweet, don't you? Think I could get you to ride my face just like this? Grind that gorgeous pussy down on me until I can't breathe? If your cunt was the last thing I tasted, I'd die a happy man, wouldn't I, wife?"

"Linc—" I gasped, shuddering as my pussy clenched around nothing, for the first time in a long time desperate to be *filled* completely.

He gripped the chair so hard, his knuckles turned white. But still, his words, dark and filthy, kept coming. Kept cranking me higher. "Come on, wife. Soak my pants. Show me how fucking good it feels when you lose control."

I had absolutely no hope of staying grounded after that. Not when his panting breaths matched mine. Not when my nipples were tight points, tingling with sensation. Not when I could feel him, hard as stone beneath me...right where I needed him.

I pressed my forehead against his as I rocked harder. Faster. Seeking more, even as my thighs shook and my stomach coiled tight, preparing for something I wasn't sure I'd survive.

"Every time you roll that sweet pussy over me, I can feel how close you are. How bad you need to come. And you know what, hellcat?" He stared between us, his gaze locked on where I soaked the front of his sweatpants. "You're gonna do it. My pretty girl is gonna come just like this—still dressed, still in charge. All over your husband's cock. And you're gonna fucking love it."

Everything centered to one point inside me before the explosion hit, bright and vibrant and earth-shattering. My orgasm tore through me so violently, I couldn't speak. I just collapsed against him, bit down on his shoulder, and cried out as my body broke apart. Lightning crashed through me, every inch inside me going hot and tight before coming completely undone.

"*Fuck.*" Lincoln's head dropped back on a savage groan, his hips surging up to meet mine.

And this time, I was sure I felt it—his cock pulsed against me as he came, his body rigid beneath me, one long, drawn-out curse spilling from his lips.

Only then did he release his hold on the chair to cup my jaw and tug my face to his. He kissed me. Gently. Reverently. So different from the filth we'd just partaken in.

And I couldn't do anything but kiss him back because I didn't trust my thoughts or my voice. Didn't trust how hard my heart was galloping in my chest or how my whole body felt wrecked and ravaged and yet somehow completely new.

Not because of what he'd done to me, but because of what he *hadn't.*

He hadn't touched me. Hadn't taken over. Hadn't demanded anything in return. And still, I'd unraveled in his lap like a ball of yarn knotted too tight with one string pulled just right.

Something I'd never done before in my life. Not with a partner... Not with anyone.

So I kissed him because I couldn't look at him. Not yet. If I did, I was scared I'd see something I wasn't ready for.

Or worse—something I already felt that I didn't want to admit.

CHAPTER TWENTY-ONE

LINCOLN

A FEW HOURS after the hottest thing I'd ever been lucky enough to witness, I lay next to Willa in the dark. Since falling apart on top of me, she'd been scarce. She'd scurried off my lap and immediately headed up to shower. Then she'd kept herself busy being anywhere but around me.

This was the first time in hours she'd been in my vicinity for more than thirty seconds. I was surprised her stubborn ass had crawled into bed instead of setting up camp outside just so she could avoid me a bit longer.

Apparently, though, the cloak of darkness was avoidance enough.

The lights were off, she'd put away her book, and she lay as still as a corpse beside me. The room had settled into the kind of quiet that usually put me to sleep in thirty seconds flat. But tonight? I couldn't stop grinning.

I could still feel the imprint of her fingers digging into my shoulders, her breath hot against my lips, and the sounds she'd made when she'd shuddered and shaken above me, grinding her way to the kind of orgasm people wrote books about. All while we were both fully clothed.

So, yeah. I was pretty damn proud of myself.

"I can feel your smugness all the way over here," she muttered, breaking the silence.

I smirked toward the ceiling. "That obvious?"

"You're basically vibrating with it."

"Can't help it. I have a hell of a lot to be smug about." I tucked the arm closest to her behind my head and turned my face in her direction. "You remember. You were there."

There was a long, quiet pause. Then she muttered, "You don't even know the half of it."

I raised one brow, my interest piqued. "What's that mean?"

"Nothing," she said. Way too fast for it to *actually* be nothing.

"Oh, come on. I just watched you come all over me, and you felt me blow my load in my pants like I was fifteen—"

"Oh my *god*. Would you stop?"

"Nah. All the walls are down now, hellcat. Might as well tell me."

"Why are you like this?"

"Charming and irresistible? Some of us are just born with it, I guess. Now, come on. Give me a hint."

Willa blew out an irritated sigh. "Lincoln—"

"One word. I can guess with one word."

"I swear to god, I'm going to—"

"How about just a syllable, then?"

"Fine, you giant man-child! *God*." She huffed, slamming

her arms down on the bed, clearly sick of my shit. "That was the first time that's happened, all right?"

"Oh *really*," I said, unable to tamp down just exactly how pleased that made me. The first time she'd come from a dry hump? Hell yeah, I'd take that honor all the way to the bank.

"You are the *worst*," she snapped. "And, great, now that I've told you, I'm going to be forced out of my own home by your ego *and* your exceptionally large head."

"Which one?" I asked, grinning into the darkness. "The one on my shoulders or the one you came all over?"

"Lincoln!" She tugged the pillow from beneath her head and hit me in the face with it.

"I'm kidding," I said on a laugh. "So it's the first time you've come from dry humping and the first time we've come together. I'm not mad about either one of those. And I definitely wouldn't be at all mad if we did it again."

She didn't respond. Not even a huff of irritated breath.

"Hellcat?"

Still nothing. Was she even breathing? I had no idea.

"Willa? What's—"

"Fine! I'll tell you," she snapped. "You don't have to *harass* me about it."

"I wasn't—"

"It's the first time I've come with someone else, all right?" she blurted, like she couldn't hold the words back anymore. "Are you happy now?"

I blinked, sure I'd heard her wrong. I turned on my side to face her, able to just make out the shape of her in the darkness. "Wait... First time, like...this month?"

"Would I be freaking out if that were the case?" She

heaved out a sigh that sounded like it carried the weight of the world. "I mean first time, like, *ever*."

Those words hung in the air as the room fell silent and my brain short-circuited. A beat passed. Then another.

"You're telling me no one else has ever made you come?"

She huffed, and I could practically hear her eye roll. "Could you not sound so damn pleased about it?"

"Oh, I absolutely could not."

"Maybe it didn't even have anything to do with *you*! Did you ever think of that?"

I barked out a laugh. "Nice try, but it was *my* cock you were grinding all over. Pretty sure it had a big something to do with me."

"I should've kept my mouth shut," she muttered.

"Too late now, wife."

I grinned into the dark, something other than masculine pride sparking in my chest. Not smugness like she'd claimed —though I definitely felt a bit of that too. But this was something more like awe. Like I'd somehow stumbled onto something elusive and rare.

And she'd let me have it.

I was the first person to witness Willa Jameson fall apart —to watch those walls crumble as she shook and shuddered through release. *Willa.* The same person who'd been holding herself out of reach since we were teenagers. Who'd been looking at me for half our lives like I was the physical embodiment of a migraine.

Willa...who'd climbed into my lap like she was tired of resisting and then come so hard she'd undone *both* of us.

She was quiet, a heavy awkwardness hanging between

us. It was the kind of silence filled with tension I didn't want between us anymore.

So instead of letting it linger, I slid my arm around her waist, tugged her into my chest, and settled my chin on top of her head. "Since I'm batting a hundred right now, you wanna do it again?"

"I hate you." She smacked my chest less forcefully than I was used to and muttered, "Jackass."

"That's not a no," I said, smiling into her hair.

Even though I'd half expected her to push away or shove me to my side of the bed, she didn't. Instead, she settled in, her forehead on my sternum, her nose brushing my chest, her hands folded together between us.

It wasn't the first time we'd been close like this in bed. We'd somehow always managed to end up in this position at some point in the night, waking up closer than either of us had intended.

But this was the first time we intentionally started this way.

CHAPTER TWENTY-TWO

WILLA

BEAU:

No video call again this week? You been busy?

WILLA:

Yeah. You know how strawberry season is… Hopefully we can catch up next week.

BEAU:

Counting on that.

THIS WASN'T the first time I'd been to Lincoln's childhood home—far from it. I'd been over countless times when we were kids, Beau, Lincoln, and me causing hell for poor Holly. At least until high school when Lincoln and my brother had veered off in a different direction from me and I'd spent most of my time with my nose buried in a book or helping Dad on the farm.

But still, this felt different.

Because now, I was walking into Holly's home under the guise of being Lincoln's *wife*, and I absolutely hated having to lie to that woman.

I was mulling over the different excuses I could give to bail when Lincoln squeezed my hand as we walked up the driveway toward the back door.

"Relax, wife. We've got this." He grinned down at me. "Besides, this is what all the practicing has been for."

His gaze turned heated as he stared at my lips, then slid his attention down my body. No doubt remembering everything that had transpired between us.

No doubt also remembering what I'd confessed.

And the worst part? I felt his stare all the way to my toes and every damn traitorous inch in between. My clit pulsed, my stomach flipping as I recalled the words he'd rasped while I'd ridden him, how hard he'd felt beneath me... How I'd made him come undone too.

Before I could say anything in response, he turned the knob on the back door and opened it, forcing me out of my memories and leading the way to pure madness.

The sharp, smoky scent of something burned hit first, followed by Chloe's muffled curse as she pulled out a very-well-done pan of cookies from the oven.

Declan stood in front of the open fridge, expertly dodging Holly swatting at him with a towel as she muttered about how dinner was in ten minutes and to stop filling up on snacks.

Just through the wide archway into the living room, Xander's daughter, Emma, was in full five-year-old prowess, shrieking out a song I didn't recognize while digging through a box labeled *Imagination Station*.

In front of her, both Xander and Atlas sat perfectly still, draped with feather boas and topped with a plastic tiara—Xander—and ostentatious fake earrings—Atlas—like it was just a normal Sunday.

At the dining table, Sutton sipped a glass of wine, watching Atlas play dress-up while Laurel hunched over her phone, thumbs flying, her entire posture screaming *I don't know these people.*

And right in the middle of all the chaos, Holly stood at the stove. She ladled gravy with one hand, shooed Declan away from the fridge with the other, and managed the entire circus like it was second nature.

My stomach tightened as I took in everything, my nerves churning while I considered where exactly I'd fit into this little farce.

"Willa! Oh, thank god," Chloe said, her hair pulled back, cheeks flushed. "You think I can salvage these cookies?"

Holly waved an unconcerned hand through the air. "Of course we can. We'll just scrape off the brown parts."

"Try *black* parts," Declan muttered. "She really burned the shit out of those."

Chloe reached up and smacked the back of Declan's head just as Holly said, "For the love, Declan, we wanted to make a good impression on Willa tonight!"

"Why?" Declan lifted his chin toward me in greeting before turning back to his mom. "She's not new here."

"She's new here as your brother's *wife*, which means she's new here as my *daughter-in-law* and your *sister-in-law*. Some manners, please."

Those words were like a giant boulder landing in my stomach with all the subtlety of a grenade. I was someone's *wife*...someone's *daughter-in-law*. I was a lot of someones' *sister-in-law*.

I was a *liar*.

"Afraid manners are a lost cause with that shithead, Mom." Lincoln bent to kiss Holly on the cheek.

"That's a dollar in the swear jar, Uncle Linc!" Emma called from the living room, not even glancing away from Xander's tiara, which she adjusted with the seriousness of a royal coronation.

"I thought it was fifty cents?" Lincoln yelled back.

"Not anymore," Emma said. "Infration!"

Lincoln snorted. "Inflation, you mean?"

"That's what I said." Emma's *duh* came through loud and clear.

"Oh Jesus," Lincoln muttered. Then louder, "Stop letting her spend so much time with Laurel, Xan! The teenage snark is brushing off on my little bean."

"Better than the overgrown frat-boy vibes she gets from you," Laurel muttered without even looking up.

"Hey," Lincoln said, offended. "I'm a married man now, thank you very much."

"I think you have me and our bet to thank for that." Sutton smirked at him over the rim of her wineglass, her brow raised.

"What bet?" I asked, splitting a glance between the two.

"We made a bet, and if I lost, she told me I had to delete my dating apps."

"And you did lose. Spectacularly," she said. "Good thing, too. You'd been missing what's been in front of you all along."

Lincoln glanced down at me, his eyes soft, lips curved up in that half grin I hated to love. "Guess I just needed to wait for the right moment to catch her."

It was a line. That was all it was—just a line because we were putting on a show for his family. For *everyone.*

But my stomach hadn't gotten that message. It flipped over itself, unable to tell the truth from a lie. Something it'd been having a difficult time with more and more lately.

Lincoln settled his hand on the small of my back and guided me to the table. Then he sat down next to me, his arm going to the back of my chair and brushing his thumb softly against my shoulder like it was the most natural thing in the world.

And that was the problem—it *felt* natural.

Too natural for something that was made up entirely of lies.

DINNER UNFOLDED the way I would expect in a family with four rowdy boys—now men. It was all loud voices, second helpings, overlapping stories, and at least three arguments over who grilled the best burger.

Through it all, Lincoln kept touching me—a hand on my knee, his fingers brushing mine, his arm resting on the back of my chair while he played with the end of my braid.

It was all so easy. *Too* easy. The kind of easy that made the lie simple to forget.

And the worst part was, it worked.

The longer I sat there, surrounded by warmth and commotion and people who egged one another on but clearly loved one another without question, the harder it became to remember this was fake.

Nothing more than a temporary fix dressed up as forever.

I was still trying to come to terms with that when a sudden scrape cut through the noise—metal against glass, aggressive and not at all subtle. Atlas was digging into a jar of my jam, scraping the bottom of it like a man starved.

Chloe stared at him in horror. "You ate it *all*?"

Atlas didn't even look up as he smothered his roll with the last remnants of lemon blueberry basil. "Fuck yeah, I ate it all. Have you tried this shit? It's delicious."

"Two dollars, Uncle Atlas!" Emma chimed in, munching on her own roll.

Chloe threw her hands up. "I know it's delicious! But you weren't supposed to use the whole thing!"

Atlas shrugged, eating half the roll in one bite. "Then why'd you put it out here?"

"Because I thought you'd have a *normal* amount like a *normal* human!"

"Well, that was your first mistake," Sutton said dryly, tipping her wineglass in Chloe's direction.

Chloe huffed out a sound that was half groan, half whine. "But I was saving the rest for waffles tomorrow."

Atlas popped the other half of the roll into his mouth.

"Fine. Tell me where to buy it, and I'll stock up with a whole fucking case. Two, actually."

Emma opened her mouth, but Atlas held up a hand. "Another buck. I got it, little bean. How about I just give you a twenty at the end of the night and call it good?"

"Deal!" Emma beamed at him with a toothless grin.

Which was quite different from the fiery stare Chloe was pinning him with. "You can't stock up, you big oaf! It's handmade by Willa." She threw an arm in my direction. "And it's *special*. She only gives them to her favorite people a couple times a year. And you just downed my only jar like it was keg beer at one of your sportsball parties!"

Atlas turned his attention to Lincoln, eyes narrowing. "How come you've never shared her jam with us?"

Lincoln smirked, leaning back in his chair. "You think I'd waste this on you? It's fucking delicious, and you're an animal."

Declan raised a brow. "Or maybe it's because she only shares it with her favorite people, and you're not one of them."

Lincoln held up his left hand, his black wedding band stark against his finger, and my stomach swooped just like it always did when I caught sight of it. "This ring says otherwise. Besides, I'm the certified taste tester at home." He turned to me, his eyes dipping deliberately to my mouth. "Isn't that right, wife?"

Lincoln's voice had dropped low, and I prayed I was the only one who'd noticed. Prayed, too, that no one was paying close enough attention to me to catalogue my flushed cheeks or my glare that was actually hiding my persistent arousal when it came to this man.

But that hope fled the second Laurel said, "Don't make it weird, you horny perverts."

Emma cocked her head to the side, her gaze curious on her cousin. "What's a horny peevert?"

Laurel cringed and glanced at Xander. "Shit. That's on me."

Emma gasped and bounced in her seat, delighted. "That's a dollar in the swear jar, Lolo!"

"You're gonna have more money at the end of the night than I made all week," Xander said.

"I know, Daddy!" Emma grinned. "I *love* Sundays!"

Laughter erupted around the table. Even Lincoln's broody, grumpy brothers cracked some grins.

"Will I get money out of you, Aunt Willa?" she asked, those wide eyes staring up at me, and I nearly lost my breath.

"Um…" I cleared my suddenly dry throat. "I—"

"You'll have more luck getting paid from me, little bean. The only time Aunt Willa really swears is when she's yelling at me."

That earned another round of chuckles, and I forced a smile, pretending my world hadn't tipped on its side thanks to one word from a little girl.

I'd thought it would be easy to come here and stay on the fringes. Hold myself back. But the Steeles didn't half-ass anything. And they had no intention of leaving me out in the figurative cold.

After the plates had been cleared, the kitchen had been

cleaned, and we'd played four rounds of charades with Emma leading the game, everyone headed out for the evening.

Lincoln was just ahead of me, laughing and joking with his brothers, and an ache settled in my chest as I watched the four of them. I missed *my* brother. Missed laughing with him and teasing him and yelling at him. I missed movie marathons and ATV races on the farm. I missed the everyday moments I hadn't had with him since he'd left.

And now, especially, I missed him. Ever since I'd made it a point to dodge his calls and reply sporadically to his texts.

Before I could start crying right there in my fake mother-in-law's kitchen, Holly stopped me with a gentle hand on my arm. She smiled and placed a stack of warm containers in my hands.

"Just some leftovers," she said. "I'm sure you and Lincoln are exhausted at the end of the day, so the last thing you want to think about is making something for dinner."

"Oh..." I said, breath catching. "That's really thoughtful. Thank you."

Holly waved away my gratitude. "No thanks needed. I also packed up the blueberry crumble you liked. You make sure my bottomless pit of a son doesn't eat the whole damn thing before you get any, okay?"

I breathed out a laugh, though I wasn't so sure it didn't sound like a sob with all the emotion clogging my throat. My mother hadn't called me in over six months. Didn't even know I was "married." And here Holly was, taking care of me without a second thought.

Her eyes softened as she wrapped an arm around me, tucking me into her side. "I'm so happy to have you in the family, Willa. Truly. I've always hoped someone would see Lincoln the way he deserves. I'm just so glad that person is you."

My smile felt brittle...fragile.

Fake.

"Me too."

CHAPTER TWENTY-THREE

WILLA

THE STRAWBERRY FESTIVAL always made Starlight Cove feel like we were living in a picturesque postcard. Fairy lights were strung overhead, creating a canopy of magic. It smelled like sugar, sunscreen, and ocean air. Residents strolled Main Street, where dozens of booths were set up. A band played in the gazebo at the park with families strewn on the lawn, soaking it all in.

While the farm had participated in the Strawberry Festival every year for as long as I could remember, this was the first year our stall wasn't a simple white tent. Instead, we were stationed in a wooden stand Lincoln built with his bare hands along with the help of a friend from high school, Ford McKenzie.

Instead of working at One Night Stan's today, Lincoln had gotten up with me at the crack of dawn and helped me set up here. Wooden crates were filled with our wares—fresh strawberries, strawberry syrup, honey, and my latest jam batches.

I'd brought every last jar of jam I had on hand—less the crate I'd dropped last week when I'd had my back spasm. But even without that, we had way more than I could hope to sell.

We were also stocked with fresh honey stored in old whiskey bottles and our newest addition—mini honey sticks my child of a husband had decided to name things like *Bee-hind Closed Doors*, *Spread 'Em*, and *Honeypot*. He'd suggested *Drizzle Me, Daddy*, and I'd told him if he ever said that again, I'd drown him in honey and make it look like an accident.

I'd been focused on getting everything laid out just so that I'd let Lincoln handle the signage. But I about tripped over my feet when I stood out front and glanced at our booth. The wooden stand—lined with stacked crates that overflowed with jars, berries, and bottles—looked downright professional. Rustic and polished all at once, like something out of a farmers market ad.

The only problem was he'd priced everything like we were selling our items out of a boutique in Manhattan and not on Main Street in Starlight Cove.

"You think you can get *twenty-five dollars* for this tiny

thing?" I asked, holding up one of the four-ounce glass jars of jam. "Are you out of your mind?"

Lincoln flashed me a grin, his dimples winking at me and making my traitorous stomach flip. "I actually think we can get thirty-five, but I didn't want to give you a heart attack."

I strode behind the booth, rolling my eyes. "I can't wait to watch you explain to every person who asks that there is, in fact, *no* edible gold in these recipes."

"What you're going to watch is me selling you out, wife."

"Selling me out?" I huffed out an incredulous laugh and shook my head. "You think you're going to be able to sell us out of strawberry tomato and strawbanero jam? Be serious."

"I don't just think. I *know*." He stepped close—closer than necessary—placed a hand on my hip, and lowered his head until his lips brushed my ear. "Then I'll collect my thank-you however you wanna give it to me, wife."

My brain short-circuited from his words and his nearness and that maddening path his thumb took under the hem of my T-shirt. And by the time it was back online with a retort, the line was five people deep.

And Lincoln's brother was leading the pack.

Atlas stood at the front of the line, eyes hidden behind dark sunglasses, those massive arms crossed over his chest, and a don't fuck with me scowl carved onto his face.

He jerked his chin toward the booth. "I'll take all the jam."

Lincoln didn't even blink. "I'm afraid the limit for pain-in-the-ass older brothers is two."

Atlas's jaw hardened. "Ten."

"Three."

Atlas braced his hands on the table and leaned toward Lincoln, his teeth clenched as he bit out, "*Five.*"

"Best I can do is four."

"Are you shitting me? I can't even get one of each flavor? That's bullshit, Linc."

Lincoln just shrugged. "Take it or leave it, bro. You're holding up the line."

There was a long, tense pause before Atlas growled, slapped a hundred-dollar bill in Lincoln's palm, and snatched four jars before stalking off in a cloud of irritation.

I didn't know what surprised me more—our very first customer asking to buy us out, or Lincoln *turning him down.*

"Why didn't you just sell everything to him?" I asked. "You could've proven me wrong in the first five minutes."

He exchanged a jar for cash with another customer and shot me a smile. "I'm building demand. Bet I can get him to pay fifty bucks for the next jars. Hell, I can probably charge him a hundred."

I snorted and shook my head. "Now you're just delusional. Maybe I should take over."

"Not before I can get some honey sticks from my sweet little honey!" Mabel strolled up, her red-sequined jumpsuit sparkling in the sun, along with her matching lipstick, stark against her pale skin. Her short gray bob was curled loosely, and a strawberry hat sat perched on her head. The self-proclaimed Starlight Cove Strawberry Queen.

"There's my favorite sex toy dealer." Lincoln winked as he handed her a mini honey stick. "You're looking good enough to drizzle, Mabel."

"Don't you tempt me, sugar. Besides, George gets first taste."

Lincoln grinned, his dimples flashing. "Well, second in line ain't so bad."

Mabel eyed my husband head to toe, her lips pursed to the side. "Boy, I'd break you in half."

I sputtered out a shocked laugh as Lincoln's smile only grew.

With a shrug, he said, "Can't blame a guy for trying."

"Quit flirting with me, and give me a dozen of those little honey sticks. Gonna conduct some...research tonight."

"Research?" I asked, brows raised as I grabbed a few of each flavor.

"Of course. Meltability, stickiness, which flavor pairs best with skin... The usual," Mabel said, her tone deadly serious. "Any interest in exploring a wholesale partnership? These would fly off the shelves at Wicked Little Things."

I blinked at her, then at Lincoln, then at the long line forming behind her. We'd been open fifteen minutes. *Fifteen.* And somehow, with Lincoln by my side, we'd been offered a booth buyout *and* a wholesale deal. Him standing here with that apron wrapped around his waist, luring customers in, was obviously witchcraft. Either that or my husband was some kind of farm-stand Casanova.

"You know what, Mabel?" Lincoln said, handing over her purchase. "We just might be. Let me talk to the missus, and we'll be in touch next week."

"Sure, sure. Oh! Speaking of the missus..." She winked at me, reached into one of her bags, and pulled out a handful of small square packets. "For the newlyweds. George's personal favorite is the chocolate strawberry, but I prefer the strawberry vanilla. You two try them out during your abundant evening—or daytime—activities, and let me know what you think!"

With that, she strolled away, passing out strawberry lube samples to every adult she came across like she was the fairy lube mother of Mardi Gras. And I tried not to remember, in great detail, how it'd felt to come apart in Lincoln's lap. I also diligently ignored the look he sent my way as he pocketed all those samples, clearly recalling the same.

CHAPTER TWENTY-FOUR

WILLA

THE MORNING BLURRED TOGETHER with barely a breath between customers. Every time I looked up, the line had doubled. Through it all, my husband was selling the shit out of everything we had while I tried very hard not to stare at his ass.

Everything was going great...except for the fact that he'd been right. We were sold out of jam before noon.

"Well, well, well," he said, smugness oozing from his tone as he handed a bag to a customer. "I do believe that was our *last* jar of jam, hellcat. You know, the jam without any edible gold that you didn't think would sell."

I rolled my eyes as I exchanged cash for a pint of strawberries. "Probably had something to do with the novelty of a hot guy in an apron saying how delicious everything tastes."

A slow grin spread across his mouth. "You think I'm hot?"

"I think all this heat is getting to you."

"Whatever you say, wife."

The crowd never waned as the sun climbed higher, and Lincoln somehow got smugger with every sale, though I had no idea that was possible. Not only had we sold out of jam, but three-quarters of our strawberries were gone, we were down to less than half a dozen jars of honey, and even the cheeky mini honey sticks were running dangerously low.

One thing was clear—Lincoln was having the time of his life.

He was in his element and loving every minute of it. Flashing his dimples, charming anyone who walked by, and flexing those obnoxious biceps just enough to make the older ladies fan themselves and the younger ones linger a bit too long.

And then there was the one who just wouldn't go away.

Blond and sun-kissed and wearing a dress so thin I could make out her lacy bra beneath it, she held a to-go cup of strawberry sangria in one hand and touched my husband with the other. Just a light stroke against his wrist as she leaned in, laughing like the two of them were sharing an inside joke.

I hated it.

Which was ridiculous. First of all, it was her fingertips she was brushing all over him, not her tits. And second of all, what Lincoln and I had was *fake*.

So why the hell did this unwanted sensation crackling in my chest feel incredibly real?

The line was stacking up as Sangria Barbie asked about everything we had available, wanting to sample each and every good.

My husband included.

But what surprised the hell out of me was the way Lincoln didn't lean into flirting back. Didn't give her even half the wattage of the smiles he'd handed out to the rest of the crowd. Wasn't even a flicker of light compared to the ones he sent *me*.

But he didn't shut her down either.

He stepped back every time she leaned in closer, his expression polite but bland as he pointed to each item she asked about with his left hand. As if purposely flashing his wedding ring.

Still, the woman didn't get the hint.

If anything, Lincoln's disinterest only made her bolder. More determined. She dragged her cup, slick with condensation, across her collarbone like she was oh-so very hot. Then she placed one hand on the table and leaned over to give him a not-so-subtle view straight down her dress like she was starring in a porno no one else knew was being produced.

His placid smile stayed in place, but I also clocked the way his mouth tightened just a bit and a tiny tic of irritation in his jaw. His response should've soothed this wild, unwanted thrum beneath my skin.

Instead, that weird twist in my gut only pulled tighter.

It wasn't jealousy. Obviously.

It was just irritation.

This woman was holding up the line. Interfering with our sales. Wasting Lincoln's and my and everyone else's time.

Finally, I couldn't take it anymore.

"Give me just one second," I said to the older man who

was next in line before stomping over to Chatty Cathy and my husband who was too nice to tell her to fuck off.

"Do you need help with something?" I asked, voice sharp, eyes sharper.

She startled, a bit of her sangria sloshing over the side of her porn glass. "Oh! Um, no. Thank you."

"Really? Seems like maybe you do. You've been standing here longer than it takes our chickens to lay eggs."

She breathed out a nervous laugh, her eyes darting between me and Lincoln, who'd stepped in close behind me —close enough his heat seeped into my spine. "I'm just having a little trouble deciding what to get. I was wondering if I could sample the honey."

"We don't serve samples of honey." I flashed her my teeth, my smile more *I will cut you* than *let's be besties*. "Or husbands."

Lincoln's feet bracketed mine as he slid his left arm around my waist, palm splayed across my stomach, his chin resting on top of my head. Solid. Steady. Possessive as hell. I didn't even have to look to know he was grinning like the smug jackass he was.

Sangria Barbie breathed out what barely passed for a laugh, made an excuse about meeting a friend, and scampered off. Probably to flirt with someone else's fake husband.

I blew out a heavy breath and turned to face Lincoln, ready to tell him to get back to work, but the look on his face stopped me cold. His cheeks were flushed, his eyes dark and hooded. And now that my rage fog had receded a bit, I realized I'd felt the solid weight of him against my back while he'd been standing behind me. One flick of my gaze down to the front of his jeans confirmed as much.

My brows flew up as I met his eyes, then dropped my voice to hiss, "Are you seriously turned on right now?"

His grin spread slow and easy, just like the honey he was selling so well. "You low-key telling another woman to fuck off while standing in front of me like I'm already yours? Yeah, wife. That kinda did it for me."

Before I could respond to him, he dropped a kiss on my lips. Then he stepped around me and greeted the people waiting in line—now a dozen deep.

That was how the rest of the day went, minus any more Sangria Barbies. And Lincoln was enjoying every second.

He was effortlessly smooth, smiling like the damn sun was shining out of his dimples and somehow flirting with every single person in line without *actually* flirting. That might've had something to do with the fact that every word, every wink, every compliment somehow circled back to me.

I'd never heard someone say the word *wife* so many times in one afternoon, but he managed to fit it into every single conversation like he was competing for the world record.

His *wife's* strawberries were delicious.

The honey his *wife* harvested was the best in New England.

The jam his *wife* made was already sold out, and he'd been lucky enough to taste-test every batch of his *wife's* recipes.

And forget about the number of times he'd touched me.

He kept brushing against me when he handed off bags. His fingers lingered on the small of my back when he was close. And every chance he got, he looped an arm around my waist to tug me into his side like that was exactly where I belonged. Pressed kisses against my temple. Told me how great I was doing and how much I was killing it.

The real problem wasn't that he was doing any of those things. It was that I was *letting* him.

I didn't step out of his grasp, didn't move out of his reach. Found I couldn't.

Because every time he touched me like I belonged to him and every time he looked at me like he couldn't wait to get me home, I forgot to breathe. And when he said wife with such possession and pride, the grumpy cat inside me that usually lashed out with hisses and sharp claws just curled up in my chest and purred.

Through it all, I tried to keep my face neutral. Focused on what needed to be done. Tried to pretend this was perfectly normal and none of it was getting to me. Not even a little.

But my cheeks were flushed and my panties were wet and my nipples were hard enough to cut glass. And, by the knowing glances Lincoln kept sending my way, that smug bastard knew it.

CHAPTER TWENTY-FIVE

LINCOLN

WILLA HADN'T SAID a word since we'd started packing up the booth once the festival was over. Didn't so much as breathe in my direction on the drive home. Didn't spare me a glance as I threw the truck into park or when she climbed out and yanked open the tailgate or when she grabbed a stack of empty crates from the back.

Nope. She just stomped up the porch like a hurricane with hips. And goddamn was I ready for this storm.

She'd been like this since the moment Blondie had touched my wrist—steely eyed, more short-tempered than usual, and so fucking hot I'd had to hide behind the booth more than once just to rearrange my dick.

The funny thing was, I hadn't even intended for us to land here.

My inability to keep my hands to myself had started because I couldn't *not* touch her. Because every time I looked at her—flushed from the sun, her cheeks freckled and rosy, her full lips twitching in the way that said she was holding back a bark of laughter—made me want to wrap a hand around the back of her neck, tug her into me, and kiss the ever-loving shit out of her.

And then keep her. Right there, just like that.

That was how it *started*.

But once I'd seen Willa's reaction to all those subtle touches—the hitches in her breath, the way she swayed slightly closer to me, then how much sharper her sass got when it was clear her body was wound too tight to think straight?

Well. Then it became a game I was all too willing to play.

She'd been simmering by midafternoon, surly by early evening, and downright seething by sundown. And now?

Now, she was stomping into the silo like a woman one breath away from combusting, and I was all too willing to light the match just to see how hot she burned.

Whistling, I strolled inside behind her, the rest of the crates stacked in my arms. After setting them down, I stretched my back and groaned, then headed to the sink and took my sweet-ass time washing my hands.

Meanwhile, she stormed around the kitchen like a pissed-off teenager—jerking drawers open, slamming cabinets, and scrubbing invisible stains off the countertop.

After drying my hands, I leaned back against the counter, arms crossed, and enjoyed the show.

My wife was about three minutes away from cracking. And I wasn't just going to sit by and watch—I was going to make sure she *shattered*.

I pushed off the counter and stepped up behind her, my hands settling on the island to bracket her hips. Leaning down, I skimmed my nose up the column of her neck, then pressed a kiss below her ear.

"You good, wife?" I murmured, just loud enough to carry over the sound of her violently reorganizing the silverware drawer.

She stiffened her spine before slowly turning to glare at me over her shoulder. "Fine."

I barely smothered a laugh at her curt response, but somehow I managed. "Really? You don't seem fine."

Eyes narrowed, nostrils flared, and mouth pinched tight, she turned around and gave me the full force of her ire. "You're mistaken. I'm great."

She said *great* like most people would say *dead*.

"You sure?" I placed my hands on her hips and slipped my thumbs beneath the hem of her T-shirt, brushing soft circles against her skin. "You seem a little...tense."

"And you seem like you're three seconds away from being murdered."

This time, I couldn't stop the smile from sweeping across my mouth. She was so goddamn cute like this—all pissed off and horny. My demonic little ball of fury.

"It looks to me like you're a bit worked up. Like maybe you've got some energy you need help...releasing."

She opened her mouth—no doubt to toss back something scathing—before she snapped it closed and narrowed her eyes. Not in a pissed-off way, but like she was studying me. I could practically see her wheels turning, no doubt replaying the entire day, and then that pissed-off demeanor turned downright deadly.

"Oh, I see," she said, her voice deceptively calm. "You

wanted to play a game today. But it'll have to wait because I'm late for a date in the shower with my battery-operated friend."

That got my attention.

My grin dropped. My cock did not.

Images of her inside the tiny little shoebox made up of tile slammed into me, each one hotter than the last. Her, leaning back into the corner, one leg up on the ledge, while she held a silicone toy against her clit. Then it flashed to her holding the detachable showerhead there instead. In both fantasies, her head was tossed back, her tits full and pushed out like an offering, nipples tight and begging for my mouth as she got herself where she needed to go. While I was nowhere in sight.

No. *Fuck* no.

If she wanted to get off while we were married, I'd give her exactly what she needed.

"You're not taking a shower," I said, voice rough.

Willa huffed out an incredulous breath. "The hell I'm not. I'm taking one right now. And that's *not* an invitation."

She tried to slip around me, but I stepped into her path, one hand on her hip, holding her steady. "Lincoln..."

I leaned down until our mouths were just inches apart, meeting her gaze. "You can take a shower. *After* I've made you come."

She blinked. "Excuse me?"

I settled my other hand around the base of her neck, gripping firmly. "If you need to get off while we're married, you come to your husband. Not a toy. Not the showerhead. *Me.*"

Her nostrils flared as she clenched her jaw, shoving once against my chest. "You think you're the patron saint of orgasms just because you got lucky once?"

My grin started slow and wicked as I recalled how she'd looked riding me straight into oblivion. "It wasn't luck that made you go off, hellcat. It was focus and my dirty mouth that got you there."

She muttered something that sounded a hell of a lot like *jackass*, but she didn't back away.

"I'm dying to do it again. Been thinking about nothing but you coming apart on top of me." I leaned down until my lips brushed her ear. "Now I wanna taste that pussy I've been dreaming about, wife. Wanna see if it's as sweet as I think it is."

I pulled back enough to catalog her features. Her cheeks were flushed, her lips parted, her eyes dark. And her tits were heaving beneath her T-shirt like she couldn't hold enough air in her lungs.

"What do you think, hellcat?"

"I think you're infuriating," she said, her words harsh but her voice weak.

"And I think you're soaked. Bet if I slid my hand inside your panties, I'd find out just how much, wouldn't I?" I tucked my fingers into the front of her waistband and tugged her close, reveling in the hitch of her breath. "Now the real question is, are you gonna let me do something about it?"

She stood frozen for a second...two...as she studied me. Trying to get a read on me. So I put every ounce of desire I had for her into my gaze as I stared right back, just fucking dying to have her again.

"Fine," she snapped. "Do it. Eat me out and get it over with."

I chuckled long and low. "Baby...that's not what's gonna happen. I'm not going to eat your pussy to *get it over with*." I undid the button of her jeans and tugged down her zipper one notch at a time. "I'm going to devour your cunt like it's my last fucking meal and I've been waiting my whole life for a taste."

She gasped as I yanked down her shorts, dragging her panties along with them, before guiding her back until she had no choice but to collapse into the armchair.

Then I dropped to my knees, spread her thighs wide, and stared at the heaven between them like it was the only thing in the world worth praying to.

"Jesus Christ, look at you," I managed through a tight throat, my voice scraped raw as I ran my thumb through her slit. "Dripping and desperate and fucking perfect."

"Lincoln..." she whispered, shifting like she was uncomfortable with the attention. But she was going to have to get used to it.

Because from this moment on, I planned to worship at the altar of her cunt and do my daily devotionals on my knees.

"Shh...quiet now while I get to work." I reached around, cupped her ample ass in my palms, and tugged her closer to the edge of the cushion. Then I leaned in, spreading her thighs wider with my shoulders, and watched as her pussy bloomed open for me.

"Don't be a jackass," she said, though her tone was

breathy, and she gripped the arms of the chair like they were a lifeline.

"Jackass? Nah, wife. I'm about to be the happiest man on the planet when I finally get to lick up all this sweetness."

I closed my eyes and ran my nose up the inside of her thigh, inhaling when I got close to all that pink. "Fuck, you smell good."

I did the same to her other thigh, taking my time and working her up until her legs were quivering, her breaths coming out in sharp pants.

When I was poised above her pussy, my lips millimeters from her clit, I murmured, "Bet you taste even better..."

And then I couldn't wait another second. No more warming up. No more holding myself back. She was already squirming, and I'd barely even touched her.

It was time to put us both out of our misery.

I licked one long path from her entrance to her clit, unable to stop the groan tearing from my throat. I was right— she did taste even better than she smelled, all sweet and tangy. She jerked against me, a gasp flying out like she hadn't been expecting this, and that only made me hungrier.

"I know I'm the only one to make you come, wife. But am I the only one who's tasted this sweet cunt?" I circled her entrance with my tongue before spearing it inside her, groaning when she clenched around me. "Tell me."

"Yes," she whispered, like she didn't want to admit it. Like she was embarrassed by that fact.

Meanwhile, I was riding high like a fucking king and drunk on the taste of her.

"That's fucking right," I said, brushing her clit with my

thumb. "I'm the only one who's had his tongue inside your pussy. Only your husband knows how fucking good you taste."

I dove in again, flattening my tongue as I licked her, slower this time. Dragging it up her slit and savoring the tremble in her thighs before latching on to her clit and sucking hard.

That was all it took for the thread holding Willa back to finally snap.

With a gasp, she shot her hands to my head, threading her fingers through my hair as she rode my face from below. Every shuddered breath was a confession, every oath of my name a claim, every moan a symphony I wanted to hear each night for the rest of my life.

"That's what I love to hear. You, fucking begging for it. Only your husband knows the sounds you make when you come. Isn't that right, wife?"

"God," she choked out. "Fingers—Linc, please. I need—"

I dipped my fingers just barely inside her, not sinking them deep but giving her a taste. She groaned, hips rocking, pussy clenching around nothing.

"Look at you—so fucking greedy," I said, voice thick.

I finally gave her what she was desperate for and sank two fingers deep, watching as her cunt swallowed them. Imagining exactly what this would look like with my cock stretching her wide.

"This pussy's starving for me, isn't she? She's been wet for hours, and now she's just begging to be filled. But I'm only going to give her a little taste tonight."

I pumped my fingers inside Willa, curling them to hit

that spot while I flicked my tongue against her clit. The moan she loosed shot straight to my cock, making me throb in my goddamn jeans. And fuck me, but I was in danger of blowing right there like a fucking teenager. Again.

"You've got me so hard, hellcat. So fucking hard." I brushed my lower lip against her before tucking it into my mouth and dragging my stubble over her clit. "All from eating you out. From licking up everything you're giving me. You taste so goddamn good."

"What do I taste like?" she asked, cheeks ruddy, eyes heavy lidded, her lips parted as she stared down at me from my throne between her spread thighs.

I sank my two fingers deep then reached up and brushed them against her bottom lip. "Open for me."

Instead of sassing back, she did as I asked, sucking my fingers into her mouth, her eyes locked with mine. She swirled her tongue around my digits, making my cock jerk. Then she moaned, her hips bucking like she didn't know which one she needed more—my mouth or my cock.

"Told you, didn't I? You taste like cinnamon and honey." I dragged my tongue through her slit again. "All spicy sweet. So fucking good."

She let my fingers go with a soft, wet gasp, her head tipping back as I licked her again, slower now—claiming every drop.

With my mouth against her, our eyes locked and my chin wet from her arousal, I murmured, "You taste like my *wife*."

She whimpered, her hips rolling, her fingers tangled in my hair, and I couldn't hold myself back anymore. I tossed one of her legs over my shoulder, held her in place with an arm braced over her stomach, and devoured her.

I groaned against her with every sharp tug of her fingers in my hair, flicked my tongue harder when her thighs squeezed my head. And when I felt her cunt start to flutter around my fingers, I didn't fucking move. Didn't change my speed or my pressure or my direction. I stayed right fucking there while she climbed the peak, her breath held, her entire body as tight as a guitar string.

At least until it snapped.

She choked out my name as she broke apart, her pussy squeezing my fingers, her clit pulsing against my tongue. And I savored every fucking drop. Knowing *I* was the first one who'd had the privilege of tasting her come.

The darkest, most secret parts of me wishing I'd be the *only* one.

I wanted to see if I could work her toward another orgasm, but before I could try, she pushed against my shoulders, her entire body convulsing when I ran my tongue across her swollen clit.

Multiples would have to wait for another night.

I sat back on my heels and let her look her fill, knowing the lower half of my face and my neck were wet from her. Hell, I could feel her arousal soaking into the neckline of my T-shirt, and I wasn't sure I was going to wash this before I wore it again. I wanted to be able to smell her on me and remember her just like this—completely blissed out with her legs spread wide, staring up at me like I'd just given her the entire fucking world.

"I think I proved my point, wife." I leaned forward until

our lips brushed, letting her taste exactly how much she wanted me. "You need to get off while we're married, you come to me, and I'll handle it with pleasure. Every fucking time."

I stood, adjusting my cock as it strained against my zipper, desperate to sink inside that gorgeous cunt while it was all flushed and swollen. "I'm gonna go take a shower and think about you crying out my name while your pussy flooded my mouth. See you in bed, wife."

CHAPTER TWENTY-SIX

WILLA

I COULDN'T FEEL my legs.

That probably should've been concerning, but my brain was too busy short-circuiting over the fact that Lincoln Steele had just made me come so hard I saw stars.

Again.

And he'd done it without so much as unzipping his pants. *Again.*

This time, he'd been able to do it with just those dirty promises and that mouth—*God*, that mouth—that he'd used like a weapon. Feasting on me like he got off on the taste of me alone.

Meanwhile, I was wrecked. Ravaged. My legs still shook right along with my foundation because what the *fuck?*

Lincoln was almost to the stairs when my brain finally rebooted and I registered what he said. This jackass thought he was going to take a shower to get off when he hadn't let me do the same? I didn't fucking think so.

"The hell you are," I said. I'd been going for sharpness in

my tone, but that was tempered by the raspy quality of my voice thanks to all the screaming he'd made me do.

Lincoln stopped and turned, one brow raised as he eyed me like I was dinner. "You have something else in mind, wife?"

On shaky legs, I stood from the chair, crossed the room like I hadn't just had my soul delivered to me by my husband's tongue, and dropped to my knees in front of him. His brows flew up as I fisted the waistband of his jeans and yanked him closer.

"I don't do double standards," I said. "If I'm not allowed to get off solo, neither are you."

Lincoln blinked down at me, his lips parted, eyes as dark as I'd ever seen them. Then he tipped his head back on a groan that bordered on a laugh. "If you so much as flick your tongue against the head of my cock, hellcat, I'm gonna embarrass myself."

Normally, I'd call bullshit, but there was nothing fake about the rigidness of his shoulders or the tense set of his jaw. He actually *would* lose it. And I found that realization more heady...more potent than anything I'd ever experienced.

Somehow, I'd reduced Lincoln Steele to *this*.

"Fine." I sat back on my heels, bit my lower lip, and looked up at him from my perch on my knees. "Then I'll just watch."

His throat bobbed as he swallowed hard, his gaze skating over every inch of me. And though I felt ridiculous sitting here, bare-assed with my shirt still on, Lincoln was looking at me like his sanity hung on the curve of my hips.

"You want a show, wife?" he asked, his voice pure gravel.

"You want to see me stroke my cock while I'm thinking about you?"

"That's exactly what I want." I reached up and unbuttoned his jeans, tugged them and his boxer briefs down just enough to free him, then leaned back to take him in.

Sweet Jesus.

The man was packing, though I'd known that from my ride the other night. But feeling it and seeing it were two very different things. He was thick and hard with a vein I wanted to drag my tongue over mapping a path up the underside of his cock. The head was flushed a deep purple and already leaking, precome dripping down his length.

When the hell had I ever looked at a penis and thought, *god, that's pretty?* Exactly never. Until now. I should've known every single inch—and there were a *lot* of inches—of this infuriating man would be pretty.

My mouth watered at the sight of him, and I was feeling some kind of way about the fact that I wasn't going to get a taste.

At least not tonight.

I made a noise in my throat—half whimper, half moan—and Lincoln's composure snapped. He wrapped his thick fingers around his cock, gripping firmly and giving himself one slow stroke, his eyes never leaving mine.

"Look at you. On your knees for me. Pouting because you can't taste my cock. Goddamn, wife, you're a wet dream, you know that? *My* wet dream come to life."

He increased the speed of his strokes, his grip tighter than I would've dared. "I can still smell you on me. Can still taste that sweet pussy. You were soaked, weren't you? Dripping down my chin and still begging for more."

My cheeks flamed with heat, the automatic embarrassment flooding me before I could stop it. But with how he sounded—reverent and undone—he didn't just enjoy it. He *loved* it. Enough that he was using those memories to get himself off.

He shuddered out a breath, his shoulders quaking and abs rippling while his forearm flexed with each tug of his cock. "All I can think about is how pretty your pussy was. How your clit pulsed against my tongue and how your cunt gripped me like she never wanted me to leave. You coming apart because of my mouth was the hottest fucking thing I've ever seen."

He wasn't teasing now, no snark in his tone. Instead, he was unraveling, his strokes harsh, his gaze darting all over my body—to the parts he could see and the ones he couldn't.

"I want to see you like that every goddamn day. Want your thighs squeezing my head while you try to drown me with your cunt. Want to fucking *own* every single orgasm your perfect body gives up. And I want to do it all after you claim me in public like you did this afternoon."

Jesus, my pussy was throbbing. *Again.* What the hell was happening to me? I shifted on my knees, desperate for some relief.

"Wish I could see all of you. I just know those tits are fucking perfect. More than a handful and topped with strawberries, aren't they? I'd be ruined the second I got my mouth on them."

He dragged his eyes from my face to my chest, then down

to the apex of my thighs, his gaze hot and wild. I froze for only half a second before I was tugging off my shirt and tossing it to the side along with my bra.

"*Fuck*," he groaned, his hand a blur as he soaked in everything new. "Look at you. Jesus Christ, *look* at you."

"I don't do double standards, remember? If I get a show, so do you."

I sat back, allowing him to take me in. Trying really fucking hard not to get in my head about it. Not to worry how I looked from this angle or if my stomach roll was obscene or how much of my cellulite he could see.

Not when Lincoln was looking at me like he'd just seen his very first *Playboy* and I was the centerfold.

"Fuck. *Fuck*." His voice was low, scraped raw, his gaze locked on me. "Look at those perfect tits. I fucking knew they'd be that gorgeous. Fucking knew all of you would be this goddamn gorgeous."

"Don't stop," I said, barely recognizing my own voice. I lifted up onto my knees, bringing myself closer to him, my hands resting on his hips. "I want to see you come. I want to feel it this time."

"Shit," he bit out, his eyes locked on me even as his rhythm faltered and his cock jerked. "You're gonna fucking wreck me, aren't you, wife?"

"I'm gonna try. Now, let me feel it, Linc. Come on me," I said, having no idea where in the hell that had come from. But I couldn't deny how my clit throbbed at the thought of him spilling himself all over me. *Because* of me.

"Fuck, *Willa*. I'm gonna—" On a guttural groan that echoed around the silo, he did exactly what I'd asked him to.

He came, hot and messy, all over my breasts while he stared down at me like I was every fantasy he'd ever had come to life.

And I loved every second of it.

The feeling was intoxicating—the power I felt, even on my knees in front of him. How he couldn't seem to hold himself back. How he couldn't look away.

Lincoln staggered back a step, collapsing onto one of the stools at the island, his chest heaving, watching me like I was magic. As he caught his breath, he slid his gaze over every inch of me, his eyes lingering on my chest and the white stripes he'd left all over it.

He reached out, swiping a finger through the mess he'd made, dragging a wet path down my body. He traced one of my nipples with his come-covered finger, circling it twice before he pinched the tight peak between his thumb and forefinger and tugged hard enough to make me gasp.

"So fucking gorgeous," he muttered, almost to himself.

Shaking his head, he tucked his once-again hard cock inside his boxer briefs and grabbed a towel from the counter before cleaning me up with gentle hands.

"You better cover up, wife," he said, his voice low and lethal as he tugged my shirt over my head. "Or I'm gonna give you something you're not ready for."

"Who says I'm not ready?"

He grinned down at me, all slow and seductive. "Is that so, hellcat? You think you're ready?"

For him to fuck me? My pussy gave an involuntary squeeze at the thought, and I had to remind myself I'd already come once tonight. I *should've* been satisfied.

Should've been, but I wasn't.

I wanted him. Inside me. Over me. Everywhere.

And I ignored the whisper in the back of my mind wondering if that was a good idea. Not *everything* had to be a good idea. Maybe this could just be a *feel*-good idea...

Instead of responding with words, I just nodded, not quite trusting my voice.

He studied me for long moments, then hummed low in his throat and offered me a hand. "Not quite yet, but soon."

I didn't know if it was relief or disappointment that flooded me, and I was too chicken to study it.

Once I stood, he tugged me to him. Then he reached up and cupped my breasts, his thumbs brushing across my nipples and tightening them into stiff peaks. "Just so we're clear, if you want to start including a benefits package in this marriage, I wouldn't say no to daily access to this view."

I huffed out a laugh and rolled my eyes. "You would be a boob man."

He wrapped his arms around me and held me to him as he kissed me. *Really* kissed me. No teasing, no buildup, no filthy promises. Just him and me and this chemistry that always crackled between us.

He pulled back just enough to murmur, "No, wife. I'm not a boob man. I'm a *Willa* man."

With one final kiss on my lips, he tugged me upstairs like he hadn't just rewritten my hold on reality.

We didn't talk about what was building between us. Didn't mention the jealousy or possession. Sure as hell didn't breathe a word about the trust it took to get on our knees for each other.

Because if we did any of that, we might have to admit this was real. And if we admitted it was real, we might have something to lose.

So instead, I followed behind him, knees still weak and pussy still wet, heart tripping over itself in the wake of his admission. Wondering just what the fuck I'd gotten myself into.

CHAPTER TWENTY-SEVEN

WILLA

Group text with Chloe, Sutton, and Willa
2:12 p.m.

CHLOE:

A little birdie told me you and Lincoln were looking awfully cozy at the Strawberry Festival. Mentioned something about how you'd probably go straight home and tear through all those lube samples…

WILLA:

Gee. I wonder who that horny old birdie could be.

SUTTON:

Did *everyone* come home with a year's supply of lube? I thought it was just Atlas.

WILLA:

That woman was passing out those packets like she was Oprah.

CHLOE:

Have you cracked into your stash? What's
your favorite flavor?

WILLA:

We...talk about our sex lives now? That's
weird.

CHLOE:

Um, hello? I got to know you at a party
where tentacle peen was the guest of
honor, and you think this is weird?

WILLA:

It kind of is.

CHLOE:

It is not! Sutton and I dish all the time. It's
how I know Atlas bought a Ghostface mask
and hid in their bathroom to scare her. And
then fuck her. Honestly, a true king.

SUTTON:

I swear, smut is the key to kink exploration.
Especially if you can get him to read
them too.

WILLA:

Lincoln doesn't need any encouragement in
that department. Holly's his smut dealer.

CHLOE:

Mine too.

SUTTON:

Same tbh. The woman knows her stuff.

WILLA:

Isn't that…awkward? Considering you're exploring all that with her sons?

CHLOE:

Not as awkward as when she told me which book made her figure out she was into light bondage.

WILLA:

WHAT

SUTTON:

Oh yeah. That was a few months ago at brunch. Mabel nearly choked on her mimosa. And you know how hard it is to surprise that filthy pervert.

CHLOE:

Speaking of spilling dirty secrets while inebriated before noon… Who's up for brunch next weekend?

SUTTON:

I'm in

WILLA:

I can't. I'll be at the market every weekend for the foreseeable future.

CHLOE:

Then a weekday. Or weeknight. Or early morning breakfast. Literally any time of day. We just need you to spill wtf has been going on between you and Lincoln.

WILLA:

Um…let me get back to you. I'm just so busy at the farm.

SUTTON:

Don't think we don't know when someone's avoiding a group session.

CHLOE:

Seriously. Did you forget who you're talking to? I'm the queen of avoidance. I have a crown and everything.

WILLA:

I really am busy at the farm!

SUTTON:

Uh huh.

CHLOE:

Guess we'll have to pounce when you least expect it.

WILLA:

Can't wait.

CHAPTER TWENTY-EIGHT

LINCOLN

TAKING my wife to the grocery store while I was starved for her pussy and recalling, in great detail, exactly how she'd tasted probably wasn't the best idea. Not when everything I looked at suddenly became a pairing to the most intoxicating flavor I'd ever had the pleasure of experiencing.

Willa wore old jeans that were nearly as soft as her tits and my flannel, the sleeves rolled to the elbows. As if that pairing weren't making me hard enough, her hair was pulled up in this lazy, messy knot that made me want to drag it all down. Or grip it while she sucked me off. Or while I fucked her from behind. Or, hell, just while I kissed the ever-loving shit out of her.

The problem I was facing wasn't just that I wanted her with a single-minded intensity. It was that I craved her like a goddamn addiction. And every look, every reluctant laugh, every brush of her fingers against me only made it worse.

And to top it all off? She didn't even realize what she was doing to me.

I was strolling behind her in aisle three, mentally mapping all the places I wanted to put my mouth on her, when the universe smacked me in the face with an offensive-as-fuck display.

"Are you *kidding* me?"

"What?" Willa stopped, glancing back at me before taking in our surroundings. No doubt wondering why I was losing my shit in the PB&J aisle.

"This is goddamn criminal," I said, nodding toward a shelf of overpriced hipster jams that looked like someone had overstock from Etsy they needed to get rid of. "Fifteen bucks for that pathetic little jar."

She huffed out a laugh. "You sold mine for *twenty-five*."

"Yeah, but yours taste delicious. These probably taste like disappointment and regret."

Willa snorted, grabbing a jar of peanut butter and tossing it into the cart. "You have to say that. Pretty sure it's in the unofficial rule book of being married."

"I say it because it's true, wife." I grabbed one of the offensive jars of jam and scanned the back, gasping at what I found. "This isn't even *real* small batch! This is made by another fucking multibillion-dollar company! Forget disappointment and regret—this probably tastes like greed and lies."

"Okay, calm down." Willa grabbed the jar from me, replaced it on the shelf, and dragged me along next to her. "Don't start a fight with that company. We can't afford that kind of lawsuit."

"We could if you'd listen to me," I said, wrapping an arm around her and letting my fingertips brush the generous curve of her ass. "We could have you stocked in stores like this. Shit, I bet I could have it done in a month."

Huffing out a breath, she rolled her eyes and strode out of the aisle. "You're being ridiculous."

She tried to sound dismissive, but I didn't miss the way her lips twitched or her eyes went soft as she looked at me. She liked that I believed in her, even if she couldn't say it out loud. And I was all too happy to be cocky as fuck for her.

Hell, for her? I'd be anything she needed me to be.

"I'm just saying," I said, strolling up behind her, lowering my voice as I leaned in close. "If you let me handle this, you'd be outselling every jar in that aisle by fall."

She gave me a look over her shoulder. "In what world do I let you handle anything?"

My gaze dropped down her body, a slow caress as I pictured her spread out in the chair, my mouth on her cunt. And then her on her knees, staring up at me like I was the hottest thing she'd ever seen.

"I've been handling some things pretty damn well, I think," I said, my voice a low rasp that didn't allow for any misinterpretation.

"Control yourself, jackass," she said, though my nickname sounded a hell of a lot more affectionate than it used to. And there was no mistaking the rosy tint to her cheeks.

"I've got good ideas besides how to make you come," I whispered in her ear then expertly dodged the smack she aimed at my stomach. With a laugh, I said, "Honey sticks? Me. Laurel on the farm? Also me. Pricing your jam at triple your usual cost and still selling out? All me."

"Settle down, Linc. We're not going to be able to fit all these groceries in the house if your head keeps growing."

A slow grin spread across my mouth. "You are an expert at that, aren't you, wife?"

"Would you stop?" she hissed, glancing back at me as she strode into the produce aisle. "Go grab me a bottle of ginger peach iced tea and quit acting like a middle school boy."

I flashed her a grin and a wink, but I did as she asked, strolling to the end cap a few aisles down and grabbing three teas since they were her favorite. When I made it back into the produce aisle, I spotted her right away in front of the eggplants.

And beside her? Jeff *I thought about asking him to build me a tub* Morris. Enemy Number One.

He was gesturing to a particularly large specimen like he was about to give a TED Talk on phallic-shaped produce.

My jaw clenched. My eye twitched.

This motherfucker.

Willa was laughing—*laughing*—and I couldn't make out what they were saying, but I didn't need to. There was one reason and one reason only a man stood that close while making hand gestures at eggplants. He sure as fuck wasn't talking about dinner.

Before my brain could talk me out of it, I stalked over and dropped the bottles of tea into the cart. Then I stepped up behind Willa and slid my hand over her stomach, tugging her gently but firmly back into me. She stiffened for half a second, but then she relaxed against me like it was exactly where she belonged.

"Believe me," I said, voice deceptively calm as I met Jeff's eyes. "She knows all about good eggplants. I make sure of it."

Willa sputtered and glanced back at me with a *what the fuck* look, and Jeff just froze, eyes wide, his entire face flaming pink.

"Oh, um, definitely," he said, clearing his throat. "Yeah, I was just telling Willa the selection's really good this year..."

"Whatever you say." I sent him a grin that was less invitation and more threat. "Let us know if you need a recipe."

He gave us a tight-lipped smile before slinking off with his giant eggplant in his basket.

What a tool.

Willa turned slowly, her eyes narrowed. "Did you seriously just *growl* at someone over an eggplant?"

"It wasn't over an eggplant, Willa. He was talking about his dick."

She scoffed. "Only you would think that."

"Because I'm right. I'm a guy, hellcat. Believe me, I know when another dude is trying to get his *eggplant* handled."

"You are absolutely *ridiculous*." With a glare, she stalked off, her ass jiggling in the most tantalizing way and making me want to drop to my knees right here and bite it.

Probably not what she was going for, but I took what I was dealt. And I was dealt a feisty wife with a killer ass and tits for days. She was dealt a husband who was deceptively sweet but actually possessive as hell when it came to her.

And I refused to apologize for it.

CHAPTER TWENTY-NINE

WILLA

ONCE WE WERE BACK at the silo, we unloaded the groceries in silence. Tight, blistering silence. The tension between us was thick, practically tangible.

It didn't matter how far Lincoln was standing from me. I could *feel* him. And I knew if I turned around, I'd find him watching me the way he had in the store. Like he wanted to bite me. Or brand me.

Or both.

Honestly, the *nerve* of this man. Acting like that just because he was my husband. *On paper*, mind you.

Not for real.

Not forever.

I set a bag of zucchini onto the counter with a little more force than necessary and huffed a breath. Lincoln would probably lose his shit if he knew Jeff had suggested those too.

"Something on your mind, wife?" he asked, breaking the silence. His voice was low, controlled in a way that absolutely was not fair.

I was anything but controlled.

"Nope."

"You sure? Cause you've practically drop-kicked the squash and slammed every cabinet door in less than a minute."

"Fine. You want to know what's on my mind?" I slammed another door and turned to glare at him. "You don't get to mark your territory and pee a circle around me just because we filed some paperwork. I'm not a fucking fence post, Lincoln."

His expression didn't falter, but the corner of his jaw ticked. The only outward sign of his irritation.

"No," he said, stepping toward me. "But you *are* my wife, and I'm your husband."

I scoffed and backed into the counter without meaning to. "What does that—"

"You didn't seem to mind marking your territory with that flirty blonde at the Strawberry Festival."

I blinked, jerking back. "That was different. She was shoving her tits in your face and practically licking your neck!"

He stepped even closer, his voice low. "So you admit it bothered you."

"I—" I started before snapping my mouth shut. Fuck *yes*, it had bothered me. She'd been all over him, and I'd wanted to climb him like a tree and hiss at her from the top. "I don't care."

He braced his hands on the counter on either side of my hips and leaned down until we were eye to eye. "You, my lovely wife, are a beautiful little liar."

I shoved against his chest, but the big jackass didn't move. "I'm *not* lying. There's no reason for that to bother me. This isn't real, Lincoln."

His eyes darkened, his jaw ticking. "No?"

I swallowed hard, my breathing rough as I met his gaze. "No."

He lowered his face, ran his nose along the curve of my jaw, down my neck and back up again. Against my ear, he whispered, "I don't believe you."

Pulling back, he flicked his gaze down to my lips before meeting my eyes once again. "You know why? Because your cheeks are all flushed and your breathing is ragged and your nipples are hard as fuck. And I bet if I slipped my hand inside your panties, I'd feel just how fucking wet you are. Tell me that's not real."

"It's not—"

He huffed out a laugh and shook his head. "It sure as hell felt real when you came in my lap and when you rode my face like you couldn't get enough. And how about when I was wiping my come off your perfect tits? Was that real, hellcat?"

Heat blasted through me like wildfire, igniting every nerve ending in my body. My pulse was a feral, reckless beast, and my pussy throbbed for his touch. Every inch of me recalling, in great detail, just how good he'd made me feel.

"Say it again," he said, stepping into me until barely a breath of space was left between us. "Tell me it isn't real."

I opened my mouth to do just that but found I couldn't. For years, I'd been fighting this thing between us, and I was so tired. Of lying to him. Of lying to myself.

"That's what I thought." He wrapped a hand around the back of my neck and crashed his mouth down on mine.

And that was it—a spark to the gasoline that we'd been soaking in for days…weeks.

Years.

There was nothing gentle about this kiss. It was hunger and want and years of built-up tension finally detonating. He kissed me like he had something to prove, and every bite to my lip was a promise, every stroke of his tongue a declaration. I moaned into him, furious with how much I needed this— needed *him*.

No more waiting. No more holding back.

I growled—actually growled—grabbed the front of his shirt, and shoved him against the counter. Tired of playing this game.

The smug bastard just laughed against my lips. "You gonna punish me, wife?"

"Shut. Up." I yanked his T-shirt, tugging it up and off like it was solely responsible for all my sexual frustration, before dragging his mouth back to mine.

He kissed me back just as hard—openmouthed, desperate. *Real.*

There was no pretending now. No faking. No acting. Because this wasn't about the marriage.

This was about Lincoln and me and this burning need that had been smoldering between us for years. The one I'd ignored. The one I'd lied to myself about.

The one here to finally demand the oxygen we'd been denying it for years.

Our clothes hit the floor like falling sparks, leaving a trail of heat in their wake. I wanted him to take me right here, right now. Against the wall, bent over the island. Hell, right on the hardwood floor. I didn't care how uncomfortable it was or how much I'd inevitably pay for it later.

I just needed him immediately.

Before I could climb straight up his body, he lifted me into his arms, his fingers digging into my ass, his mouth still hungry on mine. I didn't know where he was taking me, but I didn't care. Not when I could feel him, hot and hard right where I needed him.

I rolled my hips, dragging a groan from his throat. One second, we were upright, and the next, I was flat on my back, the mattress soft beneath me with Lincoln braced above.

"What—"

"I didn't want to fuck up your back if you had to stand there too long." He sank to the floor next to the bed and slid his hands up my inner thighs, spreading me wide for his greedy gaze. "And I'm not getting off my knees any time soon. This pretty little cunt got her first taste of worship, and now she's gonna learn what being spoiled really means."

I exhaled a shaky breath, and then he was there, licking a path through my slit and groaning into my flesh like he'd been starved for his favorite meal. Dropping my head back, I moaned to the ceiling, my thighs already trembling.

"Been dreaming about this sweet pussy since my last taste," he rasped, brushing his lips against my clit before sucking it into his mouth. "Can't even go a single goddamn night without waking up hard as a fucking rock, thinking about the sounds you made when you came on my face."

"God, Lincoln—"

He licked a path through my pussy, slow and deliberate. Memorizing me. *Savoring* me. He flattened his tongue against my clit, letting loose a low groan like the taste of me short-circuited his brain. And I couldn't say I was faring much better. Not when his mouth was this good, his attention this focused.

With one hand anchored on my thigh, he splayed me wide, and he slid his other hand under me to grip my ass. Tilting me just how he wanted. Driving me wild with every flick and stroke of his tongue, with every hum vibrating against my skin.

"You gonna try to tell me it's not real while my tongue's on your pussy?" He licked me again, slower this time, his eyes locked on mine from his perch between my spread thighs. "Gonna try to lie to me again while your cunt's dripping down my chin?"

God. *God.*

I couldn't think. Could barely breathe as I stared down at him. He looked so fucking hot like this—his eyes dark and feral, cheeks flushed, hair a mess from my fingers, the bottom half of his face wet from what he was doing to me.

"You think anyone else could make you feel this good? Could lick your pussy this well?" His voice was low...rough... paired with an edge of something I couldn't quite name.

I wasn't sure if he wanted or even needed an answer, but I gave him one anyway, shaking my head quickly as I curled my fingers in the sheets just to anchor myself to earth. To stop myself from floating away thanks to the pleasure he was stoking inside me.

"That's right," he said, nothing but pure male satisfaction in his tone. "I eat this perfect cunt like I'm hungry for it, don't I, hellcat? Because I am. I've been fucking *starving* for it."

And then he was done playing with his meal. He gripped the backs of my thighs, pushed my legs toward my chest, and buried his face against my pussy.

A constant stream of moans and unintelligible sounds left my throat as he licked broad, possessive strokes through my slit. Teased my entrance with a finger before sinking one, then two, deep inside me. Flattened his tongue and dragged it from my entrance to my clit before sucking hard enough to make me cry out, my entire body seizing in pleasure.

"There you go, wife. That's my girl." He groaned, long and low as he curled his fingers, stroking that spot inside me. "I can feel you, so fucking desperate to come."

I whimpered, rocking my hips against him. Needing... something. More, faster, harder...I didn't know. Just that I was so close but not close enough.

"Relax, baby. We're not gonna rush it." He continued curling his fingers inside me as he flicked my clit with his thumb. When his pinkie brushed against my back entrance, I damn near shot off the bed.

"Linc—" I gasped, eyes wide, cheeks flushed, pulse a galloping racehorse in my chest.

He hummed, a self-satisfied sound. "Feel good, wife?"

"Yes," I breathed, rolling my hips, so damn needy for more.

Reaching up with one hand, he cupped my breast, brushing his thumb across my nipple before pinching it and giving a sharp tug. I couldn't hold in my moan, not when he was working my body like he knew exactly what I needed. Working it like he owned it.

"Look at you. Those fucking wet dream tits and this cunt... All pink and swollen and ready for me." He worked his fingers inside me, the sounds filling the room wet and filthy and perfect. "I'm the only one who's done this to you, aren't I?"

Whimpering, I nodded because I couldn't do anything else. He was right. He was the only one who'd ever seen me like this—strung out and desperate and aching for more.

"Your mouth, Linc—" I reached for him, slid my fingers into his hair, and tugged him close. "Please. I need your mouth."

Instead of teasing me, he gave in immediately, leaning in and adding his tongue in tandem to his thumb, creating a jumbled mess of sensation that drove me wild. All while he pressed more insistently against my tight hole, and my pussy pulsed an erratic rhythm, desperate to come.

He kept his eyes locked on mine as he flicked his tongue across my clit, and then he slid a third finger inside my pussy, his pinkie just breaching my back entrance, and I shattered.

The orgasm ripped through me before I could brace for it. It wasn't soft or slow, no rolling waves of bliss. No, this was wild and volcanic, molten heat searing through my veins as my pussy clamped down on his fingers and my thighs locked tight around his head. He groaned against me like I was the best thing he'd ever tasted.

The only thing he wanted to taste for the rest of his life.

It wasn't our reality, but it was easy to trick myself into believing it was true. Especially when I looked down at him and found him staring back, eyes dark and hooded, his mouth soaked with my come. He looked feral. Desperate. On the brink of losing control.

He looked like *mine*.

CHAPTER THIRTY

WILLA

I NEEDED HIM INSIDE ME. *Now*. With a desperation that was altogether foreign to me. Sex had always been fine. Something I'd done with a few people, but nothing I'd ever craved.

But this? With Lincoln? This was something else entirely.

I reached for him, my body still shaking, my pussy throbbing for more. "I need you inside me."

He groaned against me, gave my clit one final flick of his tongue, and stood. His cock was thick and hard, sticking straight out from his body and looking intimidating as fuck.

Shit.

What was the sex equivalent of my eyes being bigger than my stomach? Because I was pretty sure I was living that reality, except my pussy was the one in danger now.

"Fuck, you're big," I breathed, unable to drag my eyes away from him.

He huffed out a pained laugh and gave one firm stroke up

his length, precome spilling from his head and over his fingers. "You're already saying that, and I'm not even inside—"

His words cut off, and he froze, eyes snapping to mine. "Fuck."

"What?"

He dragged his other hand down his face, squeezing his eyes shut. "*Fuck.*"

"*What?*" I asked again. "What is it?"

Exhaling a deep sigh, he met my gaze. "I don't have a condom."

I stared at him, mouth agape, eyes wide. "Seriously? You didn't bring one?"

"You don't have to sound so shocked about it. I wasn't exactly expecting to rail my wife this afternoon."

I braced myself on my elbows and glared at him—standing there looking all hot and gorgeous and ready for me. "Well, I wasn't expecting to want your dick inside me either, but here we are."

He darted his gaze down to my pussy, then back to my face. "You still have an IUD?"

I froze for half a second, then swallowed. Gave a short nod. "You been tested recently?"

"It's been a while." Giving himself a slow, lazy stroke, he stepped closer. "But I'm clear. And I haven't been with anyone in a long time."

I didn't know what *a long time* was in Lincoln speak. And at the present moment, I wasn't exactly in a place mentally to break down that statement or ask him for clarification. All I could do was stare at him—hard cock in hand, chest rising fast, jaw clenched like he was *this close* to snapping.

"You trust me?" he asked, voice low. Serious.

Lincoln's and my relationship was a lot of things—tumultuous, volatile, messy. But he was one of very few people in my life I trusted implicitly. Even with all our history and baggage. Maybe even *because* of it.

"You know I do."

He was on me in a heartbeat, climbing onto the bed as he trailed kisses down my neck, across my collarbone. He sucked one nipple into his mouth before moving his attention to the other, his hands just as busy. "You gonna take me bare, wife? Let me feel how tight you get when you come around me?"

"If you think you can make that happen," I said, half taunting him just because. "We're in uncharted territory now."

"Hellcat, I'm the one mapping this uncharted territory." He sat on his heels, gripping the backs of my thighs and spreading me wide for him.

"Your smugness is choking me."

"I have every reason to be smug." He ran the head of his cock through my slit, groaning like he was already half undone. "I made you come without even touching you. Drank every bit of your pleasure when you fell apart against my tongue. So if you think I'm going to settle deep inside this cunt tonight without feeling you come around it, you don't know me as well as you thought, wife."

"That's just talk and a lot of lofty promises."

His lips curved up in a grin, deliberate and so fucking sexy. "I don't make promises I can't keep."

And then he was there, the blunt head of his cock pressing against my entrance, and my breath caught.

Oh shit. *Shit.*

He was thick. Devastatingly thick.

With ragged, panting breaths, I locked my gaze on his as he pressed deeper, stretching me to that delicious edge where pleasure met pain. "Lincoln—"

"I've got you," he murmured, one hand braced beside my head, the other splayed across my hip like he was grounding me. Claiming me. "You're so fucking wet for me, aren't you? And I'm gonna go nice and easy. Just breathe, baby."

The stretch was slow. Relentless. All while Lincoln kissed me everywhere he could—my mouth, my neck, my breasts, sucking on my nipples like they were his favorite candy and he couldn't get enough.

And through it all, my heartbeat thrummed in my ears, matching the pulse of my clit as he sank inside me, inch by deliciously thick inch.

"Almost?" I asked on panting breaths, my fingers curled tight around his wrist.

He slipped his hand down, brushing his thumb against my clit and pulling a moan straight from my throat. "There you go. Let me in, wife."

"You *are* in."

"Not even halfway yet, hellcat."

"*What?*" I snapped my head up and stared between us, my gaze focused on the sight of my pussy stretched so wide around his cock, more than half of it still outside my body. "Oh my god. Oh my *fuck*, you're going to kill me with your monster cock, aren't you? That's been your plan all along."

He breathed out a laugh—half wild, half smug. "You're the one who begged for it."

I gasped, partially from indignation, but mostly thanks to him sinking another inch inside. "I did *not—*"

"You did," he said. "No use lying now, wife. Fuck knows I've been begging for you for longer than I want to admit."

He pushed in another inch, and I groaned, my entire body arching beneath him like it was trying to pull away and suck him deeper all at once.

"Jesus, Linc..." I glanced between us, seeing how much of his cock he'd sunk inside me.

"Told you," he growled against my throat, pressing an openmouthed kiss there. "We'll make it fit."

And we did. Inch by unrelenting inch, until the push and pull and drag of him in my pussy made me dizzy with want. Until my walls clamped down on his cock like they weren't ready to give up a single part of him.

"Feel that?" he rasped, not moving. Just buried deep inside me, letting me settle into the stretch and fullness. "Your sweet little cunt is wrapped so tight around me, it feels like your pussy doesn't want to let me go."

I whimpered, staring up into his eyes as he shifted his hips, pulling back before sinking deep again. My eyes fluttered closed on a moan, my pussy pulsing around him. Every pleasure synapse in my body pinpointed on the spot we were joined.

He brushed kisses along my jaw, across my cheek, before settling his lips against my ear. "This is mine now, wife. You understand? This cunt is *mine.*"

With lazy rolls of his hips, he fucked me like he had all

the time in the world. Like I wasn't seconds from breaking apart beneath him, just like he'd promised.

"No one else has felt this. No one else has *earned* this." He pulled nearly all the way out before pushing back inside in an unhurried, deliberate thrust, groaning like he was already close. "First man to watch you unravel. First to taste your come. And now?"

He kissed me slow and deep, so much possession in each slide of his tongue against mine. Then he pressed his forehead against mine and glanced between us, staring at where he was disappearing inside me.

"Now...I'm gonna be the first and only man to make you fall apart on his cock."

"Do it, then," I rasped, locking my legs around his hips and lifting mine to meet his next thrust. "Make me come all over you."

His eyes blazed, the rhythm of his thrusts stuttering. "Say that again."

"You heard me."

With a growl, he sat back on his heels and gripped my thighs, holding me open for him. And then he slammed into me, over and over, his cock hitting that place inside me only he'd been able to reach.

"Not gonna stop till you do exactly that, wife," he said, punctuating every word with a deep, punishing thrust, his thumb a blur against my clit. "Gonna work this perfect cunt till she's squeezing me so tight you forget your own fucking name."

I gripped his thighs, my nails digging in, searching for purchase. That only made him slam into me harder, grinding deeper. And when he pressed his palm flat on my lower stomach, adding pressure as he strummed my clit with his thumb, something built deep inside, wild and reckless.

"Oh my god, Lincoln—" I choked out, unable to do anything but stare up at him as he took me exactly where he wanted me to go.

"That's it," he gritted out, his gaze darting between my face and my pussy as he sank inside again and again. "Let them hear you. Let this whole fucking town know your husband fucks you better than anyone else ever could."

I didn't try to keep quiet. Even if I had, it wouldn't have mattered. I no longer had control of anything. Not my voice, not my body.

Sure as hell not my heart.

I moaned, loud and wrecked and completely gone for him.

"You want to say it's not real again? Wanna lie to me with your mouth while your pussy spills all your dirty little secrets?"

His grip on my hip turned punishing, his fingers digging into my flesh like he was trying to brand himself there.

"Tell me you feel that," he demanded, his palm pressing harder on my lower belly, thumb circling my clit even faster. "The way you're squeezing my cock... She knows, baby. Your perfect cunt knows exactly who she belongs to."

Every word landed like an electric shock, zapping through my body, sparking in all the places we were connected. I was unraveling beneath him, inch by inch, second by second, so close to falling into oblivion.

"Linc—" I gasped. "I'm gonna—"

"That's right." He sped up, his thumb flying across my clit, hips thrusting deep. Just as crazed for it as I was. "Give it to me, wife. Come all over your husband's cock. Show me no one else deserves to feel this pussy but *me*."

On a broken sob, I exploded—back arching, nails digging into his flesh, and his name falling from my lips like a prayer. My pussy clenched around him, over and over, until he cursed and sank deep.

With a low, guttural moan against my neck, he fell over the edge with me, his cock pulsing as he spilled inside me, his body shuddering with his release.

We stayed like that for long moments, both of us gasping, boneless, wrecked. My body was trembling beneath his, my heart pounding so hard I thought it might leap straight out of my chest.

Lincoln lifted his head from my neck and rested his forehead against mine, his eyes closed, our breath mingling in the space between us.

"Jesus Christ, Willa," he rasped. Proof he was just as wrung out as I was.

I ran my fingers up and down his back, relishing in the fullness of him still inside me. I wasn't sure I ever wanted him to leave.

Before I could tell him just that, he sat up and pulled out, slowly, carefully. And I felt it immediately—the warm, slick slide of his come leaking out of me. My breath caught at the sensation, but it was the look on Lincoln's face that had my lungs seizing.

Staring between us, his eyes dark and ravenous, he licked a slow path across his bottom lip. He shuffled a bit closer, swiping the head of his cock against my pussy, gathering every bit of his orgasm that had slipped out of me.

And then, with his eyes locked on mine, he pushed his cock inside me again. A slow, possessive thrust that left no doubt to his intention, filling me in the way only he could.

"Oh god," I moaned. "Again?"

"Hell yes, again. You think we're done?" he asked, his voice low, gritty, as he rocked into me. "Not yet, wife. I'm gonna keep filling you up until your greedy pussy learns to hold every single drop."

CHAPTER THIRTY-ONE

WILLA

BEAU:

Apparently newlywed life is busy as shit, but maybe text your twin once in a while? And answer your goddamn phone.

AFTER A NIGHT for the record books, I'd spent the past several days avoiding everything. The twinge in my back, the texts from my brother...my feelings.

But fuck, this was *not* supposed to happen.

I wasn't supposed to get all *gooey* for Lincoln Steele. Wasn't supposed to crave him so much it scared the hell out of me.

So, yeah. I'd avoided him. And Chloe. And Sutton.

Because I knew their little girls' date ambush was imminent, and I had no idea how I was going to handle that. What was I going to say?

Lincoln and I are married, but we're not really married. Except he fucked me like we are, made me feel things I didn't think were possible, and now I think I might be, maybe, slightly, the tiniest bit falling in love with my husband...

I was sure that would go over amazingly well.

Unfortunately, since Laurel had been helping at the farm, Sutton had the inside track on my schedule. Which was how she caught me before I could escape to the library where I'd been hiding just to get some damn breathing room from my too-hot-for-my-sanity husband.

"Girls' night. No arguments," she said from the front porch. "You've been dodging us. It's annoying."

"I've been busy," I lied.

She raised a single brow, a silent invitation to try her. "You haven't replied to the group chat in three days, and Chloe made me help her with some spell to get you to stop avoiding us. You're coming."

Since I was not, in fact, willing to try the woman who'd been a single mom to a sarcastic porcupine of a teenager for the past seventeen years, I allowed Sutton to usher me into her car and drive us into town.

And straight to One Night Stan's.

Because of course that was where we'd go. It was the best —and only—bar in town. And it wasn't like I could admit I'd been avoiding my own husband—my stupidly hot, infuriatingly attentive, somehow-also-soft-where-it-mattered *fake* husband.

The second Sutton and I walked in, Chloe looked up from behind the bar and beamed at us.

"*Finally*," she said. "I was about to file a missing person's report."

I kept my gaze locked on her because I didn't dare look around. Of course the girls would pick tonight to go out—one of only two nights this week Lincoln was working late. And there was no doubt he was here. I could feel that constant buzz beneath my skin that hummed whenever he was near.

"I think you're being a little dramatic," I said. "It's been three days."

"Have you *met* me? Xander bought me a coffee cup that says *I am the drama*."

"Most accurate mug I've ever seen," Sutton said, grabbing two of the margarita glasses Chloe passed over.

"Time for drinking and secret-spilling, ladies." Chloe grabbed the remaining glass and stepped out from behind the bar, leading the way to a booth in the back.

I started to follow them, but before I could take a single step, a finger hooked into my belt loop and yanked me back against a hard chest. My breath caught in my throat as I turned, already expecting who I'd find. Already bracing myself for it.

And sure enough, Lincoln stood there, close enough that the scent of him hit me right along with the warmth of his body seeping into my back. And then there was the grin he sent my way, all playful and amused.

"Where do you think you're going, wife?" He tilted his head, studying me like he could see straight through me. "You've been hiding from me, so I'm sure as hell gonna get my fill now."

I opened my mouth to respond—with deflection or snark,

I wasn't sure. But before I could say a word, Lincoln was there, his hand cupping the back of my neck and his lips pressed to mine.

The kiss wasn't indecent. Technically. Just the barest brush of his tongue against mine, his soft hum of satisfaction vibrating against my lips. But the shock wave it sent through me was enough to leave me reeling.

He pulled back and grinned down at me, obnoxiously pleased with himself as he darted his gaze over my face. "Time to have fun with your girls. But I'll be seeing you at home tonight, wife."

Then he swatted my ass before stepping behind the bar like he hadn't just activated every sleeper cell in my body.

I stared at him for a second too long, then shook my head to clear it before glaring at him over my shoulder. Smug jackass knew *exactly* what he was doing. Sure enough, he caught my scowl, but instead of being chastened, he just winked at me before getting back to work.

I hated his stupid face. And I really, *really* hated how much I didn't actually hate him.

I slid into the booth across from Sutton and Chloe and downed half my margarita in one go. If I had any hope of making it through the night, I needed to calm my nerves. Along with this ever-present hum in my body, reminding me my husband was far too close for my sanity.

The girls' night dishing session started off easy. Chloe talked about Mabel's latest promotion at Wicked Little Things—buy a vibe, get a cookie—and how Emma was in a kitten-only language phase. Sutton gave us the inside scoop on how much Laurel was enjoying working with me at the farm *and* the blooming crush she had on a girl at school.

This was fine. I could handle this kind of gossip since it wasn't centered anywhere near me. When they started talking about the weird, invisible tension between Penelope and Declan, I started to relax.

Rookie mistake.

Sutton reached for a chip, dipped it in some guac, and then, as casual as ever, said, "Okay, we're not grilling you..."

Chloe cut in, her smile bright. "She's lying. We're *definitely* grilling you."

My stomach flipped, my heart sinking, knowing that grilling me meant digging deep into my very much fake relationship with Lincoln. How the hell was I going to pass this test?

"What's there to grill me about?" I asked, attempting to keep my voice level.

Sutton lifted a single brow and brought her margarita to her lips. "Oh, I don't know... Maybe the fact that half the time I've seen you and Lincoln together, you've looked like you were about to claw each other's eyes out? And now you're *married*?"

Chloe nodded. "I'm with Sutton—I was just as skeptical."

Oh god. This was it. They were going to call me out on Lincoln's and my lie. Then everyone would know about our sham marriage, and Lincoln and I would be done. No more cohabitating. No more sharing one bed. No more late-night reading companion or daily verbal sparring partner or grocery store co-shopper. No more surprise deliveries of my favorite coffee or Danish, no more tickles when I had a back spasm, and no more practice make-out sessions.

And, of course, the grant would no longer be an option. The *grant* was the biggest deal here. Obviously.

A flush had worked its way up my chest, pooling in my cheeks, as I tried to get my story straight. Trying to figure out what the hell I was going to tell them.

Then a grin cracked Sutton's stony expression, and she winked. "Turns out, the only thing you wanted to claw was the clothes off his body. Honestly, been there."

Chloe nodded solemnly. "Who hasn't?"

Jesus*fuck.*

As covertly as possible, I exhaled an unsteady breath, too busy trying to regulate my galloping heart to respond with anything coherent. So instead, I took another deep breath and brought my drink to my mouth with a shaky hand just to buy myself some time.

Sutton leaned in. "Seriously, we don't even *need* to grill you. The way you look at each other? It's obvious."

"What is?" I asked.

"Like you don't know, *Mrs. Steele*." Chloe's eyes twinkled as she looked at me before glancing to her right, straight toward the bar. "You should see Lincoln right now. You've been pretending not to look at him, but he hasn't taken his eyes off you since you walked in. It's so fucking adorable, it makes me wanna puke."

I huffed out a relieved laugh that probably sounded half hysterical. "You have no idea what happens behind closed doors."

"Oh, babe." Sutton smirked at me and patted my hand. "We don't need to."

"She's not wrong." Chloe shot me a sly grin. "What we see in plain sight is enough to slap an NC-17 rating on the two of you."

"You act like a couple who's been circling each other for years, just waiting for your chance." Sutton took another sip of her margarita, eyes dancing. "And he watches you like he wants to *devour* you."

"And don't even try to act like you don't like it." Chloe swirled a finger in my direction. "You're glowing like someone getting the good D on the regular—dick *and* devotion."

Sutton snorted, and the two of them shared a laugh while I smiled and didn't say a word. What *could* I say? They weren't wrong.

And that was the problem.

The three of us talked too much and laughed too loud, and I downed my drinks like they could burn the unwelcome feelings for Lincoln straight out of my chest. Like tequila could cauterize longing.

Unfortunately, they didn't.

They only made me feel warmer. Looser. A little more like myself and a lot more like the woman I was afraid of becoming. The one who counted on someone else. Who let herself believe in things like quiet moments in the dark and a man sending his mom my favorite Danish and coffee order just because.

And that, more than anything, terrified me.

Because who would I be when this was all over and I was on my own…again?

When our glasses were empty and we were about to flag down Lisa for refills, Lincoln stepped up to our table with a smirk and a tray of three lowball glasses. "Thought you ladies could use another round."

"Ohhh…what are these?" Chloe rubbed her hands together and bounced in her seat.

"Black Cat," he said, setting the other two on the table and sliding mine in front of me. His gaze dipped to my lips, and my body lit up like a firework. "Brand new recipe. Bourbon, bitters, my wife's blackberry syrup I stole from the pantry. And a lemon twist."

He braced one hand on the table and leaned in until I could feel his breath across my lips. "Tastes like you," he murmured. "All bite at first, but it finishes sweet."

There was no doubt in my mind he was referencing our night together. When I'd attacked him in the kitchen then came all over his cock—twice—like I'd been born to do it.

He pressed a quick kiss on my lips before standing to his full height. "You ladies let me know if you need another one."

And then he walked away, and I stared after him, my cheeks flaming and my body flushed all over.

"Oh my *god*," Chloe hissed. "Did he *name a drink* after you?"

"That's what it sounded like to me," Sutton said, her tone laced with *I told you so.*

Chloe smirked, her expression positively gleeful. "Black Cat, huh? All sass, no snuggles—at least until he makes you *purrrrr*?"

"I hate you both," I grumbled.

"You don't," Sutton said. "You love us."

"No one can hate anything when they're getting the D like I just *know* he's delivering." Chloe took a sip of her drink and shook her head. "The Steele men have a certain way about them..."

Sutton nodded. "That they do. And I'm not sure NC-17 is a high enough rating for that sex-with-your-clothes-on we just witnessed between you two."

"It was *not*—"

"Tell me about it," Chloe interrupted, her head bent toward her phone, her thumbs flying over the screen. "I'm telling Xander to drop Emma at his mom's and get his ass over here. Might need to sneak off to the bathroom for a little grown-up time."

"I already texted Atlas." Sutton slipped her phone into her purse. "I give it three minutes before he comes storming through the door."

"Then it's time for a toast before they descend!" Chloe raised her glass. "To our favorite black cat and the golden retriever who finally chased her down."

"Welcome to the family, Willa." Sutton clinked her glass with mine. "The Steele men can be a real pain in the ass..."

Chloe leaned in, her voice dropping to a not-quite whisper. "But those dicks, am I right?"

I choked on a laugh and shook my head, cheeks burning hotter than the bourbon. But they weren't wrong.

"You two are the worst," I muttered, but the words came out softer than I meant them to.

That was just the booze talking, not anything else. Not

the warmth or the laughter or the ridiculous toast or feeling like I actually belonged to something…someone.

Like I was finally part of a *we*.

I blinked hard, trying to shove the feeling away. Push it back down where it belonged—out of sight and out of mind. But it stayed right there, lodged in my heart like a splinter I couldn't dig out. Small but sharp and impossible to ignore.

When I glanced over at the bar, Lincoln was laughing at something Declan said, his grin wide and carefree. He looked so damn good, all confidence and charisma. He turned in my direction then, like I was a magnet drawing his gaze. And when he caught me looking before I could pretend I wasn't, he smiled just for me. Slow and lazy and as smug as sin. Like he knew exactly what I was thinking.

Then he picked up a lowball glass filled with amber liquid, a lemon peel on the rim—a Black Cat. He raised it in my direction with a smirk on his lips that said he was toasting a secret only the two of us knew.

The trouble was, I didn't know which secret he was referring to because we shared so many.

And no matter how many times I told myself this thing between us was fake, that look on his face—the one that said *mine* without saying a damn word—was starting to feel all too real.

CHAPTER THIRTY-TWO

WILLA

I SHOULD'VE GONE HOME, but for some reason, I let Chloe and Sutton talk me into another round. And then they talked me into a game of pool, even while their bodyguards—er, boyfriends—stood watch from behind the bar.

All four of the Steele brothers were here tonight, three of them focused on this pool table and nothing else. And I knew if a certain bespectacled librarian had been in tonight, Declan would've had his attention snared too.

"Uh-oh," Sutton muttered, chalking her cue, her gaze caught on something behind me. "They've lost patience with us, Chlo."

I turned around to see both Atlas and Xander stalking toward us, the crowd splitting like the Red Sea.

"Oh, oh!" Chloe bounced on her toes, a bright grin on her face. "You know what that means! Time for three on three!"

"We're in," Sutton said, leaning into Atlas's side as he wrapped a possessive arm around her.

"Your counting's off," I said, wondering just how much

they'd had to drink tonight. "How about two on two, and I sit this one out?"

"Absolutely *not*." Chloe gave a firm shake of her head. "We need Lincoln."

Xander stepped up behind her and pressed a kiss to her temple. "Don't love that you said that as soon as I got here, chaos."

Chloe tipped her head back and grinned at him. "It's for Willa, obviously. Let's school the newlyweds since they'll be all distracted with sex eyes."

No. *No*.

The last thing I needed was Lincoln close. Not when I could already *feel* him all the way across the room. I was still too warm from the look he gave me earlier, his words murmured against my lips. And I was far too rattled from the memory of his mouth on me, his body covering mine, his cock filling me so completely.

I wasn't drunk enough for this.

I wasn't *sober* enough for this.

"He's working," I said, trying to sound cool and calm and oh-so casual. "Leave him be."

Being the good friend she was, Chloe ignored me completely and turned toward the bar, her hands cupped around her mouth. "Lincoln! Your wife needs you over here!"

"Oh my god," I muttered before downing the rest of my drink.

Sure, Lincoln ignored me completely whenever I told him I didn't need his help or that I could handle things. But, this? *This* he paid attention to.

He wiped his hands on the towel slung over his shoulder

before tossing it on the counter and stepping out from behind the bar. He strolled over to us, all cocky swagger in those jeans that were made for his ass and that T-shirt that was molded to him like a second skin.

Goddammit, he was hot.

His eyes never left mine as he walked straight to me, only stopping once he was in my space, his feet bracketing mine, his chest close enough that the hard tips of my breasts brushed against him with every inhale.

"You needed me, wife?" He wrapped an arm around me, his fingers lingering on the curve of my ass, that stupid smirk on his stupid face. "Say no more."

I didn't want to melt into his warmth. Didn't want to love how his body fit against mine or how his breath against my ear made me shudder and want things I definitely should not want.

"The only thing I need from you is to keep up," I said, forcing my voice to be steady as I stepped back and grabbed my stick. "Try not to cry when I win."

A slow grin swept across Lincoln's mouth, his dimples flashing. "Goddamn, you're cute when you're cocky, hellcat."

I narrowed my eyes on him. "You know what happens when you call a hellcat cute? Her claws come out."

He grabbed a stick for himself and stepped up behind me, his lips against my ear. "Good. Maybe she'll use them on my back tonight."

His words shot a bolt of lightning straight to my pussy as images of me doing exactly that while he filled me over and over slammed into me.

I met his gaze, unable to hide the heat in my eyes. And he was…smirking at me?

Oh, this jackass was good.

He thought he could knock me off my game? Well, two could play at that.

"Ladies?" I asked, my gaze still locked on Lincoln. "You mind if I hand my husband his ass first before we team up?"

"We'll allow it," Sutton said with a nod.

"Hell yes, we will!" Chloe settled on Xander's lap. "Watching you two is gonna be more entertaining than playing."

Then the table was ours and our audience was forgotten as Lincoln and I faced off against each other.

He racked the balls with the kind of confidence that said he could do it blindfolded. And he probably could. Probably *had*. He'd grown up in this place, had spent so much time here when he was younger that all this was second nature.

But, for years, I'd been right next to him. Playing alongside him. Getting beaten by him. *Beating* him.

Which meant this was anyone's game.

Those hot-as-sin forearms flexed as he lined up the cue, his smirk gone now and replaced by a focus that was razor-sharp. He leaned low over the table, drew the stick back, and broke.

The crack of the shot echoed through the bar, the balls scattering across the felt. A solid dropped into a pocket. Then another.

Shit.

"Well, well, well. Looks like I'm already winning, wife." He straightened slowly, that smirk back as he locked his eyes with mine. Like he knew exactly what he was doing—to the table *and* to me. "You planning to play tonight or just stand there looking pretty while I run the table?"

My blood began to boil. Not from embarrassment. Not from the crowd watching us with barely concealed grins. No, my response was all thanks to him and that cocky tone and that cockier smirk. All thanks to the sheer audacity of this man thinking I had any intention of sitting back and letting him win.

He bent for another shot, confidence rolling off him in waves. The cue slid through his fingers, smooth, deliberate— then the ball grazed the corner and spun uselessly away.

I didn't bother hiding my smile as I glanced at him. Then I made my way over, studying the table.

"I'm not just planning to play." I leaned over the table, giving him an unobstructed view of my ass and absolutely knowing his gaze was locked on it. "I plan to *win*."

I took my shot, a sudden crack splitting the air, and the striped ball sailed into the corner pocket. With a grin on my face, I straightened slowly. And sure enough, Lincoln's gaze was glued to my ass like he'd forgotten where he was.

I tapped two fingers under his chin. "Eyes up, husband. You're drooling."

And that was how the entire game went. Back and forth, like a dance.

I brushed against him on my way around the table. He murmured filth in my ear anytime he was close enough. I leaned too far across the felt, giving him a clear view down my neckline. He stared at me like he was envisioning fucking me right here, damn the consequences.

Every move we made was a dare, every glance a challenge. And somewhere between the flirting and the fighting, I forgot we weren't alone.

"You sure you're still up for this, Linc?" I asked when he had three solids on the table to my one stripe. "You're looking a little...distracted."

"Oh, I'm up, all right," he murmured, lining up his shot with maddening precision. Then he lifted his gaze to me. "And you keep bending over this table like you have been, I'm gonna forget we have an audience."

Chloe snorted from somewhere behind me. "This game is either gonna end with a bar brawl or sex on the pool table."

"My bet's on Willa beating him and Lincoln dragging her outside. Possibly by her hair," Sutton said.

Lincoln and I didn't look away from each other. The thoughts flooding my mind thanks to Sutton's words were pure filth. Lincoln's fist wrapped in my hair, him fucking me over this table or the hood of his car. And from the way he stared at me, eyes heated, lips parted, shoulders tense, I knew he was thinking the same thing.

Which meant it was my chance to pounce.

I shoved the indecent thoughts from my mind as best I could and lined up my shot. Took a deep, calming breath, pulled back my cue, and let it go. My last striped ball dropped, and then the eight ball followed, sinking cleanly into the corner pocket like it knew I needed this win as badly as I needed oxygen.

Cue in hand, I straightened and sent him a saccharine smile. "Looks like I won, husband. Time to get back to work."

With his gaze locked on mine, he crowded me against the

table, slow and deliberate, until the edge pressed against my ass and there was nowhere to go that wasn't into him. "Keep acting cocky, wife. You're about thirty seconds from being bent over the nearest surface."

Flames licked across my skin, hot and all-consuming. My thighs clenched, and my mind went blank except for his words, which repeated like a taunt, over and over.

I should've backed down. Should've laughed it off.

Instead, I met his gaze, begging him without words to make good on every filthy word. "You think that's a threat? Sounds more like a promise to me."

Lincoln didn't tear his gaze away from me, and somehow, we'd gotten closer, our noses nearly touching, our lips millimeters apart. I was three seconds away from grabbing him and kissing the hell out of him, or climbing up his body and—

"Oh my *god*," Chloe groaned. "Take it outside, newlyweds! You're gonna get everyone pregnant just by looking at you."

Lincoln didn't flinch, didn't smile. He didn't even blink. Instead, he reached down, wrapped his fingers around my wrist, and tugged me behind him. Away from the group, down the darkened hallway, and straight out the back door.

To my doom or my salvation, I wasn't sure.

CHAPTER THIRTY-THREE

LINCOLN

THE DOOR SLAMMED BEHIND US, muffling the thrum of music and conversation from inside as I steered Willa around the corner of the building.

We were alone. Technically.

The alley was quiet and dark, the lights from the parking lot casting shadows against the brick wall.

She stumbled slightly on the uneven concrete and muttered a curse. I caught her elbow, steadying her with one hand, even as the other itched to press her up against the brick and see how fast I could make her fall apart.

She glanced at me, chin tipped in defiance, eyes sparking like she knew exactly what I was thinking. "What do you want to lose at next, husband?"

Goddamn, I loved her sass.

I glanced around the alley. Shadowed. Creepy. The kind of place no sane man would bring the woman he wanted to worship.

Too bad I was a man on the brink.

"

She'd driven me wild inside. Bending over the pool table, taunting me with that lush ass hidden just beneath the flirty hem of her sundress and her insane tits damn near spilling out of the top. It was a wonder I didn't poke someone's eye out with the wood I'd been rocking the entire game, all thanks to my gorgeous-as-fuck wife.

We weren't alone out here. Not really. The sounds that poured out of the front door every time it opened—music, conversation, laughter—reminded me as much. We could be caught any second.

But that only made me harder.

And from the way Willa stared at me, her eyes dark, cheeks flushed, lips parted, she was just as turned on as I was.

"I've got a game for us, wife." I stepped into her, my front pressed to her back as I crowded her face first against the brick. "First one to make a sound loud enough to draw attention loses."

Glancing at me over her shoulder, she huffed out a noise that sounded like half laugh, half warning. "Linc—"

"Shh," I murmured, dropping to my knees on the pavement behind her and skimming my hands up the outsides of her thighs, below the hem of her dress. "Did you wear this specifically to torment me tonight?"

"Not everything is about you, jackass," she said, though the words came out breathy. Stuttered.

Already half gone, and I'd barely touched her.

"Well, it did." I wrapped my hands around her upper thighs and tugged her hips back toward me.

She stumbled a bit, catching herself on the brick wall for balance. "Lincoln. We can't do this here."

"Would you rather I fuck you over the pool table like I thought about doing that entire game?" I flipped her skirt up, groaning low at the view presented to me—generous ass, thick hips I wanted to dig my fingers into, and a pair of white panties getting in the way of the best view of all.

White, completely *soaked* panties.

"Seriously," she hissed, glancing down at me. "Someone's going to—"

"Quiet now," I said, hooking a finger into her panties and dragging them to the side. "It's my alone time with your pussy. She and I need to have a little chat."

"I swear to god—"

I cut her off with my mouth, swiping my tongue through her slit and groaning at how fucking wet she already was. My wife was a filthy little liar, pretending she didn't want this right here, right now, when she was already rocking back against my face, whimpers and moans leaving her lips.

"Shh..." I grinned against her, sliding two fingers into her cunt and going straight for her trigger. "Don't get us caught, baby."

She glanced down at me, pressing her lips together and trying to stifle her sounds.

Trying and failing.

Every time the bar door creaked open, her thighs tensed, her body going rigid. But I kept right on, my tongue focused. Relentless. Desperate to get her there.

She might've been worried someone would walk out here, but I didn't care if they found us like this. Me on my knees for my wife, her come dripping down my chin, her orgasm squeezing the fuck out of my fingers.

Hell, I half *wanted* everyone to see this. Just so they'd know she was mine. That she came for *me* and me alone.

"Linc..." she breathed, just a whisper in the night, but it made everything in me tighten, my cock jerking at the sound.

I groaned into her cunt, flicking my tongue against her clit and sinking another finger inside, curling them to brush that spot inside her.

"God," she choked out, her moan cut off as she slapped a hand across her mouth. Her thighs shook, her pussy leaking that cinnamon sweetness all over my tongue, my mouth, my chin.

"That's it, hellcat," I murmured against her. "Be a good fucking girl and give it to me."

"I'm so close..." She tipped her hips back even more, reaching behind herself and tangling her fingers in my hair like she didn't know if she wanted to push me away or hold me there forever.

She was tightening...tightening...tightening around my fingers, so fucking close to flying. And then the door opened, voices spilled out, and Willa fucking ignited.

Her entire body shook as she came apart against my tongue, her moans barely stifled by her hand. And fuck me. I had absolutely no hope of holding myself back after that.

I stood, licking my lips as I dragged the back of my hand across my chin, watching her as her legs shook, her entire body trembling. Her lips were parted as she sucked in ragged breaths, her eyes glassy like she didn't know what day it was.

She looked wrecked and wild and desperate for more.

She looked like *mine*.

"That's one," I murmured into her ear, unzipping my

jeans and pulling out my cock, already hard and aching for her. "Time to give me another one, wife. This time, I want to feel that perfect pussy squeeze my cock when you do."

She let out a tiny sound, something helpless and needy, and I was done for.

I swiped my cock through her slit before lining myself up and pushing inside. Slow and steady, my thighs quaking with the effort it took to hold myself back from slamming into her.

She sucked me in deeper, her pussy clenching around me like she wanted everything I had to give. And fuck me, but I almost gave in. Almost rammed inside her with one desperate thrust.

Instead, I gripped her hips, my fingers digging into her flesh as I slid deeper and deeper, pulling out and inching my way back in. Until finally, finally, I bottomed out.

"*Fuck.*" I dropped my forehead to her shoulder, fighting not to embarrass myself. She'd never let me live it down if I blew right now. But she was so goddamn tight, so fucking wet for me, I could barely think straight.

"Lincoln," she breathed, reaching back to dig her nails into my ass. "God, you feel so good."

"I know, baby. I know." I pulled out and sank in again, biting my lip to hold back a groan.

I started slow, filling her with deep, grinding thrusts that dragged against every sensitive inch inside her. She was soaked, her pussy still fluttering around me from that first orgasm, and the way she responded made it damn near impossible to stay controlled.

Especially because I *wanted* her just like this—desperate

and straining. Right on the edge of coming again while I fucked her in the shadows like she belonged to me.

I *wanted* her to belong to me.

"You feel how perfect we fit together?" I murmured into her ear. "Your sweet little cunt swallows me whole, doesn't she? Like your body was made to take every inch I give her. Made only for me."

Her breaths were ragged, her eyes wild as she stared back at me, those fingers digging into my ass and holding me to her. "Show me."

That was it—the moment my tenuous hold on my control snapped.

"You want me to show you, wife?" I asked, pulling nearly all the way out, letting her feel how empty she was without me inside her. "I'll show you exactly what it means to be mine."

I sank into her then, hard and deep, my hips slapping against her ass as she cried out softly with every thrust. "This sweet little cunt was made for my cock, wife. And she fucking knows it."

Willa bit her lip to keep quiet, but her body spilled every secret she tried to keep locked up tight. The way she pushed back into my pumping hips, the way she trembled around me, the way her pussy squeezed my dick like she didn't want to let me go.

"Every time I fuck you, it gets harder to stop. Harder to walk away. You keep gripping me like you want to keep me." I wrapped my hand around the front of her throat, not to squeeze but just to hold her there. Right where I wanted her.

Right where I needed her. Against her ear, I murmured, "You wanna keep me, wife?"

"Lincoln," she cried out, and as much as I wanted to chastise her for the noise, an equal part of me wanted her to do it again. Louder this time. So everyone could hear exactly what I was doing to her.

"You want everyone to know what we're doing back here?" I reached around and strummed her clit, my hips slapping against her ass as I fucked her in quick, shallow strokes. "Scream my name then, hellcat. Let everyone come. I don't care if the whole goddamn town sees what it looks like when I make my wife fall apart."

"Oh god," she breathed. "I'm—"

Her words cut off on a moan, long and low, and then her pussy was squeezing me so damn tight as she fell apart, I had no hope of holding out a second longer. Not when her cunt was pulsing around me, begging for every drop.

"*Fuck*, Willa. Gonna come so deep. Gonna fill you up, wife."

I spilled inside her with a muffled groan against her neck, my hips jerking once...twice...before I finally stilled. Every muscle taut, every thought wiped clean from my mind except one.

Mine.

CHAPTER THIRTY-FOUR

LINCOLN

LINCOLN:

You want to tell me why I had to hear about you being laid up in bed from Laurel and not my wife?

WILLA:

Because it's not that big of a deal.

LINCOLN:

Not that big of a deal? Are you serious right now?

WILLA:

I didn't get run over by a tractor, Lincoln. I sneezed too hard while feeding the chickens. That's not exactly a medical emergency.

LINCOLN:

You sneezed and collapsed and somehow that's supposed to be LESS alarming??

WILLA:

I didn't COLLAPSE! I just…folded over for a
second.

LINCOLN:

Laurel said you were walking like an injured
pirate and now you're on bed rest.

WILLA:

Laurel is a teenager and thus incredibly
dramatic. Also, it's not bed rest. It's just
some mild horizontal recovery.

LINCOLN:

You're literally *in bed*. Not moving.

That's the definition of bed rest, wife.

WILLA:

It's nothing some ibuprofen and an ice pack
won't fix.

LINCOLN:

You say that like I don't know you haven't
used either of those things.

Have you eaten today?

WILLA:

Sure

LINCOLN:

A granola bar doesn't count.

WILLA:

Then…no.

LINCOLN:

Jesus Christ. You're lucky you're hot.

Stay there. I'm coming home.

WILLA:

Do NOT come home! This is why I didn't say anything. You've got your shift at the bar tonight, and I'm FINE.

LINCOLN:

You're not fine. I'm calling Dec to cover me.

I'll be home in 15. And I mean it. DO NOT GET OUT OF THAT BED.

WILLA:

I swear to god if you show up with that pitiful look in your eyes…

LINCOLN:

Please. You love my pitiful look.

WILLA:

I love your dick. Not your pity.

LINCOLN:

Cool. I'll bring both.

WILLA:

You're infuriating.

LINCOLN:

Don't pretend you don't love it.

See you in 13.

BY THE TIME I made it back to the farm with Willa's favorite takeout and a jar of THC pain relief cream Mabel swore by, I was *this close* to tossing my wife over my shoulder and physically chaining her to the bed if it meant she'd finally take it easy.

But *take it easy* and *my wife* didn't belong in the same sentence.

Sure enough, the second I stepped inside the silo and heard the creak of the floorboards above me, I knew she'd done exactly what she wasn't supposed to. She'd gotten out of bed.

"Willa," I called, voice deceptively calm as I set the bags on the island and toed off my boots.

No answer. Not even the sound of her dragging herself across the floor and into bed like the martyring little menace she was.

I climbed the stairs two at a time and found her in the bathroom in nothing but one of my T-shirts and those husband-tormenting pajama shorts. One hand was braced against the vanity, the other clutching a glass of water like she hadn't collapsed in the chicken coop half an hour ago.

"I told you I was fine," she said before I could speak, no doubt anticipating the lecture that was coming.

"You didn't tell me shit. Laurel did. And it's a good thing, too, since you can't be trusted alone."

"Excuse you. I'm—"

"Shuffling your way to the sink when I told you to keep your ass in bed?"

"I needed water."

"You have a husband for that."

She set the glass on the sink and raised a brow at me in the mirror. "He was too busy being dramatic over text."

I didn't even blink, just scooped her into my arms, so damn tired of these games.

Willa yelped, hooking her arms around my neck. "Lincoln! You're being ridiculous. I got to the sink just fine. I could get back just fine too."

"Uh-huh. I bet you slunk out of bed the second you sent that text, and it took you the full thirteen minutes just to make your way over there."

"You're a pain in my ass," she grumbled. Noticeably not denying it.

"And you're limping."

"I'm not—" Her breath caught as I shifted her weight, her mouth pinching in a grimace.

My smile dropped as I scanned her expression. "Hurts worse than you let on, doesn't it?"

She didn't answer. Didn't have to. It was written over every tight line of her face.

I strode to the bed as fast as I dared, setting her on the mattress like she was breakable. Which, for the record, she absolutely fucking was when she was like this. Too proud to ask for help. Too stubborn to admit she needed it.

I arranged her pillows how she liked, grabbed her refilled water glass and set it on the nightstand, then headed for the stairs.

"Where are you going?" she asked.

"Getting your heating pad. And an ice pack. And a

gummy. And the takeout I brought home since I know that granola bar you said you had for lunch was actually for breakfast hours ago."

"You know this is overkill, right?"

"Maybe, but I'm good at it." I raised a brow in her direction. "Would be a shame to waste all this talent on someone who won't let me take care of her, don't you think?"

After grabbing everything from the kitchen, I made my way back upstairs. As much as I hated that she was in pain, I couldn't deny that taking care of her felt a hell of a lot better than anything else I'd done all day.

I unloaded everything on the bed, grabbing the ice pack first and tucking it gently behind her back.

She exhaled a heavy sigh—weary and exhausted. "You seriously did not have to interrupt your whole day for this, Linc. I'd be fine on my own."

I snapped my gaze to hers, my jaw ticking. "You really think I'm gonna let you suffer in silence and just go about my day? Jesus Christ, Willa."

This woman was so goddamn infuriating, I'd hate it if I didn't love her so much.

Bracing my hands on the mattress on either side of her hips, I leaned over her and met her gaze. "That's not how this works, wife. You might think the *in sickness and health* bit of our fake vows was bullshit, but they fucking mattered to me. When something's wrong, you come to me. Don't hide it. Don't downplay it. Fucking *tell me*."

"I just...hate to be a hassle."

That was it. My control snapped.

"You're not a fucking hassle. You're my *wife*. You come to

me when you're hurting. You come to me when you need something. You come to me when you're hungry or cold or pissed off or horny. Got it? *Me*."

She darted her gaze between my eyes, studying me as if searching for even a hint of a lie in my words. But she wouldn't find it.

"You got it?" I repeated, voice low and rough.

She nodded, slow and hesitant, like she still didn't quite believe it. "Got it."

"Good." I pressed a kiss to her forehead and passed her the container of chicken pad Thai. "Now stop acting like you're a burden just because you've got a bad back and the self-preservation tendencies of a deer in mating season."

She scowled at me, blinking fast as her eyes turned glassy. "Stop saying sweet shit to me while I look like an injured pirate."

I settled in next to her and brought my arm around her shoulders, tucking her into my side. "A *hot* injured pirate."

"Liar."

"Swear to god," I said. "You could be wrapped up like a mummy, and I'd still get hard."

She huffed and rolled her eyes, but her lips twitched. "Your standards are so low."

"No, baby," I murmured, pressing a kiss to her temple. "My standards are *you*."

Staring at me, she swallowed hard, her throat working like the words caught there were too big to speak. In the end, she didn't say anything. Just let her head drop softly onto my shoulder, giving in and letting me support her. And that was answer enough.

CHAPTER THIRTY-FIVE

LINCOLN

Group text with Atlas, Xander, Declan, and Lincoln
9:27 p.m.

LINCOLN:

Gentlemen. I need a little something…

DECLAN:

Fuck me

ATLAS:

Are you in jail?

XANDER:

Did you flirt with Mabel so hard that George
finally handed you your ass?

LINCOLN:

I'm wounded by your lack of faith in me.

DECLAN:

You're the one asking for a favor

LINCOLN:

It's not a favor. It's an opportunity to help your favorite brother in a noble pursuit.

DECLAN:

Nothing about you is noble

ATLAS:

Is it illegal?

LINCOLN:

No.

XANDER:

Is it dangerous?

LINCOLN:

Might be.

ATLAS:

Define might.

LINCOLN:

We'll definitely be running for our lives if my wife finds out.

DECLAN:

You're not selling any of us on this

XANDER:

I'm with Dec. I'm not interested in crossing Willa.

ATLAS:

And I'm not interested in pissing off Sutton because we did.

LINCOLN:

It's FOR Willa, dickheads.

ATLAS:

I'm listening…

LINCOLN:

She's been stressed af which means more pain flares. And since Bernice and Pearl are renting the farmhouse for the summer, Willa can't soak in the tub.

DECLAN:

So we're going to…break in to her house so she can take a bath?

LINCOLN:

I like how you think, Dec. But no.

I want to build her an outdoor soaking tub on the silo's back porch.

Big enough to stretch out.

Deep enough to soak all the way up to her chin.

Private enough so I don't have to murder anyone for looking.

XANDER:

I can get behind this.

ATLAS:

Let's circle back to "if my wife finds out."

LINCOLN:

It's a surprise. She hates being spoiled. And she's a bloodhound when it comes to secrets.

We're gonna need stealth, precision, and probably snacks to distract her.

ATLAS:

We're also gonna need a plan. And a schedule.

DECLAN:

And bourbon

LINCOLN:

I'll cover all materials, snacks, and liquor. Atlas, think you can get the football team to pitch in?

ATLAS:

If you add pizza to your list then yeah.

LINCOLN:

Done. It'll take me a bit to get everything, but I'll send out the bat signal when it's go time.

XANDER:

Do we need permits?

LINCOLN:

Absolutely not.

ATLAS:

That means yes.

LINCOLN:

What it means is if anyone asks, we're just installing porch seating with creative drainage.

XANDER:

This has disaster written all over it.

LINCOLN:

It'll be fine. I've got a blueprint drawn on a bar napkin, YouTube tutorials cued up, and an unshakable belief in our combined mediocrity.

DECLAN:

I can't wait to watch this fail in real time

XANDER:

You know you could just get her a nice candle like a normal husband and call it a day.

LINCOLN:

Candles don't say I'd break zoning laws for your comfort.

ATLAS:

I give it an hour before someone almost loses a finger.

XANDER:

A whole hour? You have more faith than I do.

DECLAN:

Just know I'm only doing this because I like Willa more than I like you

ATLAS:

Same

XANDER:

Ditto

LINCOLN:

Aww, I love you guys too

CHAPTER THIRTY-SIX

LINCOLN

BEAU:

It's been 3 weeks. No calls. No texts. That's a hell of a way to treat your best man. Oh wait…

LINCOLN:

Does this mean you're not still pissed at me?

BEAU:

You married my sister in secret, fucker. What do you think?

LINCOLN:

In that case, you're definitely not ready to hear about the kitchen island.

A FEW DAYS LATER, I made my way downstairs as I tugged my T-shirt into place, hair still damp from a shower.

After sweating through berry picking, chicken chasing, and checking the hives with Willa, I'd earned a drink before my shift tonight at the bar. All of us were still settling in with the new schedule at One Night Stan's while Tasha stepped up in a managerial role, but Trivia Night demanded all hands on deck.

It would also give me a bit of time to figure out when I could make this outdoor tub happen. Turned out, finding a chunk of time when Willa wasn't on the property was difficult as fuck. Difficult but not impossible.

I expected to find my wife relaxing in one of the armchairs, reading her latest book in the same series as the breeding one we were both so fond of. What I did not expect was to find her power walking circles around the silo like she was in a race with herself to see how fast she could wear a track into the floor.

Her hair was pulled back in a braid, her cheeks flushed, though not from arousal like I preferred. She didn't even notice me, too busy muttering to herself. Something about how so very screwed we were.

So, that was probably fine.

I stood on the bottom step, leaning against the wall as I watched her whirl past again, no sign of slowing. "I know better than to tell you to calm down. But could you maybe stop long enough to fill me in on what's got you anxiously burning a hole through the floor?"

She didn't break her stride, just scowled at me like *I* was the idiot here, and kept right on pacing.

"I'll take that as a no." I pushed off from the wall and took the last step before striding toward her. "I'm going to assume that glare was an unspoken request for my assistance."

"For your wh—" She didn't get the words out before I stepped in her path, gripped her by the waist, and lifted her onto the island. "What the hell, Lincoln?"

Stepping between her legs, I settled my hands on her thighs, anchoring her in place.

"Just breathe for one damn second, all right?" I reached over and grabbed her emotional support water bottle and handed it to her. "Here. Drink."

"Don't boss me like a child," she mumbled, eyes narrowed, but she took the bottle anyway. "I'm only drinking because I'm thirsty and not because you told me to."

"I don't care why you do it, wife, so long as you do."

She glared at me while she drank, her scowl so fucking cute I had to remind myself now wasn't the time to bend her over and fuck her into a better mood.

"Good." I darted my gaze over her face, studying her. Flushed. Irritated. And very close to hangry. "When's the last time you ate?"

"Lunch, same as you." She rolled her eyes like it was the dumbest question she'd heard all week.

I glanced at the clock—five now, which meant she'd eaten almost six hours ago.

"Don't move." I stepped back and pointed a finger at her. "I mean it."

She huffed but did as I said while I grabbed a package of her favorite peanut butter crackers from the pantry.

After opening the pack, I handed it over. "Eat. Then talk."

Her eye twitched and she opened her mouth like she wanted to argue, but she shoved a cracker between her teeth instead. I grinned, and she only pursed her lips in response. But she downed those crackers like she'd been starved for hours.

I wouldn't doubt it if she had been.

Once she finished the pack, I leaned against the sink directly across from her and crossed my arms. "All right, wife. You're hydrated and fed. Now tell me what had you running laps around the silo."

She took a deep inhale before blowing it out slowly. "I got an email that we made it through both the preliminary and secondary rounds for the grant. They've narrowed it down to the top ten applicants."

"Shit, seriously? That's amazing! That means—"

"We're *fucked*. It means we're absolutely fucked."

With a furrowed brow, I scratched my jaw, squinting one eye at her. "Not following you here, hellcat."

Willa blew out a heavy sigh, her shoulders slumping all while she picked at her cuticles—her only outward sign of nerves. "This round includes a PR interview."

"So? If I can charm the pants off you, I can charm the hell out of an interviewer."

She snorted and rolled her eyes. "Not when that interviewer is Harper Davidson."

My brows lifted as recognition hit immediately.

"Yeah," Willa said sharply. "The same Harper Davidson who spent her summers here as a kid...who moved here last year...who did an investigative piece on your *dad*. She *knows* us, Linc. She knows our history. She knows we've spent the better part of our lives at complete odds with each other."

"So does everyone else in Starlight Cove, and they bought the marriage without blinking."

"Not everyone else in Starlight Cove is a goddamn investigative reporter! She's going to be able to sniff this whole thing out. And that means we are completely and utterly fucked. We're going to mess this up. We're going to—"

"Willa," I said, my voice calm and cool but firm, breaking through her spiral. "We're not fucked. And we're not going to mess this up. Yeah, she *knew* us, but the only thing that matters is what she sees now. And what we're going to show her is a husband and wife who are happy and disgustingly in love. We're going to be fine."

"We're not! It wasn't that long ago when I couldn't kiss you without flinching!"

"It also wasn't that long ago when I had you pinned against the wall in an alley and you were coming all over my cock." I stepped into the space between her legs, gripped her hips, and ran my nose up the column of her neck. "And if I remember right, that was you riding me in our bed last night, wasn't it?"

She shivered at my words, her eyes heating as she stared at me, no doubt remembering the mind-blowing orgasm she'd had.

I trailed my fingers just under the hem of her shorts, brushing against warm skin. "If we're gonna be under investigation, I think we need to double down on our practice."

"Lincoln," she said, trying to sound stern, but her voice had that telltale hitch I fucking loved. "You're not serious."

"I'm dead serious, hellcat. If we're gonna sell this marriage, then I want Harper to take one look at you and know you've been thoroughly, repeatedly, enthusiastically fucked."

She breathed out a laugh and shook her head. "You're ridiculous."

But she couldn't hide how her thighs squeezed tight around my hips like she didn't want to let me go.

"I don't want her to wonder if it's real." I slid my hands up the wide openings of her shorts until I cupped her ass in my palms. "I want her to see how wrecked you are. Hair messy. Skin flushed. That sweet little pussy sore from how well you took your husband's cock."

Her breathing sped up as she curled her fingers around the edge of the counter like she was trying to hold herself together. Pretending like I wasn't seconds from pulling her apart.

I kissed her jaw, her throat, her fluttering pulse. "It'd be irresponsible not to prep for the interview. Think of it like a warm-up."

"A warm-up," she repeated flatly.

"Exactly." I pulled back far enough to give her a grin. "So much warm-up, it becomes muscle memory for you. I just want to make sure when she asks how married life is, you can't answer without clenching your thighs and remembering how good I fucked you the night before."

Willa attempted to shoot me a glare, but it fell flat because she couldn't hide how fast her chest was rising or how heavy lidded her gaze was or how her thighs were already twitching like she was fighting the urge to wrap them around my waist.

"What do you think, wife?"

She huffed and shoved halfheartedly at my chest. "I think you're an idiot."

"True. But I'm *your* idiot." I grabbed her hand and placed it over my cock. "And I'm currently a very hard idiot with forty-five minutes before I have to be at the bar."

She swallowed thickly, her fingers curling around my dick.

I leaned in, brushing my lips over hers. "I think we should play a game. It's called *how many times can this jackass make his wife come before he has to leave?*"

Her laugh was breathless, and the glare she shot me was entirely fake. But the way I dropped to my knees and made her scream was all too real.

CHAPTER THIRTY-SEVEN

LINCOLN

BEAU:

Nice. You're screening my calls too? Wtf?

LINCOLN:

Idk what to tell you, man. We're running a farm and a bar over here.

Keeping your sister satisfied is also basically a full time job. Not that I'm complaining.

BEAU:

I'm going to kill you for that.

IT WAS MONDAY AFTERNOON, our slowest day of the week, and I was working solo. The bar was quiet, save for the low hum of the fridge and the occasional creak of the ceiling fan that had been threatening to die since I was a teenager.

I was wiping down the counter—again—and thinking about the blackberry cardamom jam I'd taste-tested this morning. Or, more accurately, the woman who made that jam and the way she'd looked the other day, pacing our tiny home like the world was crashing down around her.

Willa wasn't the kind of woman who panicked. She was stubborn and tenacious and smart as hell. But when that email had come in, she'd spiraled. Full-on power walking in circles while muttering doomsday-level shit under her breath.

It had hit me then, like a brick to the face. This grant wasn't just a shot in the dark for her. This was *it*. Her dream. Her future. Everything she'd worked her ass off for hinged on this opportunity.

And the thought of losing that? Even just the possibility of it? Had wrecked her.

It had wrecked *me*.

I'd been racking my brain for days, trying to figure out how I could help. More than just taking her mind off it, which I excelled at.

And then I'd stumbled on something I hadn't expected to find.

I'd been in the farm office, searching for an overdue bill, when I'd found a sheet of paper shoved under the stack. At first glance, it looked like garbage—a discarded note scribbled over that she'd forgotten to throw away.

But then I'd looked closer. Saw what was hiding beneath the angry black ink and indentations from a pen pressed too hard.

It was Willa's dream, right there in black and white. A

rough sketch of a logo with what was clearly supposed to be the farm's name—rebranded to her vision.

I'd folded that mangled paper and tucked it into my pocket. Hadn't mentioned it to her. But the image had rooted itself in the back of my mind, same way she had.

I hadn't been able to stop thinking about it since—how much she wanted this. How much she deserved it.

How far we could take it, if only she'd let me run with it.

I knew she didn't believe me...didn't trust in herself. Luckily, I trusted in her enough for both of us.

And it wasn't just me believing in her—it was this whole town. The Strawberry Festival proved as much. Our line had been longer than the one for the strawberry funnel cakes, which was serious business in Starlight Cove.

Between selling out before noon, people doubling back to ask if we shipped, and Mabel damn near strong-arming Willa into a wholesale partnership, I'd realized something. Those people weren't just buying jam or honey. They were buying *her*. Willa. Her hard work and her dream, all backed by the farm everyone knew and loved.

And I couldn't stop thinking about how much bigger it could be.

The front door to One Night Stan's creaked open, and in strode Atlas. Brow creased, eyes pinched, mouth set in a firm line. Coach Asshole reporting for duty.

"Just get done with training camp?" I asked, uncapping a bottle of his favorite beer and setting it on the bar.

"What was the giveaway?"

"That Coach Asshole scowl you should trademark."

"That's what happens when I have to deal with these

feral little fucks in the summer." He sat down on the stool across from me and took a long pull of his beer. "One asshole asked if I was *retired* retired or just old."

I snorted a laugh. "I'm sure Laurel's never gonna let you live that down. Was that her murder glare I saw on the field this morning?"

He grunted in acknowledgment. "When she's not working at the farm, I've been dragging her with me to help keep the kids from getting too cocky. Five minutes in, she had a whistle around her neck and was assigning suicide sprints."

"I thought public-facing Laurel was a no-go?"

"Any other instance, I'd say that's true. But scaring the shit out of mouthy twelve-year-olds is her love language, apparently."

"Explains why she and Willa get along so well." I tossed a rag over my shoulder and braced my hands on the bar. "She's been a lot of help at the farm. Not that Willa'll say it, but Laurel's been good for her. And me. That little shit isn't afraid to tell my wife to sit her ass down and shut up so she doesn't fuck up her back more. And tattle to me when she doesn't listen. Didn't think I could love that kid any more, and yet..."

Atlas grunted. "If you could keep her a few late-night evenings to give Sutton and me some time to ourselves, I wouldn't say no."

I snorted, crossing my arms over my chest. "Sutton's mini-me has already shared just how few fucks you give about, well, fucking, no matter who's home. Something about making you buy her the most expensive noise-canceling headphones she could find?"

"Whatever. They're worth it."

"Speaking of..." I reached under the counter and grabbed a jar before setting it in front of Atlas. Willa's newest recipe I'd gotten to sample this morning.

"You going soft on me?" He stared at the jar, looked up at me, then tried to swipe it off the counter.

I snatched it back and held it out of his reach. "Not quite. How much would you pay for this?"

Atlas didn't miss a beat. He glanced at Willa's hand-lettered label for the blackberry cardamom jam, then reached for his wallet and pulled out a wad of hundreds. Without counting, he dropped all of them on the bar.

"Everything I've got on me," he said, making a gimme motion with his hand. "Now hand it over before I do something desperate."

Raising a brow, I slid the jam to him and began slowly counting the stack. "Well. That's a good start."

"Gimme a spoon," Atlas said, cracking open the jar like a fucking animal.

I passed one over, and he didn't waste any time, scooping out a spoonful. His eyes rolled back at his first taste, a grunt of appreciation leaving him.

After his fourth bite, he finally asked, "A good start for what?"

I folded my arms on the bar top and leaned toward him, a familiar spark of excitement stirring in my chest. It had been a flicker of a thought at family dinner when Atlas had eaten the last of Chloe's supply. Then that flicker had sparked and grown when he'd offered to buy out our supply at the festival five minutes after we'd opened the booth.

But now? Now, I was seeing it all a bit clearer. Seeing the future and everything it could hold. Not a fluke or a pipe dream. It was a business. With my wife's dream printed on every single jar. With me in the background, making sure everything ran smoothly and she took breaks and got the help she needed. Making sure she never again had to choose between breaking her back or keeping her farm.

She built the dream. I just wanted to help her fulfill it.

CHAPTER THIRTY-EIGHT

WILLA

BEAU:

You'd tell me if you were in trouble, right?
Or if something was wrong?

WILLA:

Nothing's wrong and I'm not in trouble. But
ily for caring.

BEAU:

You answered that text awfully fast
considering you completely ghost me when
I ask for an update on your life. Wtf is going
on over there?

I WAS EXHAUSTED. But for the first time in a long time, it
wasn't the kind of exhaustion that came with crippling pain
or delusions brought on by sleep deprivation. This was the

kind of tired that came after a long day's work—one where I gave as much as I could but no more.

And it was...enough.

Between Lincoln helping more now that he'd halved his hours at the bar and Laurel pitching in on afternoons and weekends along with a few other of the high school staff, I was no longer stretched quite so thin. Found I could actually breathe.

Which was a really nice change.

With a glass of wine in one hand, I sank into one of the armchairs just as my husband burst through the front door of the silo, looking entirely too pleased with himself.

I startled, nearly spilling some of my wine. "Jesus, Linc. You scared the hell out of me."

He bent to kiss me like it was second nature, and I ignored the flutter in my stomach that thought caused. "Sorry, wife. Too excited to tiptoe in."

Smirking, I raised a brow. "You finally beat someone at pool?"

"Not quite." He flashed me a grin before slapping a wad of cash in my lap. "I have a business proposal for you."

"Please tell me you weren't stripping on Main Street."

"Nope," he said, smiling like he could barely contain himself. "But I did sell a single jar of your blackberry cardamom jam for five hundred bucks."

I split my gaze between him and the pile of money in my lap, mouth agape. "What the hell, Linc? Did you hawk my jam on the street?"

"It was at the bar. And, yes, I did steal it from the pantry, but it was for a good cause."

"That makes it worse, not better."

"We'll see." He dragged over a stool and set a laptop on it. "Consider this my formal application to become your sex slave and jam salesperson."

"My what now?"

He opened the laptop and turned the screen to face me. A PowerPoint presentation flickered to life with the title *Operation: Make Willa a Household Name.* And then in smaller letters below it: *and Make Her Moan Mine Daily.*

"What is this?"

"This is my market penetration presentation. I sell the shit out of your delicious jam during the day and do unspeakable things to your delicious cunt at night."

"Jesus," I muttered. "So you'll do unspeakable things to me only at night?"

"Good point. Sex enthusiast 24/7, at your service, wife. But the rest stands."

With that, he flicked to the first slide and gestured to it with a flourish. "Slide one—market analysis. True, this was based entirely on drunk bar patrons, but I stand firm that it's accurate."

I huffed out a laugh and shook my head. "You're not selling me yet, husband."

"I figured as much." He forwarded to the next slide. "Which is why this next section is all about why you're a culinary genius."

"Linc..."

"Right, okay. You already *know* you're a culinary genius. Of course." He grinned, his smile infectious. "But this next slide is gonna hook you."

The third slide, titled *Eye Candy Sells*, featured a shirtless selfie of him holding a jar of the jam he must've stolen, giving the camera that smolder I used to swear he practiced in the mirror every morning.

"Sex appeal works," he said. "And I'm here to please, wife. Use me however you want."

I didn't miss the not-so-subtle undertones of *and not just with jam sales* dripping from his words.

"How many slides are there?"

"Don't worry about it. Just sit there and look pretty. Next up—distribution channels. We spread this far and wide—like your legs later tonight."

I braced my head in my palm and breathed out a laugh. "Oh my god, Lincoln."

"Mabel would definitely be our scandalous influencer. All it would take was one hooky video, and the honey sticks would go viral."

"Do you even hear yourself?"

"Don't want to go for the overdone shirtless angle? Bam!" He flipped to the next slide of him in a suit, looking hot as fuck, honey sticks poking out of his breast pocket. "Fake CEO vibes but make it sticky."

"When the hell did you even do this? I just made that jam this morning!"

"Almost done, hellcat. Next up is my artisanal pricing breakdown. Small batch, locally sourced, infused with hot farmer wife energy."

"Lincoln. Be serious."

"Oh, I am, wife." He turned to the next slide, his grin

cocky, his voice smug. "Slide seven—jam so good you'll want to marry the maker. Too bad, I already did."

The image was of him licking jam off his ring finger, his black wedding band prominent and his sex eyes on point like he was posing for the cover of a romance novel.

I snorted a laugh, my annoyance quickly fading to amusement. "That one was pretty good."

He flashed me his dimples before turning to the final slide. This one featured him staring straight at me, that smug look wiped off his face. No jokes, no pretenses—just him. And above him in a speech bubble were the words, *I'm serious, wife.*

It would've been easy to write this off as a stunt, but it wasn't. He wasn't smirking, wasn't having fun. He was just standing there, looking at me like this mattered. Like *I* mattered.

Doing something like this had been my dream for longer than I'd admit. But I hadn't even told my brother about it. Why would I, when I couldn't even make what I already had work?

But somehow, Lincoln had seen right through me. Through all my bluster and bravado and straight to the heart of what I really, truly wanted.

Not only that, but he believed I could. That *we* could.

"How the hell would we fund the increased production this would need?" I asked.

"You let me worry about that."

"And what if your brother is our only customer?" I said, trying to sound flippant even as my chest went tight.

"He won't be."

Of course Lincoln would say that. He didn't know how to be anything but confident. Confident enough to stand shirtless next to jam jars and lick it off his finger and make PowerPoint slides full of all the images.

But this wasn't a joke. This was my life...my livelihood. My legacy.

"What if he is?" I asked again, my voice smaller than I wanted it to be.

Lincoln just shrugged, like that wasn't a big deal. "Then we take Atlas for all he's worth. Pretty sure he can afford a hundred-dollar-a-day jam habit."

I huffed out a laugh, meeting Lincoln's gaze when he squatted in front of me, his hands on my hips.

"I know you're not used to someone betting on you, Willa," he said, quiet now. Serious. "But I've believed in you since we were kids. Just took me a while to say it out loud."

With that, he pressed a soft, sweet kiss to my lips before heading upstairs to shower. And there I sat, wineglass long forgotten as I stared at the laptop, the final slide glowing on the screen.

I'm serious, wife.

CHAPTER THIRTY-NINE

WILLA

BY THE TIME I pulled into our gravel driveway the following week, the sun was low and my head was spinning from the chaos that had been my first official book club. What I'd learned was that it was less a *book* club and more a *let's drink wine and talk about hot men and sex* club. And those women didn't hold back—especially the retirees.

Bernice and Pearl, the farmhouse renters, were just as shameless as Mabel. And they were enamored with my husband. They'd both gone on and on about how he was *such a sweet boy* and *should definitely earn Husband of the Year status*.

Which, yeah. I could see why they'd think that. He hopped on the ATV and headed over to the farmhouse anytime they couldn't so much as open a jar or figure out the remote. And last week, he'd driven them into town for their hair appointments. When they were done, he'd treated them to lunch and some Black Cats at One Night Stan's. The man oozed charm—he couldn't help it.

Still. I didn't need half the women in Starlight Cove eyeing my husband like he was up for auction.

"You've officially reached celebrity status, husband. You have actual fangirls," I called once inside the silo, kicking off my shoes by the door. "Bernice says she'd like you to help her 'move some furniture' next week. But I'm pretty sure that's code for turn up shirtless and lift things slowly. And Pearl called you their resident eye candy and asked when their next show would be."

No answer.

That was unusual, especially with the kind of material I was giving him to work with. That smug jackass was going to be strutting around here like a damn peacock, all proud and cocky at the silver-haired cougars panting over him.

I glanced toward the loft, juggling my purse and the last of the brownies Chloe had forced on me. "And Mabel—well, I'm not even going to repeat what she said, but it involved several honey sticks and a harness."

Still no response. The silo was quiet. Too quiet.

I furrowed my brow, glancing out the front door window. Confirming that, yes, I *had* seen Lincoln's car out front, so he was definitely here. And it wasn't like we lived in a mansion. It shouldn't have been difficult to locate my 6'5" menace of a husband.

"Linc?" I climbed the stairs, figuring I'd find him in the bathroom or lounging on the bed, reading with a pair of earbuds in. But the only thing up here was the subtle scent of his cedar soap hanging in the air.

Where the hell was he? It was too late for any farm chores—the sun was about fifteen minutes from disappearing below the horizon. And there weren't many—or any, really—hiding spots in our tiny home.

But that man could make mischief out of nothing but bad ideas and terrible impulse control. He was definitely up to something.

"Lincoln Steele," I called, making my way back downstairs. "If you're planning to jump out at me naked again, I swear to god—"

My words caught in my throat when I stepped through the French door onto the back porch and froze.

Nestled beneath a wooden pergola draped with fluttering linen panels was a huge, weathered-copper soaking tub. It was filled to the brim with hot water, and steam curled into the evening air in soft little wisps like in a dream. Fairy lights were strung from above, casting a soft, golden glow over the tub and the pots of wildflowers surrounding it, three sides of this little haven draped with fabric, making it hidden from prying eyes.

And right next to it all stood my Husband of the Year. Wearing a black T-shirt and low-slung jeans, the faintest smudge of dirt on his jaw, and a grin that melted me right where I stood.

"Hey, wife. How was book club?"

"How was—" I breathed out a laugh and shook my head, taking a step toward him. I couldn't decide where I wanted to look, my gaze pinging from him to the beautiful tub and back again. "What is all this?"

He didn't move, just crooked a finger, beckoning me closer. "Your new favorite spot."

"Did you..." I slowly walked toward him, glancing at the setup that had *definitely* not been there this morning. "Did you build me an *outdoor soaking tub*?"

His grin widened, his dimples winking at me. "Me and a few others—not that fucker *Jeff*, though. He was too busy fondling his eggplants."

"Oh my god." I huffed out a breath, half laugh, half sob. This man was sweet and ridiculous and absurd and mine.

At least, for now, he was mine.

"My brothers pitched in. And I bribed Atlas's football team with pizza. Teenage boys get shit done real quick when there's food on the line."

I stepped forward, my breath caught in my throat as I took in everything. The fairy lights. The soft drapes for privacy. The faint scent of lavender rising from the steaming water. "Lincoln, this is—"

"Romantic as hell?" he asked, brow raised.

I laughed. "It's *ridiculous*."

His smile widened as he tugged me to him, his hands on my hips, his thumbs slipping under the hem of my T-shirt. "Yeah, but I'm *your* ridiculous husband."

"I can't believe you did this," I whispered, my throat clogging with emotion.

He stared down at me, his gaze full of something that I could trick myself into believing was love. "You deserve it. Steaming, lavender-scented water. Peace and quiet. Your ridiculous husband, delivering drinks and orgasms while shirtless—what's not to love?"

I breathed out a laugh and shook my head, fighting the

stinging in my eyes and the lump in my throat that had no business being there. "You're absurd."

"Maybe. But I'm also right."

"About what?"

"You need this," he said softly. Firmly. "Not just when your back's killing you. You deserve to rest even when you're not in excruciating pain and your body *makes* you. Which is why I also set up weekly appointments with Luna for massage. She knows about your back and says she's confident she can find ways to help you relax, even if it won't alleviate your pain."

Fuck. That did it.

A tear spilled over as I wrapped my arms around his waist, pressed my face into his chest, and breathed him in. His heartbeat was slow and steady under me, a perfect melody I hadn't realized I'd come to depend on.

"Thank you," I murmured.

He pressed a kiss to the top of my head, running his hand softly up and down my spine. "You can thank me by getting your sweet ass in that tub."

I pulled back, glancing up at him. "That sounds to me like you're trying to get me naked outside, husband."

"You'd be right, wife."

His touch was warm and comforting as he slid his hands under my shirt to lift it up and over my head. He was slow, methodical, as he stripped me bare, kissing his way across my exposed skin. So reverent and adoring.

When he touched me like this—looked at me like this—he made it so easy to forget about the stretch marks on my hips and the belly pooch that wouldn't go away and the scars all over my skin. Made me forget all the ways my body had changed thanks to years of hard work and pain.

He always made me feel beautiful.

When I was naked, he helped me into the tub, one hand under mine, his other warm against my lower back, steadying me as I sank into the steaming water.

I groaned, allowing my eyes to close for a moment as I relaxed into pure heaven.

"Okay," I admitted with a sigh. "I take it back. You're not ridiculous. You're a genius."

Lincoln sat in one of the swinging egg chairs beside the tub, that familiar twinkle in his eyes. "I'm going to need that in writing when you get out."

"I'll make sure you get a notarized copy," I murmured as I sank deeper into the water, an involuntary sigh leaving me as my eyelids fluttered closed again.

After a moment, I cracked open one eye to find him watching me, a satisfied smile on his face. "Seems to me you picked the largest tub you could find. Definitely room for two in here."

"Don't toy with me, hellcat."

"I would never." I raised a brow in his direction when he didn't move. "What are you waiting for?"

Lincoln's shirt hit the patio first, then his jeans, his movements so fast and graceless it was comical. He cursed under his breath when he nearly tripped over his pant leg, and I couldn't stop the giggle from bursting free.

"Smooth."

"Shut up," he said without heat. Then he slid in behind me with a tenderness that made my throat burn. "My gorgeous-as-fuck wife is sitting here naked and asked me to join her. Do you blame me for my clumsiness?"

He wrapped his arms around my waist and tucked his chin against my shoulder, our bodies fitting together like puzzle pieces.

We sat in silence, watching as the sun dipped below the horizon, the sky streaked in shades of pink, purple, and gold. The linen curtains fluttered in the breeze as crickets chirped, water lapped against the copper basin, and the wind whispered through the trees.

"I forget how beautiful it is out here," I murmured, resting my head against his shoulder.

"I'm telling you—Sunset Soaks could sell the shit out of this place. Private outdoor soaking tub, fresh-picked peony bouquets, and a jam board with flavors not yet available for purchase? Plus, we could do tours—give them the whole small-town farm-life experience. We'd be millionaires by May."

I snorted, dragging my fingers up and down his bare thighs as they bracketed mine. "Millionaires is aiming a little high, husband. And where are we going to stay while strangers sleep in our bed, soak in our tub, and eat our jam?"

"The farmhouse," he said easily. "We'll be in it before the end of the year."

My chest went tight at his words.

We'll be in it.

Not you. Not someone. *We.*

I stared at the faint ripples in the water, the way our reflections shimmered and fractured in them—together, then apart. A weight settled deep in my chest.

Hope? Fear? Maybe both.

Because the truth was, I had no idea where we'd be in a few months, let alone by the end of the year. All I knew was this thing that was supposed to be a means to an end... something that had started entirely fake...felt more real than anything else in my life.

And that scared the hell out of me.

He kissed my temple, just a soft brush of his lips against my skin. Then my shoulder, my neck. He dragged his fingers down my stomach, slow and deliberate, no mistaking his intentions.

"Lincoln..."

"Shh." His voice was just a low rumble against my ear, sending a shiver skating down my spine and tightening my nipples into stiff peaks. "Let me get you nice and relaxed, wife."

His fingers dipped lower still, teasing the seam where my thigh met my body. Barely brushing my skin and nowhere near where I needed him, but I was still tingling and craving more.

"I'm already relaxed, thanks to this tub you built me," I whispered, breath catching as he drew slow, lazy circles everywhere but the place I needed him most. "You don't have to make me come too."

"*Have* to? Hellcat, I get the *privilege* of making you come. The *only* one who's ever had it." He pressed a kiss to the curve where my neck met my shoulder. "And I built this tub to spoil the hell out of my wife, so that's exactly what I'm going to do."

Without making me wait another second, he slid his hand

between my legs, cupping my pussy before running a thick finger up my slit. As soon as he made contact with my clit, I shuddered out a breath, sinking back into him, my thighs widening on instinct.

"There you go." He hummed low in his throat, the sound vibrating against my back. "Spread those legs for me, baby. Let me make you feel good."

He stroked me with purpose, precision, his fingers wicked tools that had me desperate and aching in seconds. I let my head fall back on his shoulder, my hips rocking against his touch, lost in the sensations he was dragging from my body.

"Linc," I breathed, digging my fingers into his thighs, my body already strung tight. "God..."

"That's my girl," he rasped, his voice low and rough. "One touch and this pussy starts begging, doesn't she? Like she knows I'm the only one who can make her feel this good. Like she knows she's mine."

I shuddered out a moan, my entire body going molten thanks to his touch and his voice and *him*. He skimmed his free hand up my torso to cup one of my breasts, his thumb and forefinger tugging the stiff peak. The sensation sent a bolt of lightning straight to my pussy, my clit throbbing as he teased me.

"Love this sweet little cunt," he murmured, the tip of his nose nuzzling behind my ear, his lips brushing my skin. "I want this pussy ruined for anyone but me. Want you so used to my hands, my mouth, my cock, nothing else could even come close to satisfying you."

I whimpered, the heat in my belly building fast, my body thrumming with sensation and longing and something deeper

I didn't want to name. Lincoln sped up his movements, his thumb circling my clit while he curled his fingers inside me, coaxing me higher.

"You make the filthiest noises when I touch you like this, hellcat. I don't want anyone else to ever know how you sound when you're like this. All wrecked and needy and perfect."

His words sank into me as he tugged on my nipple, his thumb a blur on my clit, fingers stroking so deep inside me. My breath held, my entire body strung taut...

And then, all at once, I shattered.

I arched against him, a sharp cry tearing from my throat as pleasure crashed through me in unending waves. My thighs trembled, my pussy pulsing around his fingers. Until, finally, I sagged back against him, boneless and breathless and so fucking in love.

Goddammit, I was in love.

With the one man who pushed my buttons more than anyone else ever could. Who challenged me, fought with me, sparred with me. Who fucked me and worshiped me and took care of me.

The one man I wasn't supposed to want. The one man I wasn't supposed to *keep*.

And I didn't want to admit—even to myself—just how desperately I wanted to.

So, instead, I turned in his arms and straddled his lap. The look in his eyes made my pulse stutter—dark, tender, and so full of want it nearly undid me. I reached between us and gripped his cock, long and thick and so fucking hard for me.

"This was supposed to be just for you, wife," he murmured, his eyes heavy lidded as he stared up at me.

"This *is* for me." I sank down on him then, slow and easy, as he groaned against my throat and gripped my hips like he needed the anchor.

Though he'd fucked me enough that I'd grown used to his size, I still couldn't take him in one thrust. So I took my time, rising up before inching down, again and again. And then, finally, he was seated so deep inside me, I wasn't sure where I ended and he began.

I shuddered out a moan, our foreheads pressed together as I clenched around his length and he cursed under his breath. And then I began to move. Up and down, slow strokes designed to torment us both.

"God, I could live right here," he said, his breath hot against my lips. "Watching you ride me like you were born to do it. Look at you—fucking gorgeous taking my cock so well."

Gripping my hips, he dug his fingers into my skin, guiding my rhythm over him, forcing me to take every inch as he ground up into me like he needed more. Like being inside me still wasn't close enough.

"You feel how deep I am, hellcat? How much this perfect little cunt stretched to welcome me inside? That's mine, Willa. All mine."

Whimpering, I rode him with slow rolls of my hips, my hands in his hair, our chests brushing, him filling me completely—as close as two people could get. With one hand guiding my hips, he cupped my face with the other and kissed me—hot and wild and yet somehow still tender.

And when he rested his forehead against mine, eyes closed as he murmured, "You have no idea what you do to me, wife," I let myself fall into the land of make-believe.

A place where he was mine, and I was his, and this cobbled-together life we'd built out of terms and conditions wasn't pretend. Wasn't something with an expiration date we'd agreed to before jumping.

Instead, it was beautiful and raw and *real*. Something that never had to end.

CHAPTER FORTY

LINCOLN

LINCOLN:

How busy are you at the shop?

DECLAN:

Busy. I'm not taking another of your shifts.
Jesus Christ, Linc. Quit fucking your wife all
the goddamn time and do some actual
work.

LINCOLN:

Excuse you. I'll fuck my wife whenever the
hell I want. Best part of being married.

And I'm not asking you to pick up a shift.

DECLAN:

Wtf is it then? Cause I already helped you
build a goddamn spa outside. Pretty
fucking sure the favor meter is tapped out.

LINCOLN:

It's for Willa.

DECLAN:

Fucker

Fine

LINCOLN:

If I give you a crumpled piece of notebook paper with a half-sketched logo and a rage scribble over it, can you work some magic?

DECLAN:

The fuck kind of question is that?

LINCOLN:

Long story, but I'm building dreams here, bro. *Willa's* dreams. Can you do it or not?

DECLAN:

Give me more details

LINCOLN:

She sketched it a while ago.

Stone & Bramble…the farm rebrand.

Except the paper did something to piss her off because she stabbed it repeatedly with a pen.

DECLAN:

Drop it off at the shop and I'll take care of it

LINCOLN:

Everyone always talks about how you're a huge prick, but they don't know what a marshmallow you really are.

DECLAN:

I can change my mind at any time, dickhead

LINCOLN:

Love you, you big softy

CHAPTER FORTY-ONE

WILLA

ONE NIGHT STAN'S looked like a bachelorette party and the library had a baby. Glitter was everywhere, giant pink neon lips hung on a backdrop made up of loose book pages, and feather boas draped every available surface.

Chloe, Sutton, Penelope, and I sat in a corner booth, watching as Mabel packed the place to its limit. It wasn't hard to believe what had started as a *tiny book event* had turned into the kind of evening that required backup bartenders, a themed drink menu courtesy of my husband, and crowd control. Especially when that unhinged woman was leading the party.

All four Steele brothers were behind the bar, pouring drinks at breakneck speed. Lincoln had his head down and game face on, those dimples flashing as he mixed cocktails. His forearms flexed with every subtle movement, his biceps looked illegal in that T-shirt, and the wife-guy energy while he kept shooting me winks was unmatched.

"You are not at all subtle," Sutton murmured, earning laughs from Chloe and Penelope.

"What?" I asked, pretending like I wasn't on the verge of drooling.

Sutton pursed her lips and raised a brow. "You're eyefucking the shit out of your husband."

"I hope I'll be just plain old fucking the shit out of him later..." I said before I could stop myself.

Penelope choked on her drink, Sutton looked impressed, and Chloe leaned across the table, her eyes dancing.

"Someone's in rare form tonight," she said with a grin. "He teased you within an inch of your life and then dragged you here without, uh, getting you across the finish line, didn't he?"

She wasn't wrong. But before I could tell her as much, Mabel stepped onto the stage and the music cut off, drawing everyone's attention in her hot-pink pants and shirt that proclaimed *I like my books how I like my men: thick and filthy.*

"Thank you for joining us at the first annual Spicy Book Showdown!" she said into her sparkly pink microphone. "Here's how this debauchery is going to work. Pick your favorite naughty passage, read it like your next O depends on it, and outdo every other literary pervert in here for a chance to win a hand-curated basket from Wicked Little Things."

The crowd cheered, hoots and whistles going up from all around.

"Now, who's our first heathen?" Mabel asked, scanning the crowd.

"Me!" Chloe stood immediately, a book clutched under her arm, and made her way to the stage.

She cleared her throat, cracked open a truly unhinged alien tentacle romance, and launched into a dramatic reading, complete with sound effects. By the end of her excerpt, I'd nearly snorted wine out my nose, Sutton was crying with laughter, and even Penelope couldn't contain her grin.

Xander, however, stared at Chloe like he was three seconds from dragging her into a closet and having his way with her.

Shocking everyone, Declan strode onto the stage next, jaw tight and eyes narrowed at Lincoln as he muttered something about losing a bet. He cracked open a weathered historical romance, cleared his throat, and began to read.

He kept it together for the first couple paragraphs—at least until he hit one of *those* lines. His tone shifted, voice going deep enough to vibrate against the microphone, and the tiniest, most dangerous smirk appeared on his face. Like he knew exactly what he was doing. He glanced up, just once, locking eyes with Penelope, whose entire face flamed bright red.

Oh, this was just too damn good not to capture. I pulled out my phone and hit record, adjusting my angle so I got

Declan reading in that deep tenor with Lincoln in the background, working the hell out of a cocktail shaker while looking like pure sex in a T-shirt and jeans.

Chloe leaned in, murmuring, "You post that, and this place will go viral, guaranteed."

Sutton nodded. "One Night Stan's—serving drinks *and* thirst traps. They'll have a line around the block by next week."

I hesitated, torn between wanting *everyone* to see Lincoln like this and wanting to keep him all for myself. But then I thought of everything he'd done for me. For the farm. How he backed me even when I didn't believe in myself, supported me even when I probably didn't deserve it, took care of me even when I resisted.

Maybe this could be a little something for him and for the bar—a way for me to give that support right back.

I posted it with the caption Sutton had suggested, and then I shoved my phone back in my purse without giving myself time to regret it.

"Who's next?" Mabel called.

Chloe and Sutton both yelled out my name, the two of them jostling me to head to the stage, while Penelope just grinned and didn't offer me a lifeline. The traitor.

"Willa?" Mabel asked with a grin. "Are you our next heathen?"

"No way," I said, shaking my head. "I make jam and harvest honey. I don't do erotic performance art."

A few boos went up around the bar—mostly from my so-called friends—before my husband's voice drowned them out.

"Guess that means I'll have to read for you, wife."

Oh. Oh no.

Lincoln reached under the bar, pulled out a very familiar book—*Bred in the Shadows*. The one we'd been reading all week. The one he'd been texting me passages from just to torment me throughout the day before unraveling me at night.

He strode onto the stage, met my gaze with a smirk, and flipped the book open straight to a scene.

The scene.

He wasn't doing this for laughs. It wasn't a joke. That much was clear as soon as he opened his mouth and that gravel-edged tone I knew all too well poured out of him.

With his eyes locked on mine like he was already inside me, he read about primal urges, surrendering, and the heroine being bred by her alpha.

And I damn near melted into a puddle of need right there on the floor.

By the end, he had everyone in the bar rapt, the entire room silent as if we were all collectively holding our breath.

Shifting in my seat, I stared at my husband as he continued to read. Heat crawled up my body, licking at all my sensitive spots. So desperate for him it wasn't even funny.

When he finished, ending his reading on a particularly indecent note, he took a bow, and the entire bar erupted in whistles and applause.

"Oh my god," Penelope murmured.

Sutton nodded. "I mean...holy shit."

"Seriously," Chloe said. "I feel weird being turned on by Xander's brother's voice, but here we are."

"Don't tell Lincoln that," I said as he strode across the

bar, heading straight for our booth. "His ego's already big enough."

Sutton elbowed me in the side. "His *ego* definitely isn't what you're thinking about."

Chloe and Penelope laughed, but I couldn't say anything in response because my eyes were locked on my husband's approach. And he looked good enough to eat.

"Evening, ladies," he said, though his eyes never strayed from mine. "Need you to look at something in the office, wife."

"Something in the *office*, or something in your pants?" Chloe asked, causing both Sutton and Penelope to snort.

Lincoln didn't answer, just raised a brow, tilted his head, and gave me that slow, infuriating, wife-wrecking smirk.

The crowd was still cheering for my husband, and the noise only got louder when I took his hand and slid out from the booth.

Sutton wolf-whistled, Chloe yelled, "Get it, girl!" while Penelope—my sweet, quiet Penelope—murmured, "Try not to break the desk."

And then my deviant of a husband looked me dead in the eye and said, "No promises."

CHAPTER FORTY-TWO

LINCOLN

BEAU:

You and I are overdue for a chat.

LINCOLN:

That sounds mildly threatening.

BEAU:

Good. It should.

WILLA WAS fifteen laps into her anxiety pacing when I decided to stop pretending I was reading. I closed the book in my lap and set my coffee aside, eyes never leaving her.

This wasn't just nerves—this was a full-blown mental hurricane, and the thrice-reorganized spice cabinet was taking the brunt of it.

This morning, we'd started our Sunday like we always did. Fed the chickens, checked the hives, walked the berry rows. Then I'd made us breakfast before I'd grabbed a cup of coffee and settled in to read the next book in what was becoming my very favorite series. It was giving me all kinds of thoughts on what I wanted to do to my wife.

Meanwhile, she paced like a caged animal hopped up on energy drinks.

Round and round she went, barefoot and unraveling, muttering under her breath the entire time. The spices had been rearranged. Then alphabetized. Then rearranged again by some system only she understood.

Her freak-out made sense, considering today was the day she'd been dreading for weeks. Harper Davidson was scheduled to arrive in thirty minutes for the final interview. The Big Interview. The one that could tank our chances or secure us the grant. And Willa's stress levels were through the roof, which wouldn't do us any favors.

"You planning to reorganize the entire pantry and the fridge before Harper shows up, or just the spices?" I asked before taking a sip of my coffee.

She glared at me and tossed a dish towel at my head. It landed on the floor two feet to my right.

"Not a great shot, hellcat," I said around a grin.

She stopped moving just long enough to rub her temples, her shoulders rigid with tension, and I decided that was my cue.

I set the mug down, closed the book I hadn't been reading, and headed toward her. No more teasing. No more watching.

Time to handle it.

I stepped up behind Willa, my chest brushing her back,

and braced my hands on the countertop on either side of her hips. "You're not gonna relax until I distract you properly, are you?"

She opened her mouth, no doubt armed with a biting response, but I didn't give her the chance to say a word.

I brushed her hair off her neck and dropped my mouth to the curve of her shoulder. Pressed a slow, openmouthed kiss to the place I knew made her knees weak.

Sure enough, she shuddered out a breath, her entire body seeming to sag like it was exhaling. "Lincoln, this isn't really the—"

"Shh," I murmured, dragging my lips up to her pulse point. "I'm working here."

I kissed her neck again. And again. And again. Hot, slow drags of my mouth against her skin, my lips and tongue making her forget everything but this. I dragged my teeth lightly along her neck—just enough to make her moan and grip the edge of the counter.

"There she is," I whispered, not bothering to tamp down my smile. "There's my girl."

She relaxed back into me and tilted her head to give me more access, her breath catching in a way that had nothing to do with nerves.

I slid my hand under her shirt, brushing my fingers over her stomach. "Still thinking about the interview?"

Glancing back at me, she tried to scowl, but the look fell short. With her lips parted and eyes hazy with need, my wife was just begging to be fucked.

"You're evil."

"You say that like you didn't know that when you married

me," I murmured, sliding my hand up until my fingertips traced the edge of her bra.

She breathed out a moan as I cupped her through the lace, her ass tucked nice and tight against my cock.

And that was when a knock sounded at the door.

"Shit." She exhaled a shaky breath, her head hanging as she braced herself against the counter.

I pressed one last kiss on her jaw and stepped back, adjusting my dick in my jeans. "Guess that's our cue, wife."

"You're the worst." She fanned herself while shooting me a playful glare as she strode toward the door.

Before she could get too far, I grabbed her hand and tugged her to a stop. "We've got this."

And then I kissed her. Soft. Steady. A physical reassurance that I was here with her.

Her cheeks were flushed, her shirt was wrinkled thanks to my hands, and her eyes were lust-drunk. But as she squared her shoulders and reached for the doorknob, she looked like a queen.

My queen.

She glanced back at me once—just long enough to meet my eyes. I gave her a nod, firm and sure. Letting her know without words that this wasn't just her fight anymore—it was ours.

And I'd be right next to her every step of the way.

WILLA

HARPER DAVIDSON WAS EXACTLY as intimidating as I remembered.

Not in a heels-clicking-down-the-hallway kind of way. But in an I-ooze-confidence-without-even-trying kind of way. She wore jeans and a blazer, and her soft, honey waves were tucked behind her ear as she scanned our home like she was mentally cataloguing every detail.

I braced myself. This wasn't exactly the glossy farmhouse I'd envisioned presenting. The real house was still rented to Pearl and Bernice for another month. This was Plan B. Cozy. Cramped. Intimately us.

Harper turned a slow circle, lips quirking. "This is cute. Super charming."

My eyebrows flew up. "It...is?"

She laughed and set her notepad on the kitchen island. "Definitely. It feels cozy. Lived-in."

"That's all Willa," Lincoln said, grinning at me. "She's made this place home."

My breath caught, that one simple word hitting harder than I expected. *Home.*

Harper slid onto the extra stool Lincoln had dragged over for her, her pen clicking as she raised a brow. "Shall we?"

We sat across from her at the island. As soon as I settled on my stool, I reached for Lincoln's hand, holding it like a lifeline. Thank god he didn't flinch at my death grip. Just smiled and laced our fingers together like this interview was no big deal.

"Let's start with the farm," Harper said. "Tell me about your current operation."

"We're a multiseason organic farm focused on community experiences," I said, repeating the pitch I'd rehearsed a dozen times. "We host pick-your-own berry events, harvest honey, run a fall pumpkin patch and a chop-your-own tree farm starting around Thanksgiving."

Harper nodded. "Sounds like a full plate."

Lincoln squeezed my knee under the table. "You should see the color-coded spreadsheet Willa uses to keep the place running. It's pretty terrifying."

"I imagine running this place without a spreadsheet would be pretty terrifying too," she said.

"It is a lot," I agreed, my heart rate slowing a bit. "Especially since we've started selling at the Main Street Market on weekends. He"—I nodded toward Lincoln—"encouraged me to launch a line of small-batch jams. And the mini honey sticks that we can't keep in stock were also all him."

"I just had the ideas," he said, squeezing my hand. "My wife makes all the delicious content."

Harper smiled. "And the grant? How do you see that being used?"

"Upgrades," I said. "Some of our irrigation lines are older than I am. I'd also love to add a small commercial kitchen, so we can expand our products and sell them year-round."

Lincoln chimed in, a grin curving his lips. "And maybe some fancy labels with her brand on them. Just so people know they're about to taste the best jam in New England."

"The best, huh?" Harper said. "That's a big promise."

"I only speak the truth."

When he looked at me like he was now, all soft and tender, like I already was the success I was too terrified to even believe in, my heart always tripped over itself before going all soft and gooey.

Harper wrote something down in her notepad before flipping to a new page. "What's your long-term vision?"

I froze, a wave of heat rushing through me at the question. I thought I'd prepared for this interview, but I hadn't thought about this. I opened my mouth to respond, but nothing came out. This wasn't a question I'd let myself think about in months... Something I'd *never* allowed myself to speak about at all.

Because vision was just another word for dream, and I'd learned a long time ago that dreams had a way of never coming true.

But, as if he knew I needed the reassurance, Lincoln curled his fingers tighter around mine, silently encouraging me.

I cleared my throat. "I'd, um...I'd like to rebrand. I want to be more than another farm driven by production. I want something more intentional and community-focused. Things like partnering with local restaurants for tasting menus and curated pairings, offering seasonal flavor releases of limited-edition jams... Beekeeping workshops. Farm tours. Make this a place families come back to every year. Not just for produce but for memories."

The words hung in the air, a little too honest, a little too big. My heart was racing like I'd said too much. But before I could freak out, Lincoln brushed his thumb over my hand, grounding me.

"You remember when your dad made us haul berry crates till our arms gave out?" he asked with a smile.

I nodded, a tight laugh escaping. "Every summer."

"He was all hustle. Always focused on increasing production." Lincoln's gaze was soft and tender as he looked at me. "But this? What you want to do here? It's all heart. It's all *you*, wife."

My throat went tight, his words landing deep in my chest. Leave it to Lincoln to say the one thing I didn't know I needed to hear. The one thing that made me believe, just for a second, that maybe this dream wasn't foolish after all.

That maybe we could create it together.

"Not just me," I murmured. "Us."

Lincoln held my gaze, all his usual teasing gone. I didn't say the words that were bubbling up in my throat, but maybe he heard them anyway.

I want this life, and I want it with you.

Harper smiled, flipping the page. "Let's shift to the two of you."

Fuck. This was it. This was what this all hinged on—our fake marriage and hoping like hell Harper bought that it was real.

Lincoln slid his hand up my thigh and gave it a small squeeze. A silent *I've got you.*

Harper's tone was light, but her gaze was razor-sharp. "When did you know this was the person you wanted to build a life with?"

Lincoln laughed under his breath and leaned back on the stool, the picture of ease. "I think I was about fourteen."

I snorted and turned to him with a raised brow. "Pretty sure you were also fourteen when you locked a rooster in my room and gave me a very loud, very annoying wake-up call."

With a grin, he just shrugged, completely unrepentant. "I contain multitudes, wife. You know this."

Harper chuckled under her breath. "And you, Willa?"

I hesitated. "Probably when he read my favorite book, even though it's not his preferred genre."

He grinned. "Oh, it's *definitely* my preferred genre now, hellcat. For very specific reasons, which we won't share with the grant committee."

"Lincoln," I hissed.

But Harper just laughed. "I have to admit I wasn't expecting to be charmed during a grant interview, but here we are."

"Sorry about that." I hooked a thumb in Lincoln's direction and rolled my eyes. "This one can't help it."

"I'm not gonna apologize for that," he said, grinning at Harper. "If charming you helps my wife get what she deserves, I'll turn it up to eleven."

The grin lingered on Harper's face, but her gaze sharpened just a touch as she flipped to the last page of her notes. "One final question. What's been the most challenging part of being married so far?"

"Watching her carry more than she has to," Lincoln said before I could even open my mouth to respond. "And learning whether to step in or back off."

"How about you, Willa?" she asked.

But my gaze was locked on my husband, and I couldn't look away. Because for all the ways this marriage wasn't supposed to be real, he'd never treated it that way. Not when it came to me. He'd shown up, day in and day out, like a man who'd meant every word of our fake vows.

Until this—until him—I'd never felt so cared for. So cherished.

I swallowed thickly and admitted, "Trusting someone enough to help carry the burden."

He rubbed his thumb across my skin, giving me the steady presence I'd come to rely on more than I could admit.

Harper clicked her pen again and flipped her notebook closed before sending us a smile. "This was really helpful. And surprisingly lovely." She stood, tucking her things into her bag.

"That's it?" I asked, walking her to the door.

"That's it," she confirmed. "Someone will be in touch soon."

Lincoln stood behind me, his warmth a comforting presence at my back. "Before you go, can we bribe you with some jam?"

"Tempting," Harper said on a laugh. "But I'll pretend I didn't hear that. I might swing by the market next week, though."

With that, she headed out, and Lincoln and I stood shoulder to shoulder in the doorway until she drove out of sight.

Then he shut the door, turned to me, and pulled me into his arms. "I'm so fucking proud of you, hellcat," he murmured into my skin. "You did it."

"*We* did it," I corrected and exhaled for what felt like the first time all day.

"Yeah, we did. We fucking *nailed* that shit."

I laughed, but it sounded half delirious. My cheeks hurt from smiling. My eyes burned from holding back tears.

We stayed like that for long moments, his lips against my neck, arms locked tight around me, and his chest solid and warm beneath my cheek. Maybe it was leftover adrenaline, maybe it was the steady thrum of his heartbeat that I'd come to know so well... Maybe it was the whisper of hope that had started to take shape weeks ago and only bloomed brighter today, but I'd started to believe that maybe this wasn't fake for him. That maybe this didn't have to end.

That maybe, just maybe, I wasn't the only one who'd fallen.

CHAPTER FORTY-THREE

WILLA

WHEN WE PULLED up to Holly's that night, laughter spilled through the open windows, and my heart warmed at the sound. I used to brace myself for these evenings with Lincoln's family.

Not because of *them*, but because of me. Because I didn't know how to exist in this place without feeling like an impostor.

But tonight, with my fingers twined with Lincoln's as we walked toward the back door, my shoulders were loose, my pulse steady. And for once, I wasn't calculating an exit.

"I'm giving us five minutes before someone brings up sex or swears in front of Emma," I murmured as Lincoln turned the doorknob.

"Five? That's generous."

I laughed. "You're probably right."

He gripped the doorknob and sent me that slow smile that did unspeakable things to my insides. "Ready to face the wolves?"

"They're *your* wolves," I said, though my voice came out soft. Affectionate.

He brought our hands to his mouth and kissed the back of mine. "*Ours.*"

That single syllable made my entire body hum with a want so visceral it would scare me if I examined it too closely. Thankfully, that usual Steele-brand of chaos erupted as soon as we walked through the door, not allowing me to linger on that thought.

"If you don't want me to burn things, stop leaving me unattended!" Chloe said from the stove, waving an oven mitt through the air to dissipate some of the smoke.

"I learned that one the hard way," Xander called from the living room, and Chloe laughed, loud and carefree.

"How many times do I have to tell you, Chief?" she asked. "The shed was an *accident.*"

"Just like you made bananas Foster and *accidentally* flambéed a placemat?" Laurel asked dryly, not even glancing up from her phone.

Chloe gasped. "You little traitor! That was supposed to be between us."

"No...I said it *would* be between us if you paid me twenty bucks. You didn't." Laurel shrugged. "The details were fair game."

"Um, hello?" Lincoln said, our joined hands raised between us. "Your favorite son is home, and everyone is stealing my thunder."

Holly glanced at us from the stove, a bright smile on her face. "And the saint of a woman who puts up with him." Her gaze landed on me, and her whole face softened. "There's my sweet girl."

At her words and that look she sent my way, my insides went warm and gooey in a way that had nothing to do with the berry cobbler I was carrying.

"Why the hell don't I get a welcome like that?" Lincoln asked, grabbing the dish from my hand and setting it on the counter.

"Because you didn't bring dessert," Holly shot back without missing a beat.

"I distracted Willa while she was making it this afternoon." He winked at me, a slow, sinful grin spreading across his mouth. "That should count for something."

I flushed instantly, my face heating at the memory of his lips on my neck and my chest against the island as he bent me over it, doing things to me no cobbler should have to witness.

Sutton made a choked noise. Chloe just smirked. Laurel gagged.

"Oh no," I muttered, already bracing for their inevitable ribbing.

"I'm not sure I want to eat that cobbler," Sutton said, all faux innocence. "My eyes are still trying to recover from what I witnessed in *public*, so I'm not sure I want to have anything to do with what goes on in private."

"Seriously," Chloe said. "You two had an awful lot of fun in the office."

"In the *office*?" Laurel asked. "You're animals."

Chloe grinned. "It hasn't been the same since the Spicy Book Showdown."

"Why wasn't I invited to have fun in the office?" Emma

asked with the kind of innocence only a five-year-old could muster.

"That was the night you stayed with Mimi," Holly cut in, only amplifying my mortification. "Remember? When we made our special crowns?"

"Oh yeah!" She beamed at Holly before turning her gaze on us. "But next time you have fun in the office, I wanna come."

"I promise you don't, little bean," Declan muttered, handing her a purple marker and offering his tattooed arm up for coloring practice.

While Lincoln just kept grinning like the smug jackass he was, I tried to sink into the floor. Unfortunately, it remained very much solid and not at all cooperative.

Dinner unfolded with the usual beautiful absurdity that came with being part of this family. Laurel muttered about having to deal with "the fucking chickens" at the farm, which cost her a dollar in the swear jar from a delighted Emma. Declan, Xander, and Lincoln kept devolving into a heated argument about the best kind of bourbon for an old-fashioned, while the perpetual grump Atlas silently demolished an entire plate of ribs and contributed to the conversation solely in grunts.

And somehow, through all of it, my husband kept touching me.

A hand on my thigh. Fingers combing through my hair. His palm resting on the back of my neck, thumb brushing up and down my nape like he couldn't help himself.

It was instinctual now, this thing between us. I wasn't sure when it had happened...what had been the tipping point. But there was no denying it anymore—our connection was bone-deep and impossible to ignore.

As dinner was served, the conversation never slowed. Laurel fueled Lincoln's hunger for gossip with a rundown of the latest high school drama. Atlas very reluctantly passed a jar of my strawberry basil jam down the table after only taking five spoonfuls for himself, and Emma was dumbstruck when Chloe told her I'd made it from scratch.

"Did you *really*, Aunt Willa?" she asked, eyes wide as she devoured a roll spread with jam.

"She did," Lincoln confirmed before I could say a word—the easy *aunt* that had fallen from her little lips still managing to knock the wind out of me anytime she said it. "I helped pick the strawberries."

I huffed out a laugh and shook my head. "You picked, like, *five*, and then disappeared to flirt with Pearl."

"Have you *seen* Pearl? She's a smokeshow."

"She's seventy-two," I said dryly.

"Like I've told my idiot brothers, even grandmas deserve the Lincoln flirtation treatment once in a while."

Before the conversation could devolve any further, Holly cut in, "You didn't give us part of your stock for selling, did you? You have enough jars for the market next weekend?"

I nodded. "Yeah, Lincoln's been helping with production, so I've been able to can more than usual."

"And the demand is *still* through the fucking roof," he said, leaning back in his chair with a proud grin on his face.

"That's a dollar, Uncle Linc!" Emma yelled, her delighted cackle making everyone laugh.

Holly's smile was soft and warm, her eyes filled with

nothing but love and pride. "Sounds like you two are really making this work."

We...were. Which shocked the hell out of me. From day one, I'd thought this would be a disaster. Something I had to *endure*. And now, I never wanted it to end.

"Speaking of that demand..." Atlas said, raising a brow at Lincoln, who just gave one firm shake of his head.

I wasn't sure what that was all about. Wasn't sure I cared. Not when this feeling of warmth and belonging had settled so deep in my bones.

This family was pure chaos. A full-blown circus with a swear jar as the main sponsor.

And I loved every single second of it. Loved every single one of them.

I couldn't deny it any longer—I wasn't pretending anymore. Wasn't faking a smile or bracing for the next slip or worrying about how I'd explain myself when the truth finally came to light.

Because this *was* the truth.

Me, here with Lincoln in the moment—his warm hand on my knee, his pinkie brushing mine every time he reached for his fork. With the people who'd stopped seeing me as a guest and started seeing me as theirs.

This was everything I'd never let myself want. And somehow, I had it.

My phone buzzed on the table, breaking me out of my thoughts, and I glanced down to see a text lighting up the screen.

BERNICE:

You'll want to get home. We have company.

My entire body stilled. Well, everything but my heart. That surged in my chest, racing like it knew something I didn't. The only people in Starlight Cove who would drive all the way out to the farm on a Sunday evening were all seated at this table.

Everyone except one person.

Lincoln leaned in, bumping his shoulder with mine. "Everything okay?"

I turned the screen toward him. "It's Bernice. She says there's company."

His brow lifted as he darted his gaze between my eyes, seeming to read my mind from my expression alone. "Harper?"

Hope bloomed quick and sharp inside me, and my stomach swooped. "You think they could've made a decision this fast?"

A smile swept over his mouth, slow like molasses, until his dimples were deep grooves in his cheeks. He gave me a look so smug I wanted to kiss it off him. "I don't know, wife. We nailed that interview pretty hard."

The unspoken *and that wasn't the only thing that was nailed hard* was clear in his tone. I must've been punch-drunk on anticipatory hope, because I didn't even try to hold in my snort.

"Time for charades!" Emma yelled, bouncing on her toes.

"Sorry, little bean." Lincoln stood and held out his hand

to me. "Aunt Willa and I have to get home. Someone's there to see us."

There was a chorus of goodbyes, a muttered demand from Declan that Lincoln swing by the bar later to pick up something he'd been working on, and then we were out the door, my heart in my throat and hope a wild thing raging inside me that I didn't even try to tamp down.

I WAS STILL SMILING when we pulled to a stop in front of the farmhouse. I hadn't been able to *stop* smiling—not since the second Lincoln had voiced the thought I couldn't bring myself to say aloud.

This moment might be it—the culmination of all our hard work. The grant, come to fruition.

I tried not to think about what that would mean for Lincoln and me. Tried not to read into the ticking clock that had only ever been counting down. If I could pin my hopes on this grant, I could do the same for us too.

Except when I glanced to the front porch, expecting to see a blonde bombshell waiting, my stomach bottomed out at the sight that actually greeted me. It wasn't Harper.

It was my brother.

In between a chatting Bernice and Pearl, Beau sat in one of the porch chairs, tea in hand, nodding at whatever the older ladies were talking his ear off about. But his gaze was locked on me through the windshield, unwavering.

I stopped breathing, my nerves caught somewhere

between fight, flight, and fawn, not sure what the best path of action was.

Lincoln sensed the change in the air immediately and reached out, cupping a hand on my thigh. "Hellcat? What's up?"

I swallowed thickly, never moving my eyes from my brother's. "It's not Harper."

He followed my gaze, his attention shifting out the windshield before he muttered a soft, "Fuck."

Yeah. Fuck. As in fuck me. Fuck us. We were completely, totally fucked.

Because if we thought having *Harper* in our business was bad for the grant approval? That had nothing on my twin brother being in town. The one person who knew both Lincoln and me, inside and out.

Lincoln stepped out of the truck and walked around to open my door. After helping me out, he intertwined our fingers and squeezed tight. "We've got this."

But the set of his jaw and the tension in his shoulders said he wasn't as confident as he wanted me to believe.

We walked toward the porch like we were headed to our doom. Beau's smile was pleasant enough. His eyes, though? They were knives, sharp and dangerous.

Bernice gave us a quick once-over before glancing at my brother. "Told you they'd be back before dark."

Pearl grinned as she elbowed Beau. "And didn't I say they'd be *glowing*?"

Beau hummed, his gaze assessing as he clocked our joined hands. "Must be that newlywed bliss," he said dryly.

Lincoln didn't miss a beat, tugging me closer to him. "Your sister has that effect on me."

"So," Beau said, voice mild like he wasn't about to go in for the kill. "How's married life? Seems like it's a little... rushed."

I forced a smile, but in my mind, I was strangling my brother for playing this game in front of others. "Been a whirlwind."

"Seems like it." Beau turned his attention to Lincoln and raised a brow. "You're a busy man too, aren't you?"

Lincoln offered the easy smile he was known for—all charismatic charm and dimples for days. "Your sister makes sure of that."

Bernice snorted and fanned herself. Pearl cackled. I nearly passed out.

"Why don't you all come in and stay for dessert?" Pearl asked. "I made strawberry rhubarb pie with some of your berries I picked up at the market."

"That sounds amazing, Pearl. But we were hoping to catch up with Beau before it gets too late. Maybe we can swing by tomorrow instead," Lincoln—my savior in cocky armor—said.

I could've kissed him right then and there because I did *not* want to continue this thinly veiled sibling smackdown with an audience. Especially when that audience consisted of Mabel's gossip squad.

"Sounds great. Can't wait to catch up." Beau set his teacup on the side table and stood slowly, every inch of him outwardly calm. But I could see the storm brewing under the surface.

A storm Lincoln and I were about to face head on.

CHAPTER FORTY-FOUR

WILLA

WITHOUT A SINGLE WORD, Beau followed us into the silo, the door clicked shut behind him, and then it was just the three of us in this too-small space.

He gave our home a cursory glance. "Nice, but it's a little small, don't you think?"

My spine snapped straight, that defensiveness coming out, but Lincoln settled a hand on the small of my back, his touch calming my ire just slightly.

He lifted one shoulder in a shrug. "We don't need a lot of room since it's just the two of us."

Beau hummed and slid his attention to me. "Would've been nice to know you'd rented out our childhood home and moved over here, Willa. But I guess you were too busy dodging my calls and texts to let me know." His voice was sharp, but there was an underlying edge of hurt he couldn't hide.

Fuck.

He was right—I *should've* told him. But if I'd told him

that, then I would've had to admit the reason I needed to rent out the house was because of the overdue bills. And the overdue bills were because I wasn't able to produce enough on the farm. And I wasn't able to produce enough because my body hated me. And if he'd known all that, he would've come storming back to Starlight Cove, leaving his dream behind like the hero he was. And I wouldn't have been able to live with myself.

I'd rather be the sister who shut him out than the one who held him back.

"Cut the shit," he said, his voice sharp. "You might have the retiree renters fooled, but not me. This marriage is about as real as Dad claiming he taught the goats to sort laundry."

I remembered that story. Beau and I had been maybe nine or ten, and my dad had sworn up and down for a week he'd done it. Even then when we were so young, we'd called him on his bullshit.

My heart lurched and my stomach bottomed out. I opened my mouth to respond, my words tripping over themselves. "It's not— It's not *fake*-fake—it's... Complicated. There's this grant—"

"A *grant*? Are you out of your goddamn minds?" he asked, each word landing like a blow. "This is your plan? Marry my best friend for money? Did you even think about what this would do to him? To *you*?"

I glanced at Lincoln, who stood still, his arms crossed, jaw tight. Expression utterly unreadable.

Turning back to Beau, I said, "It's not like that."

He huffed out a humorless laugh. "It's *exactly* like that. What about the future? Did you think about that? About the two of you being exes in a town this small? Spending the next fifty years bumping into each other at bonfires and farmers markets and pretending this—" he gestured around the tiny silo "—never happened?"

The thought made my eyes sting, my chest tightening over the idea of a future where Lincoln wasn't mine.

Beau turned his attention to Lincoln, his gaze narrowed. "And you. I thought you had a brain in that pretty head. You let this happen?"

Lincoln's shoulders tightened, a silent crack in his composed façade. "I didn't just *let* it happen. I *chose* it. Because I care about her."

"Then you're an even bigger idiot than I thought." Beau took a step closer, voice cold as he stared Lincoln down. "Admit it—you went along with this sham marriage for *your* benefit, not hers."

Lincoln's jaw twitched—the barest reaction, but I saw it. Beau did too.

"And what happens if the grant goes through and you get the money?" he asked. "This fake matrimony has to end sometime, so what then? You think you'll just amicably separate? Have a nice, clean fake divorce?"

"You think I haven't thought about that every damn day?" Lincoln said, his voice harsh.

Beau pressed his mouth together in a thin line and shook his head. "Not enough to make you come to your senses, apparently."

Panic clawed its way up my throat, and my pulse raced. This was going even worse than I'd anticipated, and I'd feared something bad. But this? My brother was more upset than I'd thought he'd be. And if we couldn't get him to come around...if he said one thing to the wrong person... This could all implode in our faces before the grant was approved.

"Beau, *stop*," I snapped, my composure long gone. "I'm not going to let you ruin this."

Lincoln stepped closer, settling in next to me, his hand a comforting, grounding weight against my spine.

"The grant isn't even approved yet," I continued, "and if anyone hears about this, we're fucked."

Lincoln stiffened, then slowly turned to face me, his brows drawn down. "Are you serious right now?" he asked. His voice was low, but his tone scraped against me like sandpaper over skin.

He was looking at me like I'd just happily kicked the air out of his lungs. Like I wasn't the woman who'd shared a bed with him every night for two months or laughed with his family over Sunday night dinners. Like I wasn't his wife... even if we were only supposed to be pretending.

"With everything we're talking about, the fucking *grant* is what you're concerned about?"

"That's not—" I started, then swallowed hard. Because the grant *was* what this whole thing was about. It was why we were here in the first place. Why Lincoln and I wore matching wedding bands, why we'd shared this too-tiny space for so long.

Even if I wanted it to be something else.

But that was too scary to voice right now, in the midst of everything else. So, instead, I allowed myself to give him a lie wrapped in truth.

"It was supposed to be business," I whispered.

Lincoln's entire body went still. Completely, utterly still. And then he exhaled once, a short, tired sound, and ran a hand through his hair. "I really thought we were past pretending, hellcat."

He didn't glance at my brother. Didn't kiss me goodbye. Instead, he strode toward the door, turned the knob, and walked out into the night without looking back.

The door shut behind him with a quiet finality that hurt worse than anything Beau had said. Worse than the possibility of losing the grant. Worse than the fear of everything tumbling down, of me fucking up and costing my family our legacy.

Worse than any of it. Worse than *all* of it.

I stood there, staring at the empty space my husband left behind, and found it hard to breathe.

And then the floor creaked as my brother took a step toward me, and I took out every ounce of my anger and hurt and devastation on him.

"You *asshole*." I braced my hands flat on his chest and shoved, hard. "What the hell was that?"

"That was me trying to protect my best friend and my sister from themselves," he snapped back. "You two are being stupid, and you can't even see it."

"*Stupid*? You have a lot of nerve saying that to me. You've been gone for years, Beau. *Years*. And I've been running this place alone. Breaking my back—literally—to keep it afloat. And you have the fucking audacity to show up now and lecture me like I haven't been bleeding every fucking day for this family?"

Beau's eyes flashed, shame and anger mixing in their depths. "Because you never told me you needed help!"

I laughed, but the sound came out as a sob, my throat clogged with emotion. "Because I didn't think I could! You were halfway around the world, saving babies and being a goddamn saint! You think I was going to tell you the farm was in trouble?"

Silence fell around us, both of us primed and ready for a fight. Until, all at once, Beau's shoulders slumped and he dragged a hand over his mouth, his eyes locked with mine.

"I would've helped," he said softly. "You could've told me you were in trouble. You didn't have to drag Lincoln into this."

"I didn't drag him. He jumped." I tried to blink back the tears threatening to fall, but one escaped anyway. "And now he's gone."

"Fuck," Beau muttered, stepping close to grip my upper arms. "What do you need?"

I didn't answer right away. I'd heard that question from him before, too many times to count. After Dad died. After I took over the farm. After Mom bailed and moved to Florida, leaving us. After he left me too. And every time, I'd said nothing. I didn't need anything.

I could handle it all on my own.

But I didn't have it in me to pretend anymore.

"I need him," I said, voice trembling as I admitted my worst fear aloud. "I need Lincoln."

Beau recoiled like I'd slapped him. "*That* fucking guy?"

"You mean your *best fucking friend*?" I glared at him,

even through my tears, and punched him in the stomach. "Yes, idiot!"

He doubled over with a soft, "Oof," before raising his hands in surrender. "All right, all right. I'll find him."

The second he left, the silo felt too quiet. Too still.

Too empty.

I sank onto one of the armchairs, unable to stop the tears, more lost than I'd ever been.

This was always supposed to be fake. A simple fix. A contract. A strategy. But somewhere between our first practice kiss and him building me an outdoor soaking tub like something out of a fairy tale, it became real.

And now that he'd walked out? The fear of losing the farm had nothing on this feeling inside me. Because with Lincoln gone?

It felt like I'd lost *everything*.

CHAPTER FORTY-FIVE

LINCOLN

THE BAR WAS QUIET—THE rare kind where every glass clink, every stool creak, and every muted laugh from the guys playing darts in the back sounded too loud. One Night Stan's was the community hub, a place that was never meant to feel hollow.

But tonight, it did.

Maybe because I wasn't behind the bar, mixing drinks and laughing with the regulars. Maybe because Willa wasn't with me, pretending to hate every bit of attention I poured on her while secretly loving every minute. Maybe because everything I'd been building since this thing between us started—everything I'd been *hoping* for—felt like it was teetering on the edge of collapse.

I'd come in because I didn't know where else to go. I'd told myself I needed to grab the finalized logo from Declan that he'd mentioned at dinner, but the truth was, I needed to just sit for a minute. To think. To breathe. To figure out what the hell to say when I headed back to the silo to fight for my wife.

To fight for us.

Declan slid a drink in front of me—lowball glass, amber liquid, lemon twist on the rim.

A Black Cat.

"Trying to pour salt into the open wound, man?"

"Quit being dramatic." He tipped his chin toward the folder I hadn't opened yet. "Show her that, and you'll be doing your favorite activity with your wife instead of sitting here sulking."

I snorted. "Don't think it's gonna be that easy."

"Or maybe it will be," he said, already walking away.

I pulled the folder closer and flipped it open, spreading out the two papers inside. One was the original sketch Willa had done—creased and torn with angry black scribbles all over it. The other was clean, professional, stylized but so completely *her*. A delicate vine curled around the interlocking initials, earthy and beautiful and strong. Just like the woman I—

The bells above the door jingled as someone strode inside, and I glanced over to find my *former* best friend walking toward me like he hadn't just torched my whole goddamn world.

"I figured I'd find you here," Beau said, sliding onto the stool next to mine.

"Can't get anything past you," I muttered before taking a sip of my drink.

"Fuck, man." He braced his arms on the bar and glanced over at me. "What the hell were you thinking?"

I was *done* with this bullshit. I downed the rest of my drink before setting the glass down on the bar with more force than necessary. "I was thinking she was drowning, you fucker. And I'd rather go down with her than watch her sink."

Declan strolled over, swiped my empty glass, and pinned a glare on Beau. The Steele brothers might give one another heaping doses of shit on the daily, but no one else could fuck with one of us without answering to someone else. "Everything good here, or do I need to remind Beau of his manners?"

"We're fine," I muttered.

But Declan didn't move right away. Instead, he stared Beau down, the silent *I'll kick your ass without breaking a sweat* hanging thick in the air between them. When Beau dipped his chin in understanding, Declan finally stalked off toward the other side of the bar and the customer calling for a refill.

"Christ," Beau muttered once we were alone. "I just don't get it. This was always going to blow up, Linc. It was never gonna last."

"You think I don't know that?" I said, my anger flaring. "You think I haven't thought about how this ends every damn day since the moment she said yes? *Fuck.* You think I haven't *woken up next to her* and wondered how the hell I'm supposed to let her go? I didn't care, Beau. I *don't* care. I'd marry her a thousand times over if it helped her, even a little."

Beau darted his gaze over my face, his brow pinched. "You should've come to me. I would've—"

"No, you wouldn't have," I cut in. "You weren't fucking

here. I don't blame you for that—hell, I'm the asshole who told you to go. But don't sit there and pretend you know what it's been like. You didn't see her white-knuckling that farm *and* her sanity. You didn't see her hurting, every goddamn day, and still pushing through, telling everyone she was *fine.* You didn't see how, even with all that, she still put everything on her shoulders like she had something to prove."

I braced an arm on the bar and leaned toward him, my eyes hard. "As for that bullshit you said back at the silo, I want to get one thing clear—I never once pushed her. I didn't fucking manipulate her into anything, and you're a dick for insinuating as much. I fucking *love* her."

He stared at me for long moments, eyes wide, mouth parted, like I'd just admitted to setting his house on fire. Then he cleared his throat, shifting his gaze away, before doing a double take at whatever had snagged his attention. I glanced to where he was looking—at the back wall and the chalkboard menu hanging there featuring the specials.

SHIT SO GOOD YOU'LL WANT TO ORDER 2:
JAM FLIGHT—3 ROTATING FLAVORS FROM WILLA +
BISCUITS

DRINK OF THE MONTH:
BLACK CAT (NAMED AFTER MY FIERCE BUT
INCREDIBLY LOVABLE WIFE)

His gaze drifted lower—to the collage of photos pinned to the wall. An image of Willa and me at the Strawberry Festival. One of her, Sutton, Chloe, and Penelope in the back booth at the inaugural Spicy Book Showdown. Ones of me and my brothers working behind the bar, of Mom and Emma wearing their homemade crowns, of me giving Laurel a noogie while she tried to claw my eyes out, and a dozen more snapshots filled with pure chaos. Filled with family.

When he snorted, I knew he'd found the sign I'd had to post, written in black permanent marker and underlined three times:

WILLA LIFTING BAN
IN EFFECT UNTIL FOREVER

"You had to put up a sign for that?" he asked.

I huffed out a breath. "You know how well your sister listens."

He glanced back at the chalkboard. "The jam flight. Those are hers?"

"Yeah."

"And the Black Cat?"

I shrugged.

He blew out a breath and shook his head. "She's all over every inch of this bar."

"She's all over every inch of *me*." I rubbed my wedding band without thinking. "She has been since the day I met her."

Beau studied me, his gaze assessing, and then he blew out a breath and cupped the back of his neck. "Shit, man. I knew you had it bad, but I didn't know it was *this* bad."

"Yeah, well," I said. "I did a damn good job pretending I didn't."

330

"Fuck. I'm sorry." He scrubbed a hand down his face, and I realized how goddamn tired he looked. A trip halfway around the world would do that to a person. "I just... I wanted to protect her. She's been alone since I left and—"

His words hit, knocking the air out of my lungs.

"Fuck me, she's been *alone*." I stood up too fast, the stool screeching across the floor behind me. "And I *left*."

I grabbed the folder off the bar and clapped a hand on Beau's shoulder. "Would love to stay while you pull your head out of your ass about what a dick brother you've been, but I need to get to your sister."

And then I was striding out the door and straight for my car. Because I'd made a promise—maybe not out loud, maybe not in the vows we'd recited at the beginning of all this—but one I'd meant with everything I had.

I wasn't leaving Willa. Not ever.

CHAPTER FORTY-SIX

WILLA

WILLA:

You find him? Is he okay?

Never mind. Don't answer that.

I'm not asking about him.

I need to talk to YOU.

We're not done. Text me back. Unless you're too scared.

BEAU:

Jesus, Willa. You always did punch first and ask questions later.

I'm around. Just say when.

THE SILO CREAKED SOFTLY in the breeze, like it was

breathing with me. Or for me. Because god knew I was having a hard enough time doing that on my own.

The only light came from the pendant above the island, casting a warm, golden circle over the mess I'd made. Ink-smeared paper, thanks to my tears that kept falling. An empty wine bottle. My name in shaky handwriting. A pen I kept gripping like it might save me.

And one blank line that mocked me.

All I had to do was fill in Lincoln's name. And then I could file this paperwork and be done with it. But here I sat, slumped on the stool, eyes rimmed red, wineglass in one hand, pen in the other, half laughing, half sobbing like the world's most unhinged maniac.

The only good part of my being left alone was that at least no one could see me like this. Battered. Broken.

Devastated.

"You purposely didn't think about this for weeks, and *now* it's a priority?" I muttered to myself, swiping the back of my hand under my nose. "Real subtle. A+ emotional avoidance."

The words I'd written on the paper blurred thanks to my tears.

Steele & Bramble

It was supposed to be *Stone* & Bramble. That was the plan. That had always been the plan. It was something solid. Strong.

Singular.

But now? Now, it wasn't singular, and it hadn't been in a while. This place wasn't just mine anymore.

Or at least, I didn't want it to be.

But if I filled out both lines and Lincoln didn't come back...

I swallowed down the lump in my throat and blinked back the tears that refused to quit. It was just a business name. Just paperwork.

So why did it feel like writing his name would crack me wide open? That finalizing a partnership would break me?

The door opened suddenly, a breeze floating in along with it, and I jolted, my wine sloshing dangerously close to the edge. I darted my wide-eyed gaze behind me, heart in my throat at what I'd find—

My breath caught.

Lincoln stood in the doorway, haloed in the porch light, his eyes landing on me like I was both the storm *and* the safe harbor.

"Jesus," I breathed, heart stuttering in my chest as I wiped a hasty hand under my eyes. Definitely not sobbing into a wineglass over here. "You scared me."

"Didn't mean to." He stepped inside like he belonged here—like he'd never left—and dropped something on the table next to the armchair. "I live here too, remember?"

Though I tried to hold it in with everything I had, I couldn't stop my chin from wobbling, his words undoing me more than I wanted them to.

"You came back," I whispered.

"'Course I did." His voice was soft. Steady. "I'll always come back, wife."

Tears blurred my vision again before I could blink them away, and I swallowed back the sob that was threatening to break free. This was ridiculous. I was being *ridiculous*.

He crossed the room slowly, like I was a skittish animal, and if he moved too fast, I might bolt. He darted his gaze over the mess I'd made on the island before meeting my eyes again. "What's all this?"

I opened my mouth. Closed it. Waved a hand through the air like this wasn't a big deal. Like I hadn't had an emotional breakdown because of it. "Joint LLC paperwork. For the farm. I've been, um... I've been meaning to do it for a while."

He scanned the paper, his gaze snagging on my name and the blank line below it for the joint owner.

"But I just..." I swallowed, unable to finish the sentence, emotion clogging my throat.

"You just couldn't yet," he finished for me.

I lifted a single shoulder in a shrug, my eyes filling again, all my worries and fears flooding back.

"You were scared to go all in." Cupping my face, he swiped his thumbs across my cheeks, catching my falling tears. "Because if you did, and I didn't stick around...it would've confirmed everything you're scared of."

I snapped my gaze to his, my breath caught in my throat, hope and panic both flooding my chest. "How did you—"

"Because I know you, hellcat," he murmured. "Much as you hate that sometimes. And I've been there."

I blinked as realization hit, my tears falling for an entirely new reason—one filled with guilt and shame and empathy. Because yeah. He *had* been there. When his dad left without a word. When he'd abandoned Lincoln and his brothers and their mom. Left for a reunion tour with his band and just never came back.

Lincoln knew this fear. Knew it intimately. And still, he'd been all in. And *I'd* been the one toying with his heart.

"God, I'm sorry," I choked out. "I'm a mess. But this fear is buried so fucking deep, Linc."

"I know it is, baby."

"Everything I've ever tried to make mine leaves." My voice broke, but I kept going, knowing Lincoln deserved this pure, honest, cracked-open version of myself. "My dad died and my mom left and Beau took off, and it took us ignoring his calls after a secret marriage to get him to come home. Everyone I let in finds a way out. And the stupidest part is that my hesitation with filling that out wasn't even about the business anymore. It was about *you*. Because I fell for you. And I knew—I *knew*—if I made this permanent and you left too, I'd—"

I broke off on a sob, no longer able to maintain even a semblance of composure.

"Hellcat..." He wrapped his arms around me and squeezed me tight to his chest. "This is what I've spent every damn day trying to show you. I'm not gonna leave. I'm not going anywhere."

"But you did," I whispered, my throat tight with these never-ending tears. "You left."

"No, baby." He pulled back and cupped my face, his thumbs swiping away the tears that continued to fall. "I left the room. I left the fight. I didn't leave *you*."

He grabbed my left hand and brought it to his mouth,

brushing his lips over the simple black band on my finger. "This—us? It's already permanent, hellcat. Paperwork doesn't change that. I'm your husband. You're my wife. You and I are a *we*. And that's exactly what I want."

"But it was never supposed to be forever."

He huffed out a humorless laugh and shook his head. "I've been your husband since day one, wife. It was *always* supposed to be forever."

My heart squeezed so tight, stealing my breath, that I almost missed the ache in his voice. Almost, but didn't. His words weren't just a promise. They were a vow he'd already been keeping.

He stepped back and reached for the thing he'd dropped on the side table when he'd come in. Then he placed it on the island in front of me and tapped a finger on it. "Open it."

With shaky hands, I did what he'd instructed, and my breath caught as soon as I registered what was inside.

My original sketch, the paper crumpled, the design scratched out. And another crisp sheet with my logo—the same winding vines I'd imagined, the initials interlocked like I'd doodled so long ago. Back when this dream still felt so far away. Except now, the design was refined. Polished. Perfect.

Well, almost.

"You—" My voice cracked. My fingers trembled as I traced the edges. "You did this?"

"Well, Declan did." He cleared his throat. "I found the original in the office. Asked Dec to work his magic."

I brushed my fingers over the design, a realization settling deep in my bones the longer I stared at it.

"You've always believed in this," I whispered, barely able to get the words out.

"I've always believed in *you*, Willa."

Even when I hadn't. Because dreaming meant admitting I wanted something. And wanting something only to fail was too harsh of a reality to face. Again.

But what I wanted now was so much more than ever before. My dream had expanded and grown into something bigger than I'd ever allowed myself to hope for.

Not just the farm or artisanal jams or a stand at the market.

But *him*. And *us*. Something we built together.

Something that lasted.

"I love it." I held it to my chest before setting it down. Then I pulled out the LLC paperwork from beneath the folder and handed it to him. "There's just one problem..."

He glanced at me before dropping his gaze to scan the page. And I knew the second he'd landed on it when his brows flew up.

"*Steele* and Bramble?" he asked, his voice gruff.

"It's not just my dream anymore," I said. "It's *ours*."

Emotion flickered across his face—raw and quiet but so powerful, I had no idea how I'd missed it all this time. Without another word, he reached for the pen and scribbled his name on the line below mine before signing the bottom. A messy, inky declaration that stole the air from my lungs.

And then he tugged me off the stool, cupped my face, and kissed me. His lips tender but insistent against mine—like it was the first time and the last time and every other time we'd wanted to but didn't.

When we finally broke apart, he rested his forehead against mine and breathed in deeply. "You sure about this?"

I laughed, watery and wrecked, my chest finally stitching itself back together. "I signed the paperwork, didn't I?"

He grinned. "Guess that makes it official."

"Guess it does."

He kissed me again, like he couldn't get enough. And truthfully, I couldn't either. I wasn't sure I ever would.

Thankfully, I never had to try.

CHAPTER FORTY-SEVEN

WILLA

I COULDN'T TEAR myself away from Lincoln. Not when the moment felt this heavy...this inevitable. Not when every molecule in my body yearned for him. Like gravity had a name and it was his.

One minute, we were downstairs, kissing in the kitchen. And the next, he had me spread out on our bed, naked and wanting and staring up at him like he was everything.

To me, he was everything.

"Feels like forever since I've been inside you," he murmured against my skin, kissing a path down my body.

I breathed out a laugh that turned into a moan as he licked one of my nipples before sucking hard. "You were inside me like eight hours ago."

"A fucking lifetime," he murmured, dragging his mouth lower. Kissing below my breast, over my stomach, on each hip. Then he settled between my thighs, hooking one leg over his shoulder and licking his lips like he was starving. "But first, I need a reminder of how fucking good my wife tastes."

With his eyes locked on mine, he licked a slow path straight through my center like he had all the time in the world before flicking my clit at the end. I gasped, reaching down and threading my fingers through his hair, because *fuck*. That mouth. I'd never get tired of it. Wanted to feel it every day for the rest of my life.

And I was actually going to get my wish.

He was slow at first. Lazy. He licked me with long, flat strokes of his tongue that made me arch and whimper and whisper his name like a prayer. And every time I shifted, he tightened his grip on me like he didn't want me going anywhere. Like I belonged to him.

I did. I *belonged* to *him*.

"This is mine, Willa," he murmured between licks. "I'm the first man who's tasted this sweet little cunt. I'm gonna be the last, too, aren't I, wife?"

"Oh my god," I moaned, hips rolling, heat building low in my belly thanks to his words and his touch.

He glanced up at me from between my thighs, his eyes on fire and a wicked smirk curving his lips. "Not god, baby. Just your husband. I'm the only one who knows what you need, isn't that right?"

"Yes," I panted.

He slipped two fingers inside me and sucked my clit between his lips, groaning low when I gasped, my hips rocking against his mouth. "So fucking greedy, isn't she, baby? This pussy wants to come so bad."

I could only whimper in response, words evading me. I was desperate for it—desperate for the release only he'd been able to coax out of me.

"Relax, hellcat. I always make sure you get there." He curled his fingers inside me, then met my eyes as he traced slow, lazy circles around my clit. So fucking good but not nearly enough. "I'd stay here all fucking night if that's what this perfect cunt needs. Hell, I'd *live* between your thighs if you'd let me."

At this point, with the feelings he coaxed out of my body, I might allow him to. There was no denying it anymore—I was addicted to my husband.

And I no longer had to fight it.

"Linc—*please*," I managed, my entire body strung tight with need.

He groaned, a low, filthy sound that vibrated all the way through me. Then he dove back in, relentless now—circling, teasing, then flicking his tongue exactly where I needed as he thrust his fingers inside me. I was a writhing mess, one hand in his hair and the other gripping the sheets, completely undone thanks to his lips and his tongue and his touch.

"I can feel it," he rasped against me. "You're so close, hellcat. Give it to me. Give me what's mine. *Only* mine."

I couldn't hold back a second longer. Not when he said things like that. Not with his mouth on me, his tongue working me over so expertly, his eyes molten as he glanced up from between my thighs.

So hungry and filthy and *mine*.

Everything pulled tight-tight-tight until, suddenly, the tension snapped. I cried out, my entire body shuddering as pleasure crashed over me in wild, reckless waves. Lincoln hummed and held me through it, licking me slower. Sweeter. Softer, but still there. Like he didn't want to stop.

Like he never would.

Tremors were still coursing through my body when he finally lifted his head, his lips and chin wet with me, his gaze hungry. He looked wrecked and feral and completely undone. Like watching me come—*making* me come—only reiterated just how much I was his.

And I was. I was his.

He kissed the inside of my thigh once. Then again, slower this time, his eyes locked on mine. A silent I love you written with his mouth.

I couldn't take it anymore. Needed him like I needed air. Though he'd already made me come, I was still desperate to feel him over me, pressing into me. Grounding me. I tugged him up, and he came without resistance, brushing kisses up my body as he went.

When Lincoln was braced over me, I cradled his face between my palms and kissed him. Tasting what he'd done to me. He slanted his mouth over mine, slow at first, then deeper —filthy and reverent all at once.

And when he pressed his cock against me, sliding through the slippery mess he'd made of my pussy, it only heightened my hunger for him. When he hooked my thigh over his hip and rocked into me, the head of his cock bumping my clit with each thrust, it only made me crave him more.

"Oh fuck," I moaned, eyes fluttering closed as everything in my body centered on what he was doing to me.

"You feel that?" he murmured against my lips. "Feel how fucking hard I am for you, wife? Just from making you come. You know why?"

Whimpering, I shook my head and tightened my legs

around his waist, desperate to pull him closer. To take all of him. But he just kept rocking against me and kissed me again, slower this time. Like a promise. Like a vow.

"Because I'm the only person in the world who's ever tasted it. The only one who's ever felt it." He shifted his hips back, notching his cock at my entrance. "And I'm the only one who ever will, aren't I, baby?"

"Yes," I breathed.

With a hum of satisfaction, he sank inside. Slow. So goddamn slow. Digging my nails into his shoulders, I wrapped my legs tight around his waist as he filled me inch by inch. Like he had all the time in the world. Like there was nowhere else he'd rather be than buried inside me.

A groan tore from his throat as soon as he was seated deep, his forehead resting against mine. "Jesus Christ, hellcat. Always so fucking tight for me. Like your pussy knows I'm the only one who belongs here."

"You are," I breathed, hips rolling as I gripped his shoulders, holding him close.

He stilled above me and met my gaze, his chest heaving, jaw tight. "Say it again."

"You're the only one." I dragged my hand down his back, gripped his ass, and tugged him all the way into me. "Just you. Only ever you."

Something dark and greedy sparked in his eyes—like he'd waited his whole life to hear me say that. And then, all at once, he moved.

He crashed his lips down onto mine, his tongue sliding against mine as he filled me. Again and again. Pulling nearly all the way out before giving me a deep, grinding thrust that made me cry out. He rocked into me, his strokes long and sure, every single one dragging a noise from my throat I couldn't hold back.

We didn't rush. The frantic pace that was usually present between us was nowhere to be found tonight. Instead, it was something slower. Softer. The steady rhythm of two people who were no longer racing against the clock.

Two people who knew they now had all the time in the world.

"You feel so goddamn good," he murmured into my skin, his hips rolling, cock sinking deep. "I could fuck you every day for the rest of our lives and still die wanting more. That's how fucking much I love it. How fucking much I love *you*."

My heart stuttered, my stomach flipping even as my pussy clenched around him, my body tightening and readying itself for release. "I love you too," I breathed. "So much."

"Tell me again." He rolled his hips, pressing in even deeper, his voice nothing but gravel and heat. "Say I'm the only one who gets this body. This heart. This perfect fucking cunt."

"You are. Always."

"Fuck, Willa." He rested his forehead on mine, his thrusts quickening, his muscles tight as he held himself back. "Need you to come, baby. Reach down and rub that pretty little clit for me."

I was too far gone to do anything but obey, sliding my hand between us and stroking exactly where I needed it. Lincoln pressed kisses along my neck, my collarbone, tugged my earlobe with his teeth, all while he sank inside me, again and again, and I whimpered and moaned and gasped with pleasure.

"There you go," he said, his tone threaded with satisfaction. "You make the filthiest sounds when you're falling apart on my cock. Let me hear them, wife. Let me hear you come apart on what's only yours. And then I'm gonna fill up what's only mine."

Everything tightened inside me as Lincoln whispered praise in my ear and fucked me like I was sacred. Like I was *his*. I worked my fingers in frantic circles over my clit, the pressure building with every deep grind of his hips. Until everything inside me coiled so tight I thought I might shatter from it.

And then I did.

With a cry, I came undone beneath him, my back arching as white-hot pleasure ripped through me like a lightning strike. My pussy clenched tight around him, pulsing and fluttering in relentless waves as I sobbed his name into the crook of his neck.

"Yes, fuck yes," he growled, his control breaking. "That's it. That's my girl. So fucking perfect when you come for me."

He gripped my thigh, hooking it higher over his hip, and slammed into me once, twice. Then, on a groan, he buried himself deep, his entire body shuddering as he spilled inside me.

"Fuck, Willa," he rasped, his voice hoarse and reverent. "I'm never gonna get enough of you."

His chest heaved against mine, his breath hot and uneven as he pressed kiss after kiss to my cheek, my temple, my lips.

Like he couldn't stop. Like he was reminding himself I was right here with him.

He stayed like that, buried deep and trembling, one arm braced beside my head, the other clutching my hip like he'd fall apart without the anchor. And I held him. My thighs quivering, heart racing, body still trembling with aftershocks, I held him like I'd never let him go. Because I wouldn't. Because what we had wasn't a secret or a regret or a mistake.

Because right now, in this moment, I'd never felt more his. And I'd never known a love as sweet as this.

EPILOGUE
LINCOLN

FOR THE FIRST time in recent or even distant memory, all four of us Steele brothers were seated at a table in One Night Stan's, *off duty*, during Trivia Night. Tasha was running the hell out of this evening—she'd been running the hell out of this place, period. And we... We were able to enjoy life outside this bar.

It was unsettling. Almost suspicious. Like peace and quiet were just lulling us into a false sense of security before something exploded.

Atlas had tugged Sutton's chair so close to his, she might as well be in his lap. Chloe actually *was* in Xander's lap, stealing a fry from his plate. My wife sat next to me with a soft smile on her face, her thigh warm and smooth under my hand, skin still smelling like honey from the... product sampling...we'd done earlier today. And Declan was smack-dab in the middle of three couples and trying hard to pretend like he wasn't surrounded by nonstop PDA.

"Sounds like Steele and Bramble's been busy," Chloe said, a wide smile on her face.

Willa blew out a breath and leaned into my side. "It has been. More than I could've imagined. Thankfully, we've been able to hire enough staff to manage the growth well."

"Lolo really loves working there," Sutton said.

"You'd never know it with all the snark that pours out of Miss Sassy Pants," I said with a grin.

"Oh, come on, Linc," Sutton said. "You know snark is her love language."

"She said she's managing invoices now?" Atlas asked with a raised brow.

"Yeah. Told me she wanted to build her résumé for world domination." Willa shrugged. "How could I say no to that?"

I took a sip of my beer. "I don't think I've ever seen her smile as big as she did when I told her we could actually pay her now."

Because, yeah—we'd gotten the grant. Obviously. With that interview we'd nailed, how could any other outcome have been possible?

But it turned out we hadn't even needed it—a twist of fate I was incredibly grateful we hadn't known at the beginning of all this. Otherwise, Willa wouldn't be sitting here next to me with my ring on her finger, and I wouldn't have tasted our latest honey flavors mixed with her skin mere hours ago.

My wife had finally taken my PowerPoint presentation to heart and asked how we got started. That was when I'd tapped on my jam-addicted brother with former pro-football player millions who was all too ready and willing to write a fat-ass check that jump-started production for Steele &

Bramble Artisanal Jams. And also gave him lifetime access to as many jars as he wanted—within reason, obviously. The man was an animal.

Declan had finalized the logo. Laurel had handled the branding and social media. Chloe was working on local wholesale partnerships—starting, of course, with Wicked Little Things. And Xander had agreed to pose with the jars while wearing his uniform for an ad campaign thought up by none other than my mom.

My family had shown up for Willa like she was already one of us. And she was. Woven so deep into my history, I could barely remember a time before her.

Even Beau had come around during his two week visit. We didn't talk about the exact details of Willa's and my relationship—for everyone's sanity. But Willa had her twin back, I had my best friend back, and we'd done that all without any punches, passive-aggressive texts, or anyone threatening farm burial.

"Mabel was asking when we might get some new flavors of honey," Chloe said, brow raised toward my wife.

Willa shifted in her seat, a blush staining her cheeks that made my dick twitch in my jeans. "Soon. We're testing out new flavors now."

And by testing, she meant I was spending hours drizzling them all over her body and licking them off.

Chloe grinned. "Good, keep me posted on production because the old woman's ravenous for more stock."

"I will," Willa said with a nod, pressing her lips together to hide a smile that only I knew the reason for.

Goddamn, I loved this woman.

I leaned over and murmured against her ear, "If you keep looking like that, people are gonna figure out you let me eat those new flavors straight off your thighs this afternoon."

She turned toward me, one brow raised. "Don't play chicken with me, husband. You remember what happened last time you teased me in this place? I beat you at pool."

My gaze dropped to her lips, recalling, in great detail, what had happened that night.

"Yeah, and then I fucked you in the alley," I said, voice low and rough. "Seems like I was the real winner of that night, wife."

"Wrong again," she said, leaning in until we were nose to nose. "Two beats one, husband. And I *definitely* had two."

Sutton leaned across the table toward us. "Are you two flirting or fighting?"

"Or on your way to fucking?" Chloe added.

"Yes," Willa and I answered at the same time.

"Jesus Christ," Declan muttered. "I'd kill for five fucking minutes that don't involve front-row seats to any of your sex lives."

"Ohhh," Chloe said, elbowing him in the side. "Is that a cry for help, Dec?"

Declan slid his gaze to Chloe. "No, it's a cry for maintaining my sanity. I don't need to know what my brothers do in the bedroom."

"Or maybe you just need to be preoccupied with your own bedroom activities," Chloe shot back.

"We should set Dec up with someone for next week's trivia night," Sutton said, brow raised as she split a glance between Chloe and my wife.

Willa nodded. "Might be a good idea."

"So you're not so sad," Xander said.

"And lonely," Atlas continued.

"And desperate," I finished.

"Fuck all of you," Dec said. "I'm not—"

The front door slammed open hard enough to catch everyone's attention, and in stalked Penelope. The quiet, unassuming librarian was gone, and in her place was a cardigan-clad nightmare in glasses. She stormed toward our table, her mouth pinched in a thin line, glare focused solely on my brother. And not only was Declan not at all surprised by this ambush, but he looked like he'd been... expecting it?

"Holy shit...I've never seen Penelope mad," Willa murmured. "She looks like she's going to murder someone."

"And I'm pretty sure that someone is Dec," I said, eyes on the live drama unfolding in front of us.

"We are *not* doing this," Penelope said, an accusing finger pointed at Declan.

Dec just leaned back in his chair and crossed his arms. "Actually, we are. Gotta do things by the book. Didn't think I'd have to remind you of that."

I blinked at my brother before exchanging a glance with Xander and Atlas—all three of us silently broadcasting the same *what the fuck* expression. Because Declan hadn't done *anything* by the book since he'd figured out how to escape his crib.

Atlas blew out a heavy sigh and pinned Dec with a look. "What the hell did you do now?"

"Nothing criminal," Declan said evasively.

"Depends on who you ask," Penelope snapped. "Because I'd say ruining my *life* is criminal."

"If someone could fill us in, that'd be great," Xander said, splitting a gaze between Declan—sitting in his chair, the picture of ease—and Penelope—looming over him, steam coming out of her ears.

She whirled to face us. "Oh, did your brother not tell you he got us hauled into the *Court of Mabel* like a pair of degenerates?"

We all exchanged looks of confusion. Good, so it wasn't just me.

"The what now?" I asked.

"New civic initiative," Declan said. "Mabel's apparently deputized now."

"Oh fuck," I muttered. "Who the hell did that?"

"My bet's on Luna," Chloe said with a definitive nod. "That woman can talk her husband into anything."

"Yeah, well, Mabel has a *badge* now. And thanks to Sheriff McKenzie deputizing the town troublemaker, I'm stuck with five hundred hours of community service," Penelope said, her murderous eyes locked on Declan.

"Holy shit, five *hundred*?" Sutton asked.

Declan's brow ticked up as he kept his gaze on Penelope, his expression unreadable. "Or..."

"Don't you dare," Penelope warned, voice low and lethal.

"Thirty days," Declan said. "Living together. By order of Mabel."

"Oh shit," Chloe said. "She is *such* a fucking menace."

Penelope glared at Declan. "This is *not* going to work."

Declan shrugged. "It's either that or five hundred hours

and a blemish on your perfect record. You said it yourself—this was the lesser of two evils."

Her mouth opened like she was going to argue. But instead, she just turned on her heel and stormed out the way she came. And the entire time, Declan watched her go, jaw tight, beer in hand.

The rest of us all sat in stunned silence. Then Declan took a slow sip of his beer like he hadn't just turned Trivia Night into a live reenactment of the enemies-to-lovers I'd read last week.

I leaned back in my chair and whistled lowly. "Shit, man. Seems like you're in trouble."

"Not yet," he said, his eyes still locked on the door. "But give it thirty days."

———

THANK YOU FOR READING THE MR & MRS MISTAKE! Want to find out if Lincoln and Willa broke the desk after the Spicy Book Showdown? To receive that and more bonus chapters of the happy, bickering couple spanning years delivered straight to your inbox, scan the QR code below!

AUTHOR'S NOTE

Even though I never specifically set out to, I always put a bit of my life into my books. Not always intentionally and nothing overt, but it's there in the little moments. In Mabel's personality, in a child's silly word pronunciation, in the quiet, everyday ways the hero cares for the heroine.

But I've never put as much of myself into a book as I did with *The Mr & Mrs Mistake*.

Like Willa, I've been an unwilling passenger on the chronic pain bus for a decade—something I would venture to guess the vast majority of my readers don't know.

While I was writing this book, I asked in my reader group if there happened to be anyone else who had pain similar to Willa's. I figured I'd be lucky if one or two people responded. Instead, *dozens* replied.

As much as I hate that so many of us know what it's like to experience chronic pain, it's also a stark reminder that even when we feel isolated because of our conditions, we are rarely alone. So many of us wake up hurting and choose to be present anyway—to laugh and work and love. To keep living as fully as we're able to, even when our bodies make it difficult.

Willa's story isn't only about her pain—it's also about her courage and strength to build a life around it. To love despite it. And to stop apologizing for the ways she's had to adapt.

If you live with chronic pain, I hope Willa made you feel seen. And if you don't, I hope she helped you understand someone who does.

More than anything, I want to say thank you—for reading, for supporting, and for letting stories like this matter. For Willa, for myself, and for all of us doing our best to carry something incredibly heavy that the world can't always see.

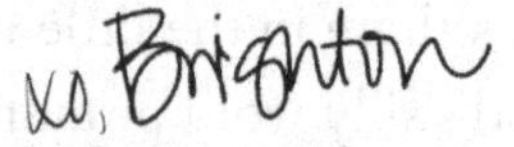

ACKNOWLEDGMENTS

This book wouldn't exist in its current form if it weren't for the help and guidance of some wonderful people I'm lucky enough to have in my corner.

Thank you to Zoe, Annika, Molly, and Selena for brainstorming these characters and this book with me and helping me figure things out anytime I came upon a roadblock.

Thank you to my editor, Lisa, for busting this out in record time (again) and making my words shine, as always.

Thank you to my amazing assistant, Erin, for taking care of all the noise in this business so I can focus on writing. I would unravel without your support.

Thank you to my readers for being as obsessed with these brothers as I am. So many new book besties have found their way to me through this series, and I'm so grateful you're here!

Thank you to the indie bookstores who've partnered with me in order to bring the Steele brothers to more readers. You're amazing!

Thank you to Jill—my personal Luna—for being not only an amazing massage therapist who takes good care of my oftentimes aching body but also an amazing friend.

Finally, to my guys. Thank you to my boys for celebrating

all my wins and for growing up into the kind of men romance heroes are made of. And thank you to Hubs for being my very own romance hero. Who loves and protects me as hard as Lincoln and only loses his patience when I'm too stubborn for my own good (like Willa). I love you all.

OTHER TITLES BY BRIGHTON WALSH

STEELE BROTHERS OF STARLIGHT COVE SERIES

The Grump Next Door

The Live-In Temptation

The Mr & Mrs Mistake

STARLIGHT COVE SERIES

Defiant Heart

Protective Heart

Fearless Heart

Reckless Heart

Possessive Heart

Rebel Heart

HOLIDAYS IN HAVENBROOK SERIES

Main Street Dealmaker

HAVENBROOK SERIES

Charmer

Troublemaker

Heartbreaker

Faker

Reluctant Hearts Series

Caged in Winter

Tessa Ever After

Paige in Progress

Our Love Unhinged

Stand-Alone Titles

Dirty Little Secret

Plus One

ABOUT THE AUTHOR

Award-winning *USA Today* and *Wall Street Journal* bestselling author Brighton Walsh spent a decade as a professional photographer before taking her storytelling in a different direction and reconnecting with her first love—writing. She likes her books how she likes her tea—steamy and satisfying—and adores strong-willed heroines and the protective heroes who fall head over heels for them. Brighton lives along the shores of Lake Michigan with her real life hero of a husband, her two kids—both taller than her—and her dog who thinks she's a queen. Her boy-filled house is the setting for dirty socks galore, frequent dance parties (okay, so it's mostly her, by herself, while her children look on in horror), and more laughter than she thought possible. Connect with her online at brightonwalsh.com/quicklinks.

www.ingramcontent.com/pod-product-compliance
Lightning Source LLC
Chambersburg PA
CBHW011550190726

48287CB00010B/2824